CW00793553

# CONTENTS

# THE ADULTERER'S HANDBOOK

A Novel

Sam Anthony

# PROLOGUE

I raise my hands to her shoulders and give her a hard shove. She stumbles away from me until her heel catches on a tree root and she falls backwards, arms windmilling, towards the setting sun.

"Lee…" she shouts before there's a spectacular splash and she disappears beneath the green, frothing water.

My first thought is, she won't be happy about me ruining her new dress.

My second is, I hope she doesn't swallow any of that slimy, foul-smelling canal water.

In a moment of panic, one thought comes to the fore: she can't swim!

Am I going to have to jump in and rescue her? I don't mind my jeans getting wet, but I'm wearing my favourite shirt. Have I got time to strip off?

Then, to my great relief, she comes coughing and spluttering to the surface. I expect to receive an earful of fully justified abuse, but, to my surprise, after some ineffectual splashing, she disappears beneath the surface again.

The water quickly stills above her.

She genuinely can't swim.

I'm about to jump into the canal and pull her to safety when I stop at the edge of the towpath.

What if I do nothing…?

# PART ONE

# CHAPTER ONE

### The Text Message

"**N**o, no, no, no, NO!" I realise my mistake milliseconds after pressing the little arrow icon. I've just sent the text message "That was incredible! God, you're so hot! xxx" to my wife, instead of my lover.

The traffic lights turn green and I drive away, searching for somewhere to park so I can figure out if I can remedy the situation. I turn into a side street and pull over. How did this happen? I'm always so careful. That will teach me not to send messages while I'm driving. I pick up my phone, type in the six-digit passcode and study the screen. Two grey ticks. My wife's phone has received it, but she hasn't read it yet. Sometimes she doesn't look at my messages for hours. Perhaps there's a way I can delete it from her phone before she even notices it. I feel sick and I'm sweating. What am I going to say if she reads it?

*For the last seven weeks, I've been having an affair with Sophia from my office. Over the course of a couple of years we'd gradually made the transition from colleagues to friends, and we increasingly used to spend our downtime together. She made me laugh, made me think and took an interest in me. I came to really enjoy her*

*company. It didn't hurt that she was also very easy on the eye. We flirted a bit, initially by email and then in person. One evening, at the tail-end of summer, after working late to finish an important project, as we and a colleague made our way to the staff car park, along a particularly dark section of the footpath, I reached out and surreptitiously squeezed Sophia's bottom. I still don't understand the strange compulsion that made me do it. What an impetuous thing to do! I had no idea how she'd react. A slap in the face would have been justified, or she could have made a scene in front of our colleague and humiliated me. She did neither. Without breaking stride, Sophia maintained her conversation with Claire from the IT department. It was as if it had never happened. I started to believe that she hadn't even noticed.*

It's my own stupid fault. I've completely ignored rule three: Always begin text exchanges with 'Hi.' It's a security feature of our carefully regulated affair, to make sure it's safe to communicate and hence to prevent situations like this one from occurring. I'm an idiot!

Two blue ticks. Tamsin has seen it! My heart sinks. What must she be thinking now? I picture her in floods of tears, staring at her phone as her world crashes down around her. There's no reply yet. Is she already throwing my clothes onto the front lawn and lighting a match? I couldn't blame her if she is.

A response at last. Just a single symbol.

"?"

*The following day at work, Sophia was still behaving as if nothing had happened. Fine by me. I'd regretted grabbing her bottom the moment I'd done it, and I was happy to forget all about the whole in-*

*cident. However, she approached me mid-morning, after being out of the office for a while, an expression of suppressed anger on her face. "I've just been with HR," she said. "I've reported you for sexual harassment and they want to see you in their office now."*

*I couldn't believe what I'd heard. "I'm so sorry, Soph. I don't know why I did it."*

*"Well I do!" she replied, her eyes steely. "I have an irresistible arse. It's always been a problem."*

*She burst out laughing. I'd never seen her so joyful. "Your face is priceless!" she gasped, trying to catch her breath as she sashayed back to her office.*

What should I do? Reply straight away? Think fast and try to come up with any old excuse on the spur of the moment? Or take my time and make sure I've got a foolproof reason why I've just sent a hugely suspicious text message to my wife? She too must have seen the two blue ticks, so she knows I've read her message. I have to reply at once. I wing it.

"Ha ha! Sorry about that. Colleague Dave got hold of my phone and thought it would be funny to send you a dodgy message!"

Two grey ticks. Two blue ticks. No reply.

Minutes pass.

I wait.

My wife is called Tamsin, and she's wonderful. I fell in love with her the moment I met her at university, and I love her more with each passing year. She's beautiful, kind, wise, classy and very, very sexy. Slightly on the skinny side of slim, she looks incredible clothed and naked. I've never met anyone who I find more alluring than her. So why am I having an affair? I've considered this a great deal. Is there something missing from our relationship that I can only obtain elsewhere? Not really. Tamsin is my dream woman. I fancy the pants off her. She's my best friend. We share many of the same likes and dislikes. She's great company and we thoroughly enjoy spending quality time together. We both appreciate fine dining and regularly go out for romantic meals. We behave like newlyweds on our summer vacation, which Tamsin meticulously researches and organises. I'd hate to do anything to hurt her, so why am I cheating on her when I'm fully cognisant of how devastated she'd be if she knew?

*For the next few days, Sophia teased me mercilessly about not being able to resist her bottom. However, our relationship continued to be professional and above board, with just some occasional flirting. That is, until my birthday.*

*At the close of business, once most of the staff had left the building, I popped into Sophia's office, as I'd begun to do several times a day, ostensibly for a chat. We often spent our break-time together and took the opportunity to gossip about and affectionately ridicule our co-workers. It was a pleasant way to spend time, and I found I was enjoying being with Sophia more and more. In fact, I seemed to be thinking about her rather more than a married man should.*

*On this particular day, my forty-fifth birthday, as I said goodbye, Sophia stood up from behind her desk, came towards me, stretched up onto her tiptoes, kissed me softly on the lips and said "Happy birthday!" in a soft breathy voice I hadn't heard her use before. I was taken aback. It was so intimate. I'd imagined what it would be like to kiss her, but it had actually happened and it was lovely. She stood there, inches away, looking me in the eye and waiting for a response. There was nobody else around so I decided to push my luck. "Any chance of a hug?" Sophia didn't hesitate. She put her arms around my neck, pressed her body against mine and relaxed into me. My arms went around her waist and I squeezed her gently. And she squeezed back. And it felt perfect. I wanted it to go* on forever, but we heard voices outside in the corridor and we leapt apart. "See you tomorrow," she waved, her eyes now on her computer screen as two people walked past her office door. "See ya," I replied as I left the room, walking on air.

There's no response from Tamsin for twelve minutes. Does she believe my feeble excuse? It's plausible. Eventually, I get a one-word reply.

"Hilarious!"

I can almost see the sarcasm dripping off my phone screen.

This is immediately followed by, "We need to talk when you get home!"

I should mention at this point that I'm heavily editing and reconstructing my wife's text messages so they make sense. She types fast and never reads them before sending. They're often indecipherable and sometimes highly humorous. This one I don't find funny at all and I'm already dreading returning home.

*For the next couple of weeks, my relationship with Sophia continued much as before, except our eyes seemed to meet more often in staff meetings, and we'd taken to hugging goodbye before we left for home at the end of each day, obviously only after we'd checked that nobody could see us. This rapidly became the highlight of my day. Sophia felt so good in my arms that I was always reluctant to stop, and these hugs became longer and longer. Increasingly, we only ended our embrace when we heard voices or footsteps in the corridor outside the room. Nothing was said, but it was obvious to both of us that something was happening between us that we wanted to*

*keep secret. How long can you maintain a hug before it starts to feel weird? Quite a while, apparently. Several times I thought these hugs were about to lead to kissing, but they never did. Until the evening of the puncture.*

I drive home, paying little attention to the traffic. This isn't going to be any fun. I don't think Tamsin has bought my story. When I walk through the front door, she's coming out of the kitchen. She must have seen my car arrive and is eager to talk without delay. With a sideways motion of her head, she summons me upstairs. I guess she wants privacy and I can hear the kids monopolising the kitchen, arguing over which songs to play while they're doing their homework.

Tamsin does not seem happy, but she's a long way from furious. This is a good sign for me. I'd place her mood somewhere between anxious and stressed. The signs are apparent: the worm-like swollen vein in her otherwise elegant neck and her hands balled into fists, but her face is nowhere near the purple shade which signifies an imminent eruption. To be fair to Tamsin, she rarely blows her top, but when she does, it's spectacular.

I close the bedroom door behind us and sit on the bed, dreading the first words out of her mouth.

"Your bloody mother is now saying she can't make it for Christmas!" she says, barely containing her anger.

"What?" What's she talking about?

"She phoned earlier to say that she and Greg are going to 'holiday in Spain' this year." She mimes air-quotes as she rants. "All those Vegan recipes I've been looking at! What a waste of time! The kids are going to be gutted."

Tamsin goes on, but I'm no longer listening. Have I got away with it? Has this new crisis superseded mine and caused her to forget that I'm supposed to be in the doghouse?

I make noises of agreement, disappointment and annoyance at the appropriate times as she continues to vent, but after a while, she begins to calm down and I tune in again.

"Well, at least we should score some devoted-family-points for inviting them, but a bit more warning would have been useful."

I concur and Tamsin opens the door and starts to make her way out of the bedroom.

As I'm beginning to let out a huge sigh of relief, she turns back to me.

"By the way, what was that weird text message about? I don't think you've mentioned Dave before. Is he new?" she asks.

"Not especially. He's been with us for a couple of years. Considers himself to be a bit of a prankster." I can't look her in the eye.

"Well, I'll be giving him a piece of my mind at your office Christmas party."

Tamsin turns and walks away. As she stomps back down the stairs, I decide to postpone my sigh of relief.

Tamsin and I have two children. Charlie is fourteen, witty, confident and as beautiful as her mother. John is eleven, tall for his age and too young to be as studious as he is. They're both addicted to their gadgets and seem to spend less and less time with their parents, to our dismay, but they're still great kids. I may be biased, but I believe we make a wonderful family, and only an idiot would do anything to jeopardise what we have. An idiot like me! However, I'm determined not to end up divorced and full of regret like my parents. I guess I'd better not get caught.

Sophia is thirty-five and has an amazing figure, somewhere between slim and voluptuous. She's undoubtedly curvier than my wife, but not as tall. The perfect hugging height. Her husband is a lucky man. Oh yes; did I mention that she's married too? They have no children yet, but they're contemplating starting a family soon.

*Eight weeks before Christmas, as I was completing a task at work, shortly after hugging Sophia goodbye, and coming perilously close to kissing her again, my phone vibrated in my pocket.*

*"I've got a puncture!" Sophia texted.*

*Sophia is the best text message writer I've ever met. She produces perfectly constructed, precise messages and even uses correct formal punctuation.*

*She'd only made it half-a-mile home before her car had begun to weave erratically across the road and she'd been forced to pull over into a lay-by.*

*On reflection, this was the first text message we'd ever exchanged, and it began a whole new era in our developing relationship.*

*"You ok?" I replied.*

*"Yeah, I'm fine, but I need a big manly man to help me!"*

*This was followed by, "I immediately thought of you."*

*Then, "Do YOU know any big manly men?!"*

*Funny!*

*"Have you tried the AA or RAC?" I responded, chuckling to myself.*

*"Not a member," accompanied by a sad face emoji.*

*"What about your husband? Can't he help?"*

*"He's away at the moment and TBH he's useless at mechanical stuff and many other things!"*

*"Where are you?" I asked.*

*Sophia sent me her location, and I set off to assist her, the way any colleague would under the same circumstances.*

Well, it looks as if I've got a temporary reprieve. Tamsin appears to believe me regarding the prank text message, so hopefully I'm off the hook, at least until the office Christmas party, which I'm now dreading. What if she confronts Dave? There's a high likelihood they'll bump into each other at some point during the evening, and the only thing she knows about him is that he's a prankster. I can already envisage the scene:

"Nice to meet you, Dave. Are you the one who sent me that dodgy message from my husband's phone?"

"Huh? I'm afraid I have no idea what you're talking about, Lee's hot wife."

"Please, call me Tamsin."

"Okey-dokey, Tamsin."

"You know! A few weeks ago you sent me a message, pretending it was from Lee to a woman he'd just been having sex with. Something like: 'That was amazing! God, you're so hot!' You must remember."

"I'm sorry, Tamsin, but that definitely wasn't me."

"Fair enough, Dave. Want to pop upstairs for a shag ...?"

Okay, so I may have an overactive imagination, and many of my daydreams involve my horny wife having sex with someone else, but I'm already terrified that the conversation will go something like that. Except possibly the last bit.

Once Tamsin discovers that my story isn't true, she'll confront me again. What new concoction can I go to next? I could accuse Dave of lying, but why would he do that? I could blame someone else in the office, but Tamsin could easily ask them. A random stranger? But she'd still wonder why I'd accused Dave in the first place. I can't see a way out of it, and I'm coming up with increasingly desperate ideas, which eventually I whittle down to just two:

Tell Dave what I've done, man-to-man, and hope that he'll back me up.

Sam Anthony

Murder Dave.

# CHAPTER TWO

*The Party*

"D ave, mate, I need a massive favour." We're alone in the staff toilet.

"Name it," he says.

"I accidentally sent a rather personal text message to my wife which was meant for someone else. Then I panicked and said you'd pinched my phone and sent the message as a prank."

"Oh cheers, mate! Why me?"

"Well, you're the biggest prat I know!" I wink. "So can you help me out? It's quite possible my wife's going to ask you about this at the Christmas party. All I need you to do is say that *you* did it."

He sighs. "I'm not going to come out of this well, am I? What about my reputation as a cool, suave, ladies' man?"

"I'm sorry, Dave. I wouldn't ask if it wasn't extremely important."

"Okay," he says. "I don't suppose you're going to tell me who the message was really meant for."

"Your mum!" I punch him lightly on the arm and head back to my office.

I love Tamsin more than anyone in the world, so why am I cheating on her? Could it be the excitement of an affair or the pleasure of passionate sex? So different from the routine, mechanical, functional sex we've been having for the last few years. We both end up satisfied because we know how to get each other off, but where's the fun? Where's the lust? Where's the passion? It's always the same. Nobody goes to their favourite restaurant and orders the same meal every time, month after month, year after year. After a while it becomes monotonous and you begin to crave variety. Perhaps I just fancy something novel. Something slightly different for a change.

*When I pulled up behind Sophia's car, she got out and pointed towards the problem tyre. It was pretty low, but not completely flat, and there was no sign of a blow-out or any obvious damage.*

*"Thanks for helping, Lee. I really appreciate it," she said.*

*"Anything for you, Soph. Do you have a spare tyre?" I asked.*

*"No idea. Where would it be?" Women!*

*"Probably in the boot."*

*Together we walked around to the back of the vehicle, Sophia opened the boot and we peered inside. She stood very close to me and I couldn't help noticing that she smelled great. Had she recently applied perfume? Surely that's an unusual thing to do while you're waiting for a wheel change.*

*"There it is. Looks in good condition to me." I lifted it out, found the jack and some tools underneath it, and got to work.*

*It didn't take long to jack up the car, take off the old wheel and replace it with the spare. I did my best to appear proficient and manly, while Sophia held her phone torch so I could see what I was doing.*

*When I'd finished the job and tidied away the flat tyre and all the tools, Sophia said, "Lee, I'm so grateful. Is there any way I can thank you?" The coquettish twinkle in her eye was something to behold.*

*"Well, I can probably come up with a few ways," I mumbled.*

*She looked around to make sure that we couldn't be seen and there were no cars coming, then moved closer to me, put her arms around my neck, pressed her body against mine and kissed me. Not the soft kiss on the lips like on my birthday. This was a proper kiss. An open-mouthed, full-on snog which went on for minutes. And I reciprocated. My lips were getting heavily involved. My hands wanted to join in the fun too, but they were filthy from changing the wheel, so my arms just hung limply by my sides while she squeezed me tight.*

*Eventually, it was Sophia who pulled away. Breathlessly she said, "Why don't you have a long, hard think about how I can express my gratitude. Try to come up with a few ideas and tell me tomorrow."*

Tamsin walks down the stairs looking absolutely stunning. Her hair is up, showing off her graceful neck to full effect. She's wearing a little black dress – which conceals only the top few inches of her long shapely bare legs – and high heels – which make her taller than all but a few men. The package is completed with some classy jewellery: diamond earrings hang from her lobes and a matching necklace draws the eye to her accentuated cleavage.

Wow! I'm trying not to salivate. She looks so hot. It's another reminder of just how lucky I am to have such a beautiful wife. I sigh contentedly until I realise that my lover and my wife are about to come face to face at the office Christmas party. This could be a disaster.

I consider myself to be an affectionate guy. I like to manifest my feelings for Tamsin physically; by holding her hand and cuddling her as much as she'll allow. For me, when we're intimate, we're not simply having sex, we're making love. I like the lights on, so I can make eye contact whenever possible. Gazing into my wife's eyes during the throes of passion can provide a deep connection between us; but Tamsin prefers the lights off, and even when they're on, she usually has her eyes tightly shut. Perhaps she's concentrating on the pleasure that she's experiencing, or possibly she's pretending it's not me that she's with. Maybe her way to attain optimum enjoyment is to fantasise that she's making love with someone else. I simply don't know.

With Sophia, it's just sex. Definitely hot sex, but I'm not expressing my feelings for her, I'm simply enjoying the mutual pleasure. I'm certainly not in love with Sophia; not the deep, overwhelming love I have for Tamsin.

*I spent a restless night, tossing and turning, and considering different ways that Sophia could thank me. Suffice it to say, they were all very, very rude and, by the morning, I was lying in bed feeling particularly horny. I reached out to Tamsin and tentatively put my hand on her thigh.*

*"We've got an early morning staff meeting today." She yawned, stretched, leapt out of bed and began to get dressed.*

We arrive at the party fashionably late. Most people are there already.

Heads turn as Tamsin enters the room. There's no doubt that she looks stunning when she's dressed up in her finery. She exudes class and style, and her cleavage looks amazing in that outfit. We find chairs and sit down. How can she not realise that every red-blooded male in the room is slyly watching as she crosses those long legs?

It doesn't seem fair that all attractive women have the power to tantalise men merely by casually crossing and uncrossing their legs, or by surreptitiously leaning forward, just a little more than is absolutely necessary, to provide a fleeting glimpse down their top. Do they realise the effect they're having? They certainly hide it well if they do. In this situation, the gentlemanly thing to do would be to avert the eyes, but it's not that easy, especially if your wife is as sexy as mine.

Tamsin is the sexiest woman I've ever met, but also my best friend. This is a problem. How can you treat someone you respect – the mother of your children, the ironer of your shirts – as a sex object? I'd love to treat her like a whore; to make sexual demands: "Here's some money. Now, these are the depraved things I want you to do to me, bitch. Sorry! I don't know what got into me then. What I actually meant was … darling, it would be really nice if you could …" It's never going to happen. I respect Tamsin too much to even ask.

*"Did you come up with some ideas?"*

*Sophia approached my desk early the next day, a spring in her step and a twinkle in her eye.*

*"You're funny," I replied.*

*"No. I'm serious. I really want to thank you properly."*

*"It was no problem, Soph. I'm always happy to help. Buy me a nice bottle of wine if you like."*

*"I was hoping you'd prefer something a bit more personal."* *She catches and holds my eye.*

*"What did you have in mind?" I enquired.*

*It felt like we were dancing around the subject, but neither of us was brave enough to verbalise what we both apparently wanted.*

*Then, out of the blue, Sophia took a deep breath, started to blush and blurted out, "You can shag me if you want!"*

*She looked away, obviously deeply embarrassed.*

*I didn't know what to say.*

The early part of the evening is spent mingling, drinking and shouting to be heard above the noise of the disco. Nobody is dancing yet, but that hasn't stopped the DJ from blaring his music at full volume and thereby stifling conversation.

Sophia's husband, Joe, chose not to come after she told him that most attendees weren't bringing their partners, so at least that's one less complication.

I've spotted Sophia. She's at the bar, surrounded by a group of five young men who are currently at the strutting-around-showing-off-their-plumage phase of their seduction technique. I expect the field will gradually get whittled down during the dance-off round of the competition, and will culminate with the last two standing locking antlers for a while before she gives them both the brush off.

Sophia keeps glancing across the room at me and smiling seductively. She's not being too subtle about it either. I hope Tamsin hasn't noticed.

There's definitely something exciting and terrifying about being in the same room as your wife and your lover, and I can't say I'm enjoying the experience.

*What's the correct response when a woman you really fancy offers to have sex with you?*

*"Hell, yeah!" if you're both single.*

*"Do you think we can get away with it without your husband finding out?" if you're single, but she's not.*

*"Do you think we can get away with it without my wife finding out?" if she's single, but you're not.*

*But what if you're both married? "Absolutely not! We're both in relationships. That would be completely wrong!" or "Yeah! Let's go for it. But we need a really good plan to avoid getting caught in the act."*

*I can imagine what it could be like if we were caught:*

*Sophia and I are* in flagrante delicto *in her bedroom when Tamsin bursts in. Her face passes through a range of distinct emotions: shock, disgust, anger, grief. As the tears begin to flow down her face, my children walk into the room looking distraught and ashamed of their once much-loved father. My mum and Greg enter from the ensuite bathroom and start tutting and shaking their heads, appalled. I see my old primary school teacher peering in the window, looking so disappointed in me. My old pet dog is there, tail motionless, she can't even look at me. With a sigh of infinite weariness, Tamsin gets a huge gun out of her handbag and shoots off my wedding tackle, with three precisely aimed shots. I writhe on the bed in agony, blood everywhere, as they all traipse out of the room without a backward glance, even Sophia.*

*Studying my shoes, I replied, "I'd really enjoy that, Soph, but I just can't be unfaithful to Tamsin. It wouldn't be right."*

*I saw tears well up in Sophia's eyes and she turned and walked disconsolately away.*

*She didn't talk to me again for two whole weeks.*

I'm starting to relax. This is okay. Tamsin is on one side of the room, Sophia on the other. Tamsin doesn't even know who Dave is, and Sophia's husband isn't present. My complicated love life is under control.

Tamsin leans in closer and shouts into my ear.

"Can I borrow your phone? I want to get Charlie to check I turned the iron off."

"Sure." I hand it to her. "Where's yours?"

"Can you see any pockets in this dress?" She gives me a twirl. It's clear that a few drinks have loosened her up already.

"Good point. Did I tell you how beautiful you look tonight?" I ask.

She smiles and kisses me on the lips. "Only about a million times."

Behind her, I can see Sophia staring daggers at the two of us. She gulps down half a glass of white wine and picks up another from the bar.

Women rarely find me attractive these days. I don't remember anyone fancying me since I hit thirty. In my youth, on a night out, when I was feeling particularly handsome and well dressed, I'd look around to see who was checking me out. I'd quickly glance behind me to see who was admiring my butt. I never caught anyone. But then, along came Sophia. She made it perfectly clear, not only did she think I was attractive, she actually lusted after me. It's a pleasant experience; very flattering. Perhaps I'm not over the hill after all.

*I was weak.*

*After fourteen days of feeling virtuous for rejecting Sophia's offer, I was back in her office.*

*"I'm so sorry, Soph," I began. "I really hate this. I miss you so much. Please, can we go back to how it was before?"*

*She looked up at me dejectedly. "I don't think I can, Lee. Since we kissed, I can't get you out of my head. Being just friends isn't enough for me any longer. I want more."*

*I couldn't come up with an appropriate reply and, after an uncomfortable silence, she continued.*

*"You're the first person I think about when I wake up in the morning and the last one I think about before I go to sleep at night," she said. "Please let me show you how much you mean to me. I truly believe we could make each other happy."*

*She paused and looked at me for a long time before saying, "I want us to have an affair."*

I've just managed to get Sophia on her own in order to apologise for kissing Tamsin in front of her. It must be hard enough for her to see me with my wife, without me rubbing her nose in it. She's quick to calm down, but is now being much too flirty for a public place. She keeps resting her hand on my arm and standing really close to me, to make herself heard over the din of the disco. Surely Tamsin must be suspicious of the smouldering looks Sophia keeps firing in my direction. How many drinks has she had?

I glance around in time to see Tamsin coming towards us. Something's up.

"Why have you changed the passcode on your phone? It always used to be my birthday," she says, ignoring my companion.

"Hi, darling. Have you met Sophia?" I sound calm, but inside I'm panicking.

They shake hands loosely and look each other up and down, the way women do when they're trying to decide which of them is the prettiest.

"Nice to meet you," they say at the same time, smiling insincere smiles which suggest that they both consider themselves victorious.

In my head Sophia is thinking: "She may be skinnier than me, but she's so old!" while Tamsin is thinking: "She's quite pretty, I guess, but she could lose a few pounds."

"I changed it!" I blurt out.

They both turn to face me, bemused by my non sequitur.

"My passcode. I changed it after Dave got hold of my phone the other day. It seemed sensible to make it more secure."

"Oh, yeah. That reminds me. I need to speak to him." Tamsin looks around the room. "Which one's Dave?"

This is it!

I'd never been unfaithful to my wife. I wasn't that guy. The guy who respects his wife so little that he cheats on her. When I made my marriage vows, I meant them sincerely. I genuinely believed that I would forsake all others. I'd obviously contemplated having sex with somebody else; show me a man who hasn't. But it was merely random thoughts which popped into my head before I promptly dismissed them. My relationship with Tamsin meant everything to me. It still does. We both trust each other to be honest, loving and faithful, as long as we both shall live. Unfortunately, in Tamsin's case, her trust is misplaced.

*"You do realise what that would mean?" I said. "If we had an affair, we'd be risking everything. If anyone ever found out, it would almost certainly destroy both of our marriages. We'd probably end up suffering through acrimonious divorces. We could lose our homes, our kids, our family and friends. We'd both take a big financial hit. Do you really think it would be worth the risk?"*

*"No one will ever find out," Sophia replied, pleadingly. "We'll be careful. We won't take any risks. We'll plan a foolproof strategy; so secure that we'll never be caught. Please, Lee. At least think about it for a few days before you make up your mind."*

Watching from the opposite side of the room, I see Tamsin weaving her way through a knot of ladies gyrating around their handbags on the tiny dance floor. I see her walk up to Dave and shake his hand. That's promising. They start to converse. Her back stiffens at one point, but it's hard to read their body language from this distance. Tamsin gestures over her shoulder, pointing her thumb in my direction, and Dave says something in response and shakes his head, looking serious.

Their conversation seems to go on forever. I wish I could lip-read, but I haven't got a clue what they're saying to each other.

Eventually, they finish talking and Tamsin makes her way back to me.

"What did Dave say?" I enquire, as casually as possible.

"I'll tell you later." I'm unable to interpret Tamsin's expression as she takes some money out of my wallet and heads back to the bar.

The rest of the night could go either way. Either I'm busted – she's seen through my charade and when we get home my happy life, as I've known it up to now, will come to an abrupt and messy end – or she's believed my feeble explanation, is still madly in love with me and, who knows, I might even get lucky later.

I wouldn't say that Tamsin never initiates sex, but it's highly infrequent and she has to have several strong drinks first. On those rare occasions, when the stars align, her legs are recently shaved, she's wearing her finest underwear, she's having a good-hair day, she's done all the ironing, I've loaded the dishwasher and put the bins out, work is going well, she's at the right time of her cycle, the kids are asleep, several men have flirted with her, and she's had the optimum amount of alcohol then maybe, just maybe, she might initiate sex. Obviously, I play my part too: I bite my tongue; knowing the smallest inappropriate comment might have a disastrous effect.

Apprehensive that I might inadvertently say something to start a distracting conversation, I stay silent and cross my fingers, because if it happens, it's mind-blowing.

Alcohol seems to make Tamsin particularly horny and uninhibited, and on these occasions, she's inspired in the bedroom. Without a doubt, the top ten sexual experiences I've ever had – with Tamsin – have been when she's initiated it in an inebriated state.

*I spent another restless night thinking about what Sophia had said; all sorts of questions jostling for attention in my mind.*

*Did I want to have sex with Sophia? God, yes!*

*Did I want to have an affair? No! I'm a nice guy.*

*What about if I could get away with it, without being caught? Perhaps.*

*What did Sophia look like naked? I so wanted to find out.*

*Should I make a list of pros and cons before I make a decision? Definitely.*

*How about a spreadsheet? Stop being such a spreadsheet nerd!*

*Did Sophia really want to have sex with me? Yes! She did. She really did!*

*Where could I research how to have an affair and get away with it? The internet.*

"I asked Dave what other pranks he'd played, but he couldn't think of any. That's a bit weird isn't it?" Tamsin asks me.

"He's probably just too embarrassed to admit them," I reply. "Some of the things he does are pretty immature."

"Like what?"

"Oh, you know … mostly schoolboy stuff like …" I'm struggling.

At that moment my phone rings. It's Charlie.

"Charlie's asking where her yellow pyjamas are," I say.

Tamsin snatches my phone and directs Charlie to the exact location of the misplaced nightwear.

The conversation goes on for so long that by the time she ends the call, Tamsin has completely forgotten what we were talking about.

It looks like I'm in the clear. At least for now.

Just before we leave the party, I find myself alone with Sophia in a dimly lit corridor. She moves in close and tilts her head upwards. Her lips are extremely tempting, but before I can decide whether to kiss her or not, a couple of inebriated colleagues stumble into us and knock Sophia off balance. The moment passes and we smile at each other and go our separate ways.

From the car, while waiting for Tamsin to complete her goodbyes – which usually take an inordinately long time – I send a text message to Sophia.

"Hi."

"Hi. You ok?" comes the immediate reply.

"Wanted to kiss you!" I quickly message back.

"Me too, you sexy hunk. X"

I turn off my phone just in time, as Tamsin opens the door and slides into the car.

"Home, James," she giggles, "and don't spare the horses!"

I'm pretty sure I'm not going to have to murder Dave. Not yet, anyway.

*Cons:*

*I might destroy my marriage and forfeit my family.*

*I might lose my home, my car and most of my money.*

*I might destroy my reputation, and no longer hold the respect of the people I care about the most.*

*I might make myself ill through stress and worry.*

*I might contract a sexually transmitted disease.*

*I might have to live with guilt for the rest of my life.*

*I might spend all eternity burning in hell, if it exists.*

*Pros:*

   *Hot sex!*

*It was a no-brainer.*

                  *I was going to have an affair!*

# CHAPTER THREE

*The Phonecall*

Christmas Day is one of my top five days of the year, along with my birthday (birthday sex), our wedding anniversary (anniversary sex), Valentine's Day (Valentine's Day sex) and every day of our summer vacation (holiday sex). Christmas Day, however, is always a special family day, even when we have to spend it with my mother and Greg. The kids look forward to our regular traditions and won't let us change anything from year to year.

This Christmas morning begins, as it has always done, with Charlie and John excitedly entering our bedroom at 7:30 a.m. carrying the present-filled stockings which have miraculously appeared at the end of their beds during the night.

They take it in turns to open their presents, and during a lull in the proceedings I check my messages and emails. Tamsin isn't impressed. "You're not going to spend all day looking at your phone, are you? It would be nice if we could just have one day without gadgets," she says.

So I dutifully switch it off. And then back on again as soon as Tamsin walks into the bathroom. But I make sure it's now on silent mode and won't even vibrate. Then I forget about my phone and just enjoy the festivities. I fully intend to eat and drink far too much, as is *my* tradition.

As usual, my mum has spent a ridiculous amount of money on Charlie and John. She dotes on her grandchildren and spoils them rotten by buying really thoughtful and expensive gifts, often overshadowing the gifts we've given them. She must put as much time and effort into carefully handpicking their presents as she does into buying something for Tamsin which she knows that Tamsin will hate. This year she's excelled herself, by giving Tamsin one of those DNA testing kits where you spit into a tube, send it off to the labs, and four weeks later you discover you're descended from Ethelred The Unready.

My mother, like many older people in this country, is slightly – unwittingly and thus unapologetically – racist, and she's mentioned a few times that Tamsin's family 'look like they come from gypsy stock!' Obviously she never says this in Tamsin's hearing, but still there's no love lost between them. I guess that this gift is my mum's way of trying to find out if her theory is correct. But it won't succeed. My expectation is that this gift, as is traditional, will go straight into Tamsin's reject-box to be donated, at the first opportunity, to one of the local charity shops.

I like to think I know my wife pretty well. While her mouth usually says something like, "Oh, how lovely! That's so thoughtful of you, Irene." By the time the words reach my brain they've become, "Well, you've done it again, you old battle-axe. Why do you hate me so much?"

Tamsin is a talented actress, and she performs brilliantly once again when Mum and Greg call our landline – two minutes after we've started our dinner – to wish us a Merry Christmas from sunny Spain. If I didn't know better, I'd genuinely believe that she's delighted with her new gift.

I've no idea why my mother dislikes Tamsin, but they've never hit it off, and it's been the same since the first time I brought Tamsin back from university to visit my family home.

On my first day at university, I found myself miserable, friendless and living in a hall of residence, in a tiny, grotty room opposite a tall, good-looking, dark-haired chap called Jake. I'd left school at eighteen to work with my dad at his building company, then returned to full-time education six years later as a mature student. Despite our age difference – I was six years older and a year below Jake – we got on really well and soon became firm friends. It was through Jake that I first met Tamsin – the love of my life – as they were undergraduates on the same course. By my second year, there was a group of seven of us who had become good pals. We used to hang out with each other all the time, and shared a student house together in my second year. For a while, we even formed a prog rock band which went by the inspired name of Prurient Curiosity. I was on lead vocals, Tamsin played keyboards and Jake made a raucous noise on the guitar. The others had little musical talent, but made up for it in enthusiasm. We were awful, and the band didn't last long, but the bond we formed at university turned out to be permanent, and the seven of us have subsequently kept in touch and tried to meet up at least once a year.

*The next day was a Saturday, so I had the whole weekend to do some research before I saw Sophia again on the following Monday, and gave her my decision.*

*I waited until Tamsin had left the house to go to the gym, then locked myself in my office, booted up the computer and set to work.*

*Unfortunately, I'm a bit behind the times when it comes to anything technical, unlike my kids who seem to perform magic on their various devices.*

*The first thing I did was type 'how to have an affair without getting caught' into a search engine. I was hopeful that I'd find something useful, but I was gobsmacked when I got 545 million hits. There were 545 million articles out there giving advice on how to have an affair successfully! It seemed like I wasn't the only person in the world who was planning to cheat on his wife.*

*The top three search results were:*

*"My perfect affair - how I'm getting away with it"*
*"10 easy ways to have an affair without getting caught"*
*"How not to get caught cheating: 14 steps (with pictures)"*

*I skimmed these three articles and realised that I'd already made one big mistake. The advice was: Use private browsing mode on your web browser. Apparently, employing this method will avoid leaving suspicious entries in the search history, like the four I'd already generated in the first twenty minutes of my cunning plan to be really careful.*

*Not a problem, I thought. I can delete my search history when I'm done. But it seems that this is suspicious too. Why would anyone delete their entire search history if they had nothing to hide?*

*With a bit more research, I discovered that I could delete selected sites and searches from my history, while leaving behind a few innocuous ones in case anyone ever looked.*

*After some cleaning, I was satisfied that I'd left no suspicious traces, and I opened a private browsing window and resumed.*

*I'd already realised that I had a lot to learn if I was going to have an affair and keep it secret.*

Jake has just left. He always pops in on Christmas Day for a brief visit. It's another part of our tradition. Twice divorced, Jake drives over two hundred miles in order to spend part of Christmas Day with each of his three children and his goddaughter, Charlie.

By 7 p.m. I'm in need of the bathroom. While I'm standing and relieving myself, my right hand is busy, but I have nothing to do with my left, so I take out my phone for the first time in several hours, and discover that I've received thirteen text messages, all from Sophia.

They start off pleasant enough, but soon take a worrying turn.

8:35 "Hi"
10:22 "Hi!"
11:12 "Hi!!!"
11:54 "Happy Christmas! xxx"
12:32 "Are you ok?"
13:03 "About to have lunch. Message me soon x"
15:40 "Why aren't you replying? I'm feeling fat and very squiffy!!!"
16:10 "I miss you! Drinking my sorrows away x"
17:18 "We should be together today. I love you! xxx"
17:49 "Just thrown up. Feel wretched!"
18:10 "Are you ignoring me?!"
18:22 "Message me now or it's over!!!"
18:32 "I'm so drunk!"

Tamsin knocks on the door. "Are you all right in there?" she says.

I leave my phone on silent, but I switch it to vibrate.

"Just coming," I reply and head back to rejoin my family.

For someone having an affair, Bank Holidays and rites of passage must be the worst. There's an expectation on a day like Christmas Day that everyone has to have a wonderful time and everything has to be perfect within the family, but anyone committing adultery is fully aware that everything is not perfect. How can it be when they're part of a disloyal marriage?

Their spouse may not be aware of it, but *they* can't hide from the fact. Couples in this position, especially those who have a closer relationship with their lover than their spouse, will inevitably feel lonely and isolated when they're unable to communicate with each other.

I can't exactly blame Sophia for missing me on Christmas Day. It's quite sweet, really.

"Aren't you going to get that?"

As we complete the third round of our traditional card game, my phone begins to vibrate in my pocket. It isn't ringing out loud, but everyone can hear the vibrations. I know it's Sophia; inebriated and unpredictable. What do I do?

"I said aren't you going to get that?" Tamsin is frowning at me as she shuffles the cards.

I take the phone out of my pocket and take a peek at the screen.

"I don't recognise the number," I lie. "But I'd better take it. You never know, it could be something important."

What's Sophia playing at? It's Christmas Day and I'm at home with my family. Has she forgotten the rules, or is she just too drunk to care?

As casually as possible, I make my way into the kitchen and close the door firmly behind me.

"What are you doing calling me on Christmas Day? It's a family day," I whisper.

"I'm sorry, Lee. When I didn't hear from you all day, I was so worried. I'll hang up," Sophia slurs in reply.

"No! Not yet," I snap. "You need to help me come up with a reason for this phone call. What am I going to say to Tamsin?"

"Just say it's a wrong number."

I pause for a few seconds.

"Actually, I can't think of any reason why that won't

work. Nice one."

"You see. I'm not just a pretty…"

"Listen, Soph. I need you to do me a favour," I say, interrupting her.

"Anything, Lee," she says, obviously aware that she's not in my good books.

"Take another look at rule seven and rule fourteen," I say, and hang up on her before she can respond.

*I decided the safest thing to do would be to compile a list of rules. If Sophia and I were going to cheat on our spouses successfully, without anyone getting hurt, we'd need to be singing from the same hymn sheet. I'd write the hymn sheet and insist she agreed with and abided by the lyrics. It would be like a contract; a set of guidelines we'd both have to follow in order to eliminate any chance of us being caught having an affair.*

*For the rest of the weekend, I spent every spare moment, when Tamsin was out of the house, using private browsing mode to acquire the best advice for having an affair and getting away with it. I compiled handwritten lists of do's and don'ts until I had several pages of guidance, then I condensed these pages as much as possible and turned them into fifteen simple rules. It took quite a while to memorise all fifteen, but once I had, I shredded all the paper I'd used and flushed it down the toilet.*

There are two distinct types of affairs: emotional and physical. Tamsin would be more distraught if I had an emotional affair rather than a physical one. If I fell in love with another woman, that would distress her more than if I had meaningless sex with another woman. Somehow, I think she'd see it as more of a betrayal; the perception of closeness, the sharing of feelings and secrets, the confiding in each other.

I take the opposite view. I'd be devastated if Tamsin had

a physical affair; sharing her body, *my* body, with another person, man or woman; I don't think I could get past it. I'd be forever comparing myself with him or her. Was he a more skilful lover than me? Did she know the secret ways to turn Tamsin on which she never shared with me? Did he have a firmer body than mine? Was he better endowed? I'd never be able to stop imagining Tamsin and her mystery lover in bed together, or in the shower, or in the back seat of Tamsin's car.

In contrast, an emotional affair which didn't lead to anything physical: no harm, no foul. Did he fulfil Tamsin's emotional needs better than me? Who cares!

I need to be clear with Sophia that our relationship has no emotional aspect whatsoever. It's entirely physical.

"That was quick. Who was it?" Tamsin asks as I rejoin my family at the card table.

"Oh, just a wrong number. Someone trying to get hold of a guy called Tony. We had a quick chat and I reckon he must have had the last two numbers the wrong way round when he dialled. He sounded pretty drunk to be honest. Whose go is it?"

"It's yours, Dad," Charlie replies, before adding, "Who's still dialling numbers in this day and age? All my contacts are in the address book on my phone. I can't remember the last time I had to physically type the individual numbers."

"Yeah, weird huh?" I say, discarding the ace of hearts before I realise that I actually need that card. "Your go, John."

John gleefully picks up the ace of hearts and the game resumes.

That was too close for comfort, but I think I got away with it again.

*On the following Monday morning, I took my lunch into Sophia's*

*office as usual. She looked particularly attractive that day in a new fitted dress and knee-high boots. She was wearing her hair up, and I couldn't help but imagine kissing her beckoning neck.*

*"Well?" She didn't beat around the bush. There was an eager expression on her face.*

*"Well, what?" I replied, nonchalantly.*

*"Can we do it? Can we have an affair?"*

*"I don't understand why you're so keen," I said. "Am I really that ravishing?"*

*"Yes! I've fancied the pants off you for ages, but it's not only that. Things haven't been great at home for quite a while. I love Joe and I'd never leave him, but we're more like housemates than husband and wife these days. He just wants to play golf all the time, but I want a regular damn good shagging." She flushed. "I was hoping you'd be the man to give me one."*

*I paused.*

*I weighed my options.*

*Sophia waited.*

*Our eyes were locked, but I blinked first.*

*"There'd have to be some ground rules," I said.*

Sometimes I worry about the way my mind works. Every now and then, I can't help wondering what my life would be like if Tamsin was to die. Perhaps a slow painful death from leukaemia after I bravely and selflessly donate some of my bone marrow. Maybe she drops dead from a brain aneurysm or is killed instantaneously in a car crash. Tamsin would be gone, and I'd be all alone, but just think of the sympathy I'd receive. Attractive single ladies would flock to my house from miles around, bringing the delicious home-cooked meals they'd prepared for me, and try to lift my spirits.

In my imagination, I'm at home watching TV when the doorbell rings. It's one of the hot young teachers from Tamsin's school – the redhead with the eye-catching arse.

"Hi, Lee. I was really worried about you – all on your own and feeling sad – so I've cooked you some Lobster Thermidor."

"Yum! That's my favourite. You're so kind and thoughtful. Would you like to come in?"

"Thank you," she says, enters and takes off her coat to reveal that she's only wearing a black lacy basque, stockings, suspenders and high heels. Her figure is stunning.

"Sorry about my outfit," she says. "I'm on my way to the pole dancing club where I work two nights a week."

"Not a problem," I say.

"You must be so miserable and lonely, Lee. Is there anything I can do to cheer you up?" she asks.

I try my luck. "It's being physically close to someone that I miss the most," I say, wistfully.

"Come here," she says and takes me in her arms.

She starts to nibble my earlobe, and it's very enjoyable.

"This is definitely helping," I encourage her.

"I think it would help even more if we have very naughty, absolutely-no-strings hot sex," she whispers into my ear. "My identical twin sister's in the car outside. Do you mind if she joins in too …?"

That's how my mind works when I allow my thoughts to roam freely. There must be something wrong with me.

I wonder how long I'd have to mourn before I could start dating again, following Tamsin's very sad demise. At least a month? I'm not being serious. In reality, I'd be absolutely devastated if I was to lose her. Tamsin is my life. My raison d'être. Nobody could ever take her place in my heart. Thank goodness she's fit, healthy and a careful driver.

"Oh, and you can tell your mother, I don't want her stupid

DNA kit, and she can jolly well give me gift vouchers from now on."

I'm in the bedroom with Tamsin and she's starting to let off steam now we're alone for the first time since 07:30 this morning.

"I can't say *that*," I reply. "She'd be devastated. Maybe *I* could use the DNA kit instead? To be honest, I'm actually quite interested in my genetic heritage. But we'd better tell my mum that you did it, and we were amazed to discover that you're actually human after all."

"Don't even attempt to be funny!" Tamsin yells.

"I'm sorry," I say, trying to placate her. "Apart from Mum's present, we had a pretty good Christmas, didn't we? The food was amazing. You excelled yourself once again. I don't know how you do it all. You truly are superhuman. Thanks for making it such a special day for all of us."

I kiss her on the cheek.

"It was a nice day, wasn't it?" She smiles, and I'm reminded of how beautiful she is and how lucky I am to be married to her.

"So, why don't we finish it off with some rumpy-pumpy?" I ask, more in hope than expectation. "The perfect end to a perfect day."

"Oh, Lee. I'm so tired," she sighs. "Maybe in the morning."

I'm pretty certain it won't happen in the morning, but I still believe that I'm the luckiest man in the world.

# CHAPTER FOUR

## *The Photograph*

I t's a warm Saturday morning in early spring. Outside my bedroom window the birds are singing their hearts out in the hope of getting some action. That was my hope too, but Tamsin got up early, before I was awake, so I didn't even get the chance to initiate sex. She left the house about ten minutes ago to go shopping for some new shoes. I'm towelling myself dry, after a shower in our en-suite bathroom, when I receive a text message.

"Hi." It's Sophia.

"Hi, gorgeous! What are you up to?" I reply.

"Still in bed. Thinking about you! Joe's out playing golf."

My interest is piqued. "What are you wearing?!"

"Guess!" comes the speedy response.

"Are you naked?!"

"I might be!! I can send you a photo if you like?"

Now, this is something of a grey area. It's not explicitly forbidden by the rules of our affair, but we both agreed that it was way too risky to send each other naughty photos.

"Yes please!" I reply, reasoning that there can't be any harm. Tamsin is out of the house, and I can delete the photo long before she gets home.

"Look, Soph, I want to get this straight from the outset. I love my wife and kids. They're my priority. I won't let anyone or anything come between me and my family. What we're about to embark upon is just an affair. Nothing more. We're both lacking sexual fulfilment in our marriages, and this is simply a way of getting a bit of extra physical pleasure and satisfaction without anyone getting hurt. Agreed?"

"Yes. I feel exactly the same way," Sophia said.

So I proceeded with my rehearsed monologue. "I've been doing some research. It's boring, but I'm afraid we have to talk about it if we're going to proceed with this."

She smiled at me patiently and I continued, enumerating the main issues on my fingers as I progressed.

"Apparently, the top way people get caught is their cell phones; things like their call log, itemised phone bills, text messages and emails. There's no doubt that evidence found on phones is the most common way affairs are exposed. Then there's the browsing history and search history on people's computers. Also credit card statements can reveal all sorts of secrets. Even something like perfume or aftershave can catch people out. There's a huge list of pitfalls: being spotted out and about together, lying about your whereabouts, changing your habits, a friend informing on you, something posted on social media ..."

I'd long since run out of fingers.

"There are so many ways to be found out, Soph. We have to be really, really careful. Can we do that?"

"I believe we can, Lee," she said, struggling to maintain a straight face in response to my long and serious speech. "Just tell me exactly what you want me to do and I'll do it."

"Okay. Please don't laugh at me. I've put together a list of rules."

She didn't laugh.

"Get a pen and your notepad, and write these down," I said.

I don't get it. Tamsin is the most important person in my life. She means the world to me. I genuinely don't understand why I'd risk everything I care about, merely because my sex life isn't perfect. I have a smoking-hot wife who I adore – who will actually have sex with me occasionally if the conditions are right – but I can't help wishing that she'd lust after me the way that I lust after her. If only Tamsin didn't make it seem as if sex is just another boring chore for her to carry out; right at the bottom of her list of priorities.

Once I put together a spreadsheet. I like spreadsheets. Don't judge me.

It was a couple of years ago. For a four-week period, I recorded, as best I could without being too obvious about it, every activity Tamsin undertook and how long she spent on each one.

It turned out that, on average each week, Tamsin spent most time sleeping (56 hours), followed by:

Work (45 hours)
On her phone (17 hours)
Watching TV (16 hours)
Socialising (12 hours)
Eating (9 hours)
Commuting (9 hours)
Cleaning the house (8 hours)
Exercising (7 hours)
Shopping (7 hours)
Playing the piano (7 hours)
Reading (6 hours)
Cooking (5 hours)
In the bath (4 hours)
Dining out (3 hours)
At the cinema (3 hours)
Ironing (2 hours)
Dressing (2 hours)
Applying makeup (2 hours)

In the toilet (1 hour)
Showering (1 hour)
Cleaning her teeth (70 minutes)
Having sex (45 minutes)

To be clear, I'm ashamed and embarrassed that I did this, but I couldn't help finding it interesting.

Sex is extremely pleasurable, fun and free. Surely, it should be higher up the list.

Tamsin probably believes that I'm some sort of sex-obsessed pervert, but I just want her to take an interest in our sex lives. How about a scintilla of enthusiasm? There aren't many real pleasures in life: fine dining, a good bottle of wine, an inspiring book, a riveting TV series and hot sex. Not only is the last one the most enjoyable, it literally costs nothing except time.

Tamsin has arrived home unexpectedly and walked into the steamy bathroom.

With one hand I'm holding a towel around my waist, with the other I'm holding my phone. On the screen is the naked photo that Sophia has just sent.

"Forgot my handbag and now I've put my phone down somewhere and I can't find it. Can I borrow your phone to ring mine?" Tamsin asks.

She reaches out to take it from me.

My peripheral vision blurs. All I can see, in the centre of my view, in perfect focus, is my phone, angled towards me, with a naked photo of Sophia right there on the screen, and Tamsin's hand right next to it, palm up, ready to receive it. There's nothing I can say to explain this away.

Is there any other way out of this potentially disastrous situation?

I could hand the phone to Tamsin and lie. Pretend the

naked photo was as much of a shock to me as it was to her. Perhaps Sophia had accidentally sent it to me instead of her husband: "Oh my God, Tam! Look what Sophia's just sent me by mistake. She's going to be so embarrassed about this at the office on Monday (chortle)." But what about the preceding text messages that I haven't had a chance to delete yet? They would definitely incriminate me.

I could refuse to hand my phone to Tamsin. Pretend I was expecting an important call from work. On a Saturday? No. Not believable.

I could feign losing my temper: "No, you can't borrow my phone! I'm fed up of you using it every time you lose yours!" Except Tamsin never loses anything. I'm the one who's always putting things in random places and then getting the whole household to help me search for them.

I'm out of ideas.

1. Never tell anyone.

2. Delete everything (text messages, emails, internet history, search history).

3. Always begin text message exchanges with 'Hi.'

4. If anyone ever has any suspicions, deny everything.

5. Change cell phone passcodes weekly.

6. Only use cash for any affair-related purchases.

7. No gifts or mementoes.

8. No contact when we're with our families.

9. No public displays of affection.

10. Always use condoms.

11. No cosmetics (perfume, aftershave, lipstick, body lotion).

12. Always shower before going home.

13. No alcohol or drugs.

14. It's a physical affair, not emotional, so no falling in love.

15. Either of us can end the affair at any time.

*"Is that all?" Sophia asked. She'd written all fifteen rules on a pad of paper as I'd dictated them from memory.*

*"Yes. Unless you can come up with any other good ones," I replied.*

*"Do you really think they're all necessary?"*

*"I do. And, if you don't mind, I'd like to explain why," I said.*

*She smiled; that special smile which is usually reserved for humouring earnest children. "Go on then, Lee."*

*I could tell she was indulging me, but in my opinion, it was vital that we agreed on the rules right from the start.*

*"Neither of us can tell anyone; not our best friend, our brother or sister, or the random stranger in the seat next to us on a plane. It's such a juicy piece of gossip that we can't trust anyone to keep it secret. If you tell your best friend and they tell their best friend and they tell their best friend, pretty soon everyone knows."*

*"Agreed," she said.*

*I continued. "Presumably, we'll arrange our liaisons by text …"*

*"Liaisons!" she interjected, laughing. "You're so old-fashioned."*

*"Sorry," I said. "But please don't interrupt. I've got a whole speech to get through. It could take a while."*

*Sophia sniggered and mimed padlocking her mouth shut.*

*"Presumably, we'll arrange our liaisons by text message, so it's vital we delete all communication promptly, just in case anyone gets hold of our phones. Also, if we begin all of our text message conversations with just the word 'Hi' then, if anybody sees them, at least they're innocuous and explainable. If the other person's in a position to continue the conversation safely, they can do so, but if it's not a good time, just don't reply."*

*"Agreed." She was still smiling.*

*"Next one. If anyone ever suspects anything untoward is going on between us: deny, deny, deny. The whole point of these rules is to make sure there's no evidence to incriminate us, so if we stick to a firm denial of any accusations, nobody can prove anything."*

*"Got it, boss." She was cheeky, and I liked it.*

*"This one might be a bit over the top, but I reckon we should change the passcode on our phones on a weekly basis; just in case we've forgotten to delete everything. I'd hate it if Tamsin or one of the kids picked up my phone, typed in my date of birth and saw a dodgy message from you."*

*"It's not really your date of birth, is it?" Sophia laughed.*

*"Possibly." It was Tamsin's, actually. "Do you think every week is too often?" I asked.*

*"Definitely. How about once a month?"*

*"Okay," I said. "I can be flexible. You haven't changed your mind about this have you?"*

*"Actually, I am starting to have second thoughts."*

*"Really?"*

*"No." She winked. "Keep going."*

Tamsin works extremely hard. Even though it's only three days a week, being a primary school teacher is an intense job. She puts so much time and effort into planning, marking and admin that she's often exhausted by the time she gets home. I try to help out by doing some of the housework. It's my job to do the vacuuming, empty the rubbish bins, make the packed lunches for school, load the dishwasher and mow the lawn. I'm useless at DIY, but my dad is very handy, and he often carries out odd jobs for us. Tamsin does everything else, and I realise it's a huge amount, but there are some things I simply can't help with, due to issues of efficiency. For example, when I iron the kids' school clothes, they get rejected and Tamsin has to do them all over again.

My ineptitude around the house adds to Tamsin's tiredness and frustration. I know I ought to do more, and I would if I could, but my motivation for this is questionable. I sometimes feel guilty for doing chores because of my hidden agenda. I'm always secretly hoping that I might get sex in return. I realise I've got this backwards. If there's a large amount of housework to be done, I've got no chance of getting lucky. But if the house is immaculate, and all the jobs are completed, I'm in with a chance. A slim one, but a chance nevertheless.

Everything stops.

Time is standing still.

I can see Tamsin, motionless, her hand out expectantly.

I can see Sophia's naked body on the screen of my phone.

I can hear my heart thumping noisily and rapidly in my chest.

And ... Action!

I start to hand the phone over to Tamsin, but my fingers are still wet from the shower. The phone slips out of my grasp and begins to fall towards the floor. I try to grab it, but only manage to fumble it further away from me and nearer to the toilet bowl. One last attempted catch is unsuccessful and, with a splash, my £600 phone plops into the toilet.

*"We mustn't use cash for any affair-related purchases and we can't buy each other any presents at all. There are a couple of reasons for this. It'll save us having to explain where the presents came from and it'll avoid suspicious items on our credit card bills."*

*"What sort of purchases?" Sophia said.*

*"Hotel bookings, condoms, whipped cream, tinned pineapple rings, lubricants, handcuffs ..."*

*"Whoa there, tiger!" she interrupted. "What kind of girl do you think I am?"*

*"Kinky?" I suggested, hopefully.*

*"Yeah, that's about right," she nodded and gave me a lascivious smile.*

*"Do you agree?" I said.*

*"Hmm. Are you saying I* shouldn't *buy you a World's-Greatest-Lover award for Valentine's Day with my credit card from the www.havinganaffair.com website using my home computer, as that might be a bit suspicious?"*

*"Now you're getting it," I said.*

What is it with my obsession with sex? Some people might say I should just count my blessings and be content with what I've got: a near-perfect marriage with regular rumpy-pumpy which happens to be not quite as often as I'd like, and lacks a bit of enthusiasm and variety. I'm an incredibly lucky guy. I should just suck it up and be grateful. Is there something wrong with me? Is my brain wired incorrectly? Am I suffering from a chemical imbalance? What's so hard about being faithful to the woman you love? I have no idea. I wish it was otherwise, because I don't like myself anymore.

"Lee!" Tamsin squeals as we stare at my phone sinking slowly to the bottom of the toilet bowl.

It's face-down. There's a small stream of bubbles coming out of the microphone-end.

"You're such a klutz!" she chuckles, shaking her head in disbelief. "Well, *I'm* not fishing it out."

I'm in no hurry. It's essential that when I retrieve my sodden phone, the screen is blank.

*"No contact when we're with our families. That's an obvious one, isn't it? It pretty much means we can only communicate with each other during work hours."*

*"What about weekends when Joe's out playing golf all day?" Sophia asked.*

*"Well, the chances are I'll be with at least one member of my family, so it's probably best if we just stick to weekdays and work hours. Don't you agree?"*

*"If you say so, Lee." Her tone of voice informed me that she was beginning to get rather bored with this process.*

*"Also, no public displays of affection," I continued. "We have to stop hugging at work. If somebody saw us, it'd look highly suspicious."*

*"What if I start hugging all my colleagues; not just you? For the sake of consistency. Once I've developed a reputation as the girl who hugs everyone, nobody would think twice about seeing me hugging you."*

*"Yes, that could work too," I replied, deadpan, stroking my imaginary beard thoughtfully. "Of course, I'd have to do the same, but I'm not convinced our colleagues would welcome my hugs as much as yours."*

*"You're probably right. Okay, no PDA. I've got it." Sophia tried, but failed, to hide her disappointment.*

*"Anyway," I said. "I'm hoping we can make up for it with some serious naked, sweaty affection when we're alone together."*

*"Me too!" Sophia replied, eagerly. "When can we start? I'm horny already."*

*"Hold your horses," I said. "I'm barely halfway through my list."*

I used to consider myself to be a good person. I'd never murdered anyone. I'd never committed rape or sexual assault. I'd been faithful to my wife. I'd tried to be kind to people and animals. I'd given money to a few charities. I'd stayed on the right side of the Ten Commandments, apart from a bit of coveting. Yes, I've broken the law a few times: underage drinking, driving at 80mph on the motorway, not being totally honest with HM Revenue & Customs. But on the whole, I'd always tried to do the right thing.

The moment I committed adultery, I ceased to be a good person.

I'm an atheist. I don't consider committing adultery to be a sin, but I do believe it's morally wrong, and I wish I hadn't done it.

It's a bit like losing your virginity. Once you've done it once, your identity has changed from one binary state to another. From virgin to non-virgin. From a good person to an adulterer. You can't be in both of these states of existence, and you can't be somewhere in between. It's one or the other.

I've had many conversations with Jake about this. Jake's parents are Jewish. According to the Bible, the Talmud and Rabbinic law, a Jew is anyone with a Jewish mother, but Jake describes himself as a non-practising Jew and an atheist to boot, but he grew up in a household in which there were regular debates about ethical and moral issues, so if ever I require moral guidance, he's the man I turn to.

Jake and I are in agreement that adultery is just plain

wrong, but I've never shared with him that a little voice in the back of my head keeps whispering, "What's the harm if nobody gets hurt?"

I fetch some tongs from the kitchen and use them to rescue my phone from the bottom of the toilet bowl, then I rinse it thoroughly under the tap and wash my hands. As expected, and hoped for, the screen is black and unresponsive.

"Should I try to turn it on?" I ask Tamsin.

I'm not worried anymore. If I can switch it on, it will boot up to the home screen, not the dreaded photo, but I suspect it won't switch on at all. However, to be on the safe side, I'd rather not have it come back to life while Tamsin is with me, as I've still got some deleting to do.

"Aren't you supposed to leave it in a bag of uncooked rice to dry out?" she said.

"Yes. Good idea. I'll do that."

I go back to the kitchen in search of rice.

"I've found your phone," I shout up the stairs.

"Where was it?"

"In your handbag."

"Oh yeah," Tamsin says.

This is getting ridiculous. Not only did my marriage nearly come to an ignominious end, but I'm also probably £600 worse off. If I've got any sense, I should end my affair at the earliest opportunity. Unfortunately, the little sense that I do have is currently being overruled by my penis.

It's only now that I consider what must be happening from Sophia's point of view. She sent me a lovely naked photo, but received no reply. Why not? Didn't I like the photo? Was it so shocking it caused me to have a heart attack and collapse unconscious? Why haven't I responded?

In my imagination, Sophia is lying in bed, naked. Always naked. She's staring expectantly at her phone screen, hoping for a compliment about how sexy she looks in the photo, or possibly a suggestion about what I'd like to do to her the next time we're alone together, or maybe a reciprocal naked photo of me. I picture her getting increasingly anxious as a reply doesn't arrive. She starts to worry about me. Am I incapacitated? Dead? She sends me text messages, but I don't reply. She tries to phone me, but I don't answer. She dials 999 and requests an ambulance and the police to go to my address. She gets into her car, still naked, and drives to my house to make sure I'm all right ...

# CHAPTER FIVE

*The Map*

As soon as Tamsin leaves the house again, I try to contact Sophia. I know she'll be wondering why I haven't responded to the naughty photo she sent me. My phone is out of action, but I could use our land line to call and reassure her that all is well. I pick up the extension in our bedroom and then realise that I shouldn't be using our home phone as Sophia's number will appear on our next itemised phone bill. A public call box should be safe though. Unfortunately, there aren't any of these near our house, so I get dressed, drive into town and park near the post office. There are two telephone kiosks located outside and neither of them is in use, unsurprisingly as nobody uses public phones these days. I keep a pot of small change in my car, primarily for buying parking tickets, and I grab a handful of coins from within it to pay for my call. I walk to the booth, pick up the phone and listen for the dialling tone. Then I feed in a few coins and stop, feeling stupid. It's just occurred to me that I haven't got a clue what Sophia's phone number is. I reach into my pocket for my cell phone so I can look up her number in my contacts list. What am I doing? I haven't got my phone. It's in a bag of rice in the airing cupboard at home. How can I get in touch with Sophia? Send an email? That requires a computer, and even if I had access to one, I only know Sophia's work email address, but she doesn't log-on to that account at weekends. How can I contact her now? Post her a letter? Carrier pigeon? Smoke signals? Go round to her house?

I realise that I've got no immediate way of getting in touch with Sophia and resolve to come up with a plan to avoid this happening in future, but in the meantime, I'm out of ideas and getting increasingly anxious.

I climb back into my car and start the engine. As I'm driving home, it slowly dawns on me that I'm completely overreacting. Nothing has happened. Nobody knows anything. The only issue is that Sophia must be wondering why I'm suddenly incommunicado. However, as long as she does nothing and I do nothing, we're still in the clear.

"We have to use condoms every time we have sex."

"But I'm on the pill," Sophia said.

"It's still best if we use condoms as well. You cannot get pregnant! My sperm are determined little blighters, desperate to pass on as much of my top quality DNA as possible to the next generation, so we can't be too careful. Two types of contraception should be enough. The pill is 99 percent effective and condoms are 98 percent effective so if we use both that's 197 percent effectiveness. There's no way you can get pregnant with those odds."

"Er ... I'm not sure it works quite like that, Lee."

"I know, but you get my point. It's better to be safe than sorry."

"Fine." Sophia said, with a sigh.

"Also, condoms are highly effective against HIV, chlamydia, gonorrhoea and many other STIs."

"I can see you've been doing your research, Lee, but I haven't got any of those diseases and I assume you haven't either."

"I don't think so, but we don't know for certain that Tamsin isn't a secret, part-time, high-class hooker, who's given me symp-

*tomless chlamydia. Or Joe might actually be a closet homosexual intravenous drug user – who shares needles – and has passed on HIV to you."*

*She laughed. "I'm pretty sure you're wrong, but I'm happy to err on the side of caution, if that's what you want."*

*"It is," I said.*

*"Okay. Who's going to buy them and where will we keep them?"*

When Tamsin and I first got together at university, we used condoms. She switched to the contraceptive pill shortly after we got engaged and remained on it until we decided to have kids. Two or three months after she came off the pill, Tamsin fell pregnant with Charlie, so I know my swimmers are pretty potent. We switched back to condoms in between kids until we started trying for our second child, and again within a matter of weeks Tamsin was pregnant with John. We agreed that we now had a perfect family – and two children was plenty – so after some discussion, Tamsin had a coil fitted. That discussion got pretty heated and led to our first real row. She wanted me to have a vasectomy, and I was adamant that nobody was going anywhere near my reproductive organs with anything sharp. I felt at the time that I had a genuine, well-reasoned argument for not having a vasectomy, but Tamsin disagreed. The main points of my rationale were the following:

THEY SLICE INTO YOUR BALLS!!!

At work on Monday morning, I go into Sophia's office first thing and apologise.

"I'm so sorry, Soph. I couldn't reply to your message on Saturday because I dropped my phone down the loo."

"What?" she says, bemused.

"It's a long story. I hope you didn't think I was ignoring you."

"No. Not at all. I just assumed you couldn't reply for some reason."

"So you're not cross with me?" I say.

"That depends." She lowers her voice. "Did you like the photo?"

"God, yes! You're so sexy."

"Then you're forgiven," she says, smiling warmly.

*"I'm on the pill, so Joe and I don't use condoms. I don't mind buying some, but it'd be extremely suspicious if he discovered I had them."*

*Sophia was correct of course.*

*"I hadn't even thought about how to buy condoms," I said. "We'd have to get them with cash, but we obviously can't use cash for online purchases, so one of us will have to buy them from an actual shop, and risk being recognised. Every time I go into the local pharmacy, I see someone I know, so a distant one would be better."*

*"I could nip up to Scotland with our big trailer and get a whole month's supply?" Sophia said and gave me a wicked smile.*

*"How about I buy some the next time I visit my mum?" I said. "She lives miles away. No one will recognise me there. Then I'll store them in a locked draw in my desk for whenever we need them."*

*"Good plan," she said. "Do you need to borrow the trailer?"*

*"Not this time. I think a couple of crates full should be enough for now. If it turns out you're completely insatiable, we can always buy more next time."*

"Where was that restaurant we went to with your mum and Greg?" Tamsin asks me out of the blue.

I'm relaxing on the sofa in the conservatory and enjoying a good book. The weather has warmed up considerably, and it's a pleasant evening. All is good with the world.

"No idea. Wasn't it about halfway between their house and ours?" I say.

"Pass me your phone. I'll have a look."

Here we go again. A squirt of adrenaline sets my heart beating faster and I can sense my anxiety levels climbing. I try to relax and breathe normally.

Surely I'm safe.

After three days in a bag of rice in the airing cupboard, to my great surprise, my phone switched on as normal as soon as I charged it and pressed the power button. In fact, it's been fine ever since, except the speaker now sounds a bit crackly.

I'm confident that there's nothing incriminating for Tamsin to discover on my phone. I've long since deleted the naked photo and the accompanying messages. Before leaving work this afternoon, as has become my habit, I removed all traces of any messages or emails from Sophia, and I scrubbed the search history. I know Sophia won't try to contact me now, not while I'm at home with my family, but I can't help feeling a touch of trepidation as I hand the phone over to Tamsin.

She starts tapping away on the screen and I pretend to be nonchalantly reading my book, although I'm merely scanning the same paragraph over and over again.

I assume that she's trying to locate the restaurant on the internet somehow, but I'm not sure why she's using my phone and not her own.

"Wasn't it around your birthday?" she asks.

"I honestly can't remember, Tam." I frown, confused. How is the date of the visit going to help her find a restaurant on the internet?

"Here it is. Told you. Two days after your birthday," she says.

I'm really confused.

"Well done. How did you find it?"

"You've got Location Services enabled on your phone.

I just looked at the map to see where you'd been on the days around your birthday, and there it was."

I'm not one for using swear words, I've never seen the point, although I'm reliably informed that a good Anglo-Saxon expletive can actually reduce the pain after hitting your thumb with a hammer, or the equivalent. I say nothing out loud, but I'm certainly thinking a few choice ones.

"The map shows where I've been?" I say, a noticeable tremor in my voice.

"Well, it actually shows where your phone has been, but, assuming you have it with you, it plots your movements. It even identifies the restaurants and shops you've visited. I find it all a bit Big Brother, so I've switched it off on my phone," Tamsin says, smugly.

Why did I not discover this in all my research? While I was assuming I was being really careful, my phone had betrayed me by keeping a record of all my movements, including my visits to Sophia's house.

"Well, I never knew that. Can I have a look?"

I reach for my phone.

"I'll show you."

Tamsin sits down next to me on the sofa, still holding my phone, and points at the screen.

*"Next rule," I said. "No cosmetics when we're together. That includes perfume, aftershave, lipstick, body lotion or anything else that'll leave a trace or an odour. It wouldn't be good if I went home with lipstick on my collar, or you walked around smelling of my aftershave. To be doubly sure, it's also essential that both of us have a shower before going home."*

*"Together?" Sophia said, hopefully, and winked at me.*

*"I like the way your mind works," I said, smiling.*

*"I always get home hours before Joe, so I can shower as soon as I get back from work."*

*"Sounds good. There's often someone in my house when I get home, but I guess I could shower at the gym if necessary," I said.*

*"Sorted. What's this rule about alcohol and drugs though?" Sophia asked.*

*"Well, I don't know about you, Soph, but after a few drinks, I tend to lose my inhibitions, and sometimes I say and do all sorts of inappropriate things. I'm even more erratic when I'm high on cocaine and heroin. I just think it'd be wiser if we remain in control of all our faculties when we're taking risks."*

*For a second, I thought she'd taken me seriously.*

*"But it's my lifelong dream to have somebody snort cocaine off my buttocks," Sophia said, pouting.*

*"Mine too. But we're going to have to make some sacrifices if this is going to work."*

◆ ◆ ◆

Why now?

I've been happily married for sixteen years. Has something changed recently in my relationship with Tamsin? Not really. The passion has been gradually waning for years, but it's been a slow process. Has it suddenly crossed some sort of threshold? Not that I'm aware of. I don't recall waking up one morning and thinking: 'The tipping point has now been reached; I'm no longer getting enough sex in my marriage, so it's time to have an affair.'

Is it related to my age? Some sort of midlife crisis?

I've seen evidence suggesting that men are more likely to have an affair when their age ends with the number nine, particularly thirty-nine and forty-nine, but I'm forty-five. I'm nowhere near the danger years, but I guess I'm around the mean age, although not the mode. Funny things averages.

I did some research into the signs that a man is having a midlife crisis. The physical symptoms can be:

Depression. No.

Lethargy. No.

Erectile dysfunction. No, thank God!

Loss of sex drive. Possibly, until I began my affair, and then: Hell, no!

Fatigue. No.

Irritability. No.

The non-physical signs include:

Buying a sports car. No.

Changing your personal appearance. No.

Replacing old friends with younger ones. No.

A desire to get into shape. No more than usual.

Making impetuous decisions. No.

Having an affair. Yes.

On balance, I think it unlikely that I'm having a midlife crisis, but I really would like to find an explanation for my recent infidelity. Just so I can have an excuse for my unforgivable be-haviour.

"This is our house here." Tamsin is holding my phone and pointing at the map on the screen. "On this particular day, you can see that you drove into town at about ten-thirty. It looks like you parked in the main car park, then went to the bank on foot, and then to the post office."

"How can it tell if I'm driving or walking?" I say.

"No idea, but it's very clever. It can also tell if you're jog-ging, cycling, flying, on a train, a boat ... Like I said: Big Brother is watching you! After the post office, you walked back to the car and came home. At 18:45 we drove to the restaurant, where we stayed until 22:34, and then we drove back to our house. It's all on here. There's a different map showing your movements on each day of the year."

I swallow.

"Most of your weekdays look pretty boring," Tamsin says, scanning through the maps. "You just drive to the office and drive home again. Sometimes you go to the gym." She pauses. "Here's a work day when you went somewhere at lunchtime. It looks as if you drove to the middle of a housing estate in town and stayed there for just under an hour. I'll zoom in." She taps my phone twice and then shows me the screen.

I feel light-headed as nausea overwhelms me.

I know where I went.

That's Sophia's house.

*"Okay, here's the penultimate rule, and this one is extremely important. We both have to agree that this is just a physical affair. We're doing it for the sex and that's all. There can be no falling in love. If I start to develop emotional feelings towards you, I have to tell you so, and we end it. The same for you. This is going to be the perfect affair, where nobody gets hurt. Not Tamsin, not Joe, not you, not me."*

*Sophia was trying not to laugh. "You think I'm going to fall in love with you?"*

*"Hey! I'm a really lovable guy once you get to know me."*

*"Don't flatter yourself, Lee. I reckon I'll be able to control my feelings. It's you I'm worried about." There was that cheeky smile again.*

*"Well, that leads nicely to the last item," I said. "Either of us can end the affair at any time, with no recriminations. If we believe it's getting too serious. If we think our spouse is suspicious. If we've simply had enough. We can just call it to a halt, and that's it. All over. Finito."*

Names for people like me are few and far between. In fact, I can only think of one:

Adulterer.

That word has a precise meaning, and I satisfy the definition. I'm a person who has had voluntary sexual intercourse with someone who is not my legal partner.

There are plenty of words to describe men who have casual affairs: philanderer, womaniser, Casanova, Don Juan, cad, cheater, Lothario, ladies' man, fornicator, two-timer, playboy, promiscuous, immoral, unfaithful, someone who plays around, fools around, sleeps around and many more. Interestingly, some of these epithets are almost complimentary.

The words to describe unfaithful women, however, are much more numerous and unpleasant: slut, whore, harlot, strumpet, tart, trollop, tramp, hussy, floozie, scrubber, slattern, slag, skank, Jezebel, seductress, temptress, man-eater, loose woman, scarlet woman, woman of ill repute and so on. None of these is complimentary.

In fact, many words for a prostitute are often used to describe a woman who's been unfaithful to her husband.

I can't think of another word that specifically describes a married man who's had sex with a woman who isn't his wife.

Hi. My name is Lee, and I'm an adulterer.

"There aren't any pubs or shops in that neighbourhood," Tamsin says. "It's just residential housing. What were you doing there?"

"I can't remember to be honest, Tam. It was weeks ago."

I'm stalling for time while I frantically try to think of a reason why I'd spend my lunch hour in somebody's house. On the spot, I come up with three possibilities of varying degree of implausibility, and I sound them out in my head:

I was helping someone move heavy furniture.
"Who?"

A colleague needed some important documents for a meeting so I gave him a lift home.
"Who?"

Dave was showing me his practical joke collection.
"Really? Dave again?"

If I *have* to name someone from work, I'm setting myself up for potential problems at the next office party.

"Hello, Dave."
"Hi, Lee's hot wife. It's lovely to see you again. You look particularly gorgeous tonight."
"We'll get to that in a minute. À propos of nothing, Dave, what's your address?"
"Erm, I can't remember. Let me just check with Lee."
"Just as I thought. Now, what were you saying about how gorgeous I look?" She takes him by the hand and leads him upstairs for a shag.

I try out a few other specious excuses internally:

I really like the herbaceous borders on that street, so sometimes I just drive there to eat my lunch and think about you, my love.
"That's bollocks!"

I was collecting something I'd bought in an online auction?
"What was it?"
"I can't tell you. It's a surprise."

I was shagging Sophia from the office.

"I want a divorce."

I'm out of time. Tamsin is looking at me, expecting a reply. I go with the least bad option.

"I was collecting something I'd bought in an online auction?" I say.

"I see."

She hands me back my phone, gets to her feet and makes to exit the conservatory.

"Aren't you going to ask me what it was?"

What am I doing? I'm an idiot. I was free and clear.

"What was it?"

"I can't tell you. It's a surprise."

"A surprise for when? You've missed my birthday, our anniversary and Valentine's Day."

"Wait and see."

"Ooh, exciting! I love surprises," Tamsin says as she walks away.

Within five minutes I've deleted my map history and disabled Location Services forever.

# CHAPTER SIX

*The Hotel*

T amsin is away for the weekend. She's visiting Nilofer, one of our friends from university. Sophia's husband, Joe, has headed up north for a couple of days at a golf resort. Thereby, a perfect opportunity has presented itself for Sophia and me to spend some quality time together, in the absence of our respective spouses.

Sophia has booked herself into a Spa hotel, twenty miles away from our home town, for a weekend of pampering.

I'm actually in Tamsin's good books for a change after buying her an antique piano stool from an online auction. I gave it to her to celebrate the twentieth anniversary of the first time I heard her play the piano. I realise this sounds a bit lame, and the date was just a rough guess, but it seems as if she believes me, and she's delighted with both the gift and the romantic gesture.

Normal order has been resumed, and the icing on the cake is that Sophia and I are planning to rendezvous in her hotel this weekend for a serious shagfest.

I'm supposed to be keeping an eye on the kids, but they're in and out of the house all the time, visiting friends and putting off doing their homework. They're quite happy to fend for themselves for a few hours and I have no doubt they won't even notice my absence.

*"If we're actually going to do this, Soph, those are the rules. All fif-teen of them are written there on your notepad. I need you to read them carefully, memorise them thoroughly, and then eat that piece of paper they're written on." Somehow I maintained a straight face.*

*"I'll tell you what, Lee; you'd better be bloody good in the sack!"*

*"Prepare to have your world rocked." I said as I stood up. "I've got to get back to work. How about tomorrow lunchtime we discuss how we're actually going to do this? The practicalities. Where should we meet? When? How often?"*

*"I've got a few ideas already," she said.*

*"Excellent. Now eat the paper and we'll talk again tomor-row."*

Private investigators claim that 90 percent of their surveil-lance cases centre around infidelity. It's hard to find exact figures about adultery because all the surveys seem to come back with slightly different results, depending on the country, the design of the questionnaire and the type of people asked.

From my meta-analysis, it appears that roughly 43 per-cent of males and 22 percent of females have been unfaithful to their spouse, by cheating with at least one person.

In a third of all marriages, one or more partner has com-mitted adultery.

So, it appears that I'm not alone. In fact, if these figures are true, there are several million male adulterers just in my country alone, and nearly a billion in the world.

Alarmingly, roughly half of the male adulterers have had affairs with five or more people, so there's a fifty-fifty chance that I'm going to do this again, several times.

These figures don't make me feel any better. I know I'm a scumbag. Being just one scumbag out of several million is not a comfort.

◆ ◆ ◆

"Hi."

It's a text message from Sophia.

"Hi, sexy. What are you up to?" I reply.

"Just had a full body massage. Now relaxing by the indoor pool. Feeling tranquil, carefree and horny. I want you now! When are you coming?!"

"John's about to go out. As soon as he leaves, I'll be on my way. X"

"Hurry up or I'll start without you! The massage therapist already offered me a happy ending and I'm tempted!!!"

"Did she?!!"

"He!!! Sven. Handsome Swedish hunk. So good with his hands!!!"

"Really?"

"Just kidding. Sadly!"

This message is followed thirty seconds later by, "It was actually a beautiful busty Brazilian babe called Isabella. She couldn't stop touching me!!!"

"Kidding again?" I ask.

"Maybe!"

"Maybe not!!!"

I hear the front door slam.

"John has just left. On my way! Where will you be?"

"Either by the pool or in my room getting warmed up with Sven!"

"Or Isabella!!"

"Or both!!!"

◆ ◆ ◆

*The following lunchtime, back in Sophia's office, she had a sugges-*

*tion to make.*

"*Lee, I think we should meet at my house. Joe is…*"

"*No way!*" *I interrupted.* "*That's far too risky.*"

"*Listen. Just hear me out. For his job as a pharmaceutical sales rep, Joe travels far and wide, selling … whatever it is he sells. He never comes home during the day. We could use the spare room. It's perfect. Definitely safer than a hotel or the back seat of your car.*"

"*He never comes home?*" *I said, not convinced.*

"*No. His sales region is miles away. He leaves before six-thirty every day, and he's never home before seven o'clock in the evening.*"

"*Well that sounds promising,*" *I said.* "*But what if I'm spotted entering or leaving your house by one of the neighbours?*"

"*You can come in the back entrance. That's not a euphemism by the way.*" *Sophia paused and jiggled her eyebrows suggestively.* "*We've got tall hedges, and the back gate isn't overlooked by any houses nearby, so nobody would be able to see you.*"

"*Where would I park though? I don't want my car to be recognised outside your house.*"

"*Just leave it a couple of streets away and walk from there. Vary the parking spot each time, to be on the safe side.*"

"*Soph, are you sure it's one hundred percent safe?*" *I asked.*

"*Absolutely. And the best thing is, our spare room has a four-poster bed. It's going to be perfect for tying you up.*"

*I swallowed.*

If so many people are having affairs, why do they do it? I've got a lot of questions about this:

What reasons or excuses do adulterers use to explain their infidelity?

How do they justify their extraordinary behaviour?

Why do they take such emotional and practical risks?

Can they simply not help themselves?

Are they merely following their animal instincts?

Do they not have free-will?

Are they pre-programmed to be unfaithful?

Is there a flaw in some people's DNA which makes them more likely to cheat on their partner? An adultery gene?

My DNA results eventually came back, and I was disappointed to learn that I'm not very interesting at all. 84 percent of my ancestors are from England and Wales, 9 percent are from Ireland and Scotland, and the rest are probably Germanic. In other words: I'm British.

I wanted to be told:

Dear Mr Bolton

Good news! We've discovered you have the adultery gene; therefore you have a strong propensity towards being unfaithful to your wife. Please don't worry if you commit adultery. It's in your genes, so you simply can't help it. Stop beating yourself up.

Yours faithfully (Oh, the irony!)

Science

I arrive at the hotel, get changed and head for the indoor swimming pool. I'm wearing my trunks, a towelling bathrobe and my flip-flops. I spot Sophia reclining next to the pool, reading a magazine and looking ravishing in a sky blue bikini. Pouring myself a glass of water, I take the opportunity to scan the room for anyone familiar. There's nobody here I recognise, which is just as well because Sophia is beckoning me over in a not very subtle way.

I join her and sit on the reclining chair adjacent to hers.

"Don't get comfortable," she says. "I've got big plans for you." She flashes me a lascivious smile and licks her lips.

"Excellent. Shall we have a quick swim first?" I ask, gesturing towards the water.

"You can if you like, but be quick. I'm gagging for it!"

"Don't you like swimming?" I say.

"To be honest, I don't know how to swim." She shrugs. "I never learnt."

"The water's not very deep this end." I point to my left.

"Actually, Lee, I'm very wet already, if you know what I mean."

I do.

I rearrange my robe.

"Where's your room?"

*And so it began.*

*The day finally arrived when I became an adulterer.*

*We'd planned, a week in advance, that on the following Friday lunchtime, we'd meet at Sophia's house and our affair would commence. It was a fairly common practice at work for the staff go to one of the local pubs for lunch on Fridays, so it wouldn't be too suspicious if we were seen leaving the building, as long as we weren't spotted together.*

*That week was one of the longest of my life. The anticipation was overwhelming. I barely slept, and when I did drop off, I had the most bizarre erotic dreams, and often woke up feeling exhausted and anxious.*

*My waking hours were spent either looking forward to some uninhibited sex, the like of which I'd rarely experienced, or wondering why I was putting myself into such a stressful situation. Many times, in the wee small hours, I'd decided that I was just going to call the whole thing off, but when morning came, and I saw Sophia at work, looking all shaggable, I'd changed my mind back again.*

At what specific point does adultery actually happen? Is it the moment you make the decision that you're going to have sex with someone who isn't your spouse? Is it the split second your penis enters their vagina? Or does oral sex count as adultery? What about phone sex with someone on the other side of the world? What about flirting?

In one survey, when asked if they considered flirting to be infidelity, 33 percent of men and 43 percent of women said yes. I definitely say no. Surely flirting is just a bit of adult banter. It doesn't mean anything dubious on its own. In fact, I enjoy it when Tamsin flirts with other men. It makes her feel desirable and that makes her horny and that makes it possible that she might initiate sex, provided she's had sufficient alcohol.

Is it cheating to send flirty text messages? 59 percent of men and 76 percent of women said yes. Utter tosh! What's the matter with these people? There must be some serious prudes out there who do nothing all day but take part in sex surveys to offset the misery of their failed relationships.

Do online relationships count as infidelity? 68 percent of men and 87 percent of women said yes. Again, I strongly disagree.

It's apparent from my research that women have a significantly lower threshold than men for what infidelity entails. I'm not sure where the cut-off is for Tamsin. Perhaps I should ask her. In my head, the conversation doesn't go well. I try out a few opening gambits:

"So, Tam, in your opinion, what constitutes infidelity?"

"Why are you asking? You're having an affair aren't you?"

She slaps my face and knees me in the testicles.

"Well, that's ridiculous," I chuckle, pretending to read an article on my phone. "It says here, 43 percent of women think flirting is infidelity."

"Have you loaded the dishwasher?"

"Yes, darling." She's not interested. "How can flirting be infidelity?" I persist, shaking my head and talking to myself.

"Well it depends, doesn't it, Lee? If you're flirting with someone you've fallen in love with, *that* would be infidelity; but a bit of shared sexual innuendo with a handsome guy you've just met at a party is fairly harmless. It's all about context."

"So, if I say, 'Your legs look amazing in that dress,' to a stranger at a party, then it's harmless flirting, but if I say it to someone I have romantic feelings for, it's infidelity?"

"No," she sighs, exasperated. "If you say *that* to a stranger, you're a sex pest."

She knees me in the testicles.

"A guy at work reckons flirty text messages count as infidelity. What do you think, Tam?"

"Dishwasher?"

"Done."

"Give me an example."

"Erm, what about, 'I had a dream about you last night!'"

"How many exclamation marks?"

"One."

"Well, that's not too bad, but you just know the follow up text message is going to be really pervy."

"Three exclamation marks?"

"That's already too pervy."

"How about 'Let's have drinks after work'?"

"That's fine. Actually, it's a bit too bland. It could genuinely mean just drinks."

"Fancy a shag?"

"If you send that message to anyone who's not your spouse, then that's definitely infidelity and you deserve this."

She knees me in the testicles.

"No. I was asking *you* if you fancy a shag," I gasp.

"Erm. Yeah, all right." She nods enthusiastically.

"I can't now. My balls…"
I collapse in agony.

"Lee, what were you doing at a Spa hotel on Saturday night?"
Alarm bells ring.
"Hmm?"
Luckily, my mouth is full of food, so if I chew slowly, I've got some thinking time.
The four of us are eating dinner around the dining room table, and Tamsin has caught me completely by surprise.
I hold up one finger, palm towards her, and continue to chew, using the universally acknowledged sign for: I have a perfectly valid reason for being at a hotel last Saturday evening, when I was actually supposed to be at home looking after the kids, and I'll give you the aforementioned reason just as soon as I've finished chewing this particularly gristly piece of beef.
I really need more information before I can answer the question.
I swallow.
"Pardon?"
"A teaching assistant from school saw you leaving a hotel at about ten o'clock last Saturday night."
That helps a bit. I try out some explanations in my head:

My muscles have been really tight since I went to the gym, so I thought I'd get a massage.
"Twenty miles away, at ten o'clock at night?"

I felt like getting my chest waxed.
"But it's still hairy …"

I wasn't there. It must be a case of mistaken identity.
"She recognised you and your car."

Which teaching assistant?

"Does it matter?"

I was buying you a surprise pampering weekend.

"Another surprise? Why didn't you book it online or phone them?"

Tick Tock.

I panic and break rule one.

"Jake was staying there for a conference and he invited me to join him for a drink."

I load my fork with a large portion of chewy looking beef.

"You were with Jake last Saturday?" From the tone of Tamsin's voice, I get the impression she doesn't believe me.

"Yeah, I thought it would be nice to catch up."

I fill my mouth with food.

"Why didn't you tell me you'd seen him?"

I'm chewing again.

I shrug.

"You're really enjoying this meal, aren't you? I'll have to cook it more often," Tamsin says.

I'm still chewing.

I nod.

I chew.

I swallow.

"Sorry, Tam. It completely slipped my mind. Jake says 'hi' by the way."

*We were exceptionally careful the first time.*

*We'd parked our cars in different car parks that morning, left the office five minutes apart, and driven to Sophia's house using different routes. She parked on her drive, while I parked two streets away and walked to Sophia's back gate. She was right; that method of access wasn't overlooked by any of the neighbouring houses. I checked to make sure that her upstairs bathroom light was on, which was the sign I'd insisted upon to confirm that everything was fine. My heart was beating like a bass drum in a disco song as I let myself in through the gate, crossed the back garden and entered the house through the unlocked door.*

*And there she was.*

*For a while, we simply gazed at each other.*

*"There's still time to change your mind," I said. "Up to this point, we haven't done anything wrong except kiss. We haven't committed adultery. We aren't having an affair. If I turn around now and leave, we're still the good, faithful people we've always been. But if I stay ..."*

*Sophia moved very close to me, pressed her lips against mine to stop me speaking, wrapped her arms around my neck, and held me tight while we kissed. Then she stood back, took hold of my hand and, without saying another word, led me up the stairs.*

I'm not going to lie. It was everything I'd dreamed it would be. Hot, sweaty, passionate sex with plenty of variety and bucket-loads of enthusiasm. I could no longer say that I wasn't sexually satisfied. My only regret at the time was that I was fulfilling my desires with Sophia and not with Tamsin.

According to research, when trying to justify their affairs, 23 percent of men blamed lack of sexual satisfaction, 14 percent said they wanted more attention, and another 14 percent wanted to experience a new sensation. Well, I'd certainly assuaged those top three issues.

It's different for women. 28 percent cited a lack of emotional satisfaction and 22 percent committed adultery purely for revenge. Now that's a scary statistic.

Other reasons both genders give for their infidelity include emotional validation, feeling unappreciated, loneliness, communication barriers, growing apart, their partner letting themselves go, and simply because it was just easy to do. I don't believe any of these reasons apply to me. Tamsin is a wonderful, supportive, communicative wife who has succeeded in staying in great physical shape. I'm the one who has the problem.

"Jake, it's Lee. Can you talk?"

"Just a minute, mate. I'll find a quieter room."

I've locked myself in the bathroom, while Tamsin and John clear away the dirty plates and load the dishwasher.

I really don't know how this is going to go. Jake and Tamsin have been friends since before I met either of them. I'm about to ask Jake to lie to Tamsin in order to save my marriage. Where does his allegiance lie?

"That's better. What can I do for you?" he says.

"Jake, I've done something really stupid."

I've never said it out loud before and the words are sticking in my throat. "I've ... been having an affair with someone from work."

"Oh my God! Why would you do that to Tamsin?" He sounds shocked and disappointed in me.

"Because I'm an idiot." I feel wretched.

"Does she know?" he says.

"No. That's why I'm ringing. I just told her that I met you for a drink at a hotel last Saturday night. I was hoping you'd back me up."

There's a long pause.

A very long pause.

I can hear Jake breathing; then the sound of a discreet beep.

"I've got another call coming in, Lee. It's Tamsin. I've got to take this."

Jake hangs up on me.

# CHAPTER SEVEN

## *The Condom*

I t's Friday evening. Neither Tamsin nor Jake have mentioned the hotel incident two weeks ago, so I'm starting to relax. My assumption is that Jake has backed me up and lied on my behalf. He's a good friend, to me if not to Tamsin, and I'm very grateful, although it hasn't passed me by that the man who had been my moral compass, I'm now utilising as a firewall to conceal my adultery.

Tamsin has just arrived home and gone upstairs to our bedroom to change out of her smart work-clothes into something more comfortable.

Tamsin always looks glamorous and gorgeous when she goes out. She makes a real effort with her outfit, her hair, make-up and jewellery. However, she's begun to wear increasingly functional clothes when she's around the house. Comfortable sweatpants, faded T-shirts, shapeless jumpers and fluffy slippers make up most of her apparel soon after she steps through the front door. She's also started going to bed in old, mismatched, cotton pyjamas … and socks. There's nothing sexy about socks in bed. It's no wonder she rarely feels desirable when she dresses in such a dowdy manner at home.

"Lee, can you come up here a minute?" Tamsin calls down the stairs.

It's the sing-song voice she uses in front of the kids when she's trying to appear calm, while in reality she's fuming inside.

I jog up the stairs.

Is this it? Has Jake told Tamsin I wasn't with him at the hotel? Has he gone even further and told her about my affair? I can't believe he'd do that to me. To us.

I'm racking my brains, trying to think if there's anything else I could have done wrong lately.

Five hours ago I was enjoying some loud, uninhibited, kinky sex with Sophia, but apart from that, I can't come up with anything.

I'm anxious, to put it mildly.

Tamsin is standing in the doorway of our en-suite bathroom, still in her work-clothes, her foot tapping.

She beckons me into the room and points down at the toilet bowl.

"Do you know what *that* is?"

This must be a rhetorical question because it's quite obvious that there's a condom wrapper suspended in the water at the bottom of our loo.

*The afternoon after I became an adulterer, I was on cloud nine.*

*Back at the office, at the staff meeting, I deliberately sat opposite Sophia, so I could gaze at her without being too obvious about it. She was thoroughly professional and businesslike, rarely glancing in my direction, but when she did, and our eyes met, we exchanged a look that spoke volumes. My internal dialogue went something like this:*

*"I've had sex with you."*

*"You have indeed."*

*"I made you climax with my tongue."*

*"Yes."*

*"Twice."*

*"It was three times, actually."*

*"And I've seen you completely naked."*

*"Uh huh."*

*"From every angle."*

*"What do you think?"*

*"I think you've got a smoking hot bod."*

*"Why thank you, kind sir."*

*"I've seen your boobs too."*

*"You sound like an adolescent schoolboy."*

*"Yes, but on the other hand ... boobs!"*

*"Good grief!"*

*"I've been inside you."*

*"Correct."*

*"Deep inside."*

*"Deeper than anyone has ever been, you well-endowed stud."*

*"What do you think, Lee?"*

*"I'm sorry, Claire, I was miles away. Can you repeat the question?" I said.*

Is it too much to expect Tamsin to be my best friend, soulmate, co-parent, intellectual sounding board and, at the same time, my red hot lover who can be instantaneously in the mood to satisfy my basest carnal desires? Yes, it is. Tamsin is amazing when it comes to multi-tasking, but I realise that this is expecting too much of her. The minute both kids are out of the house, I pounce on her and request lovemaking. I expect her to be delighted to have a break from whatever banal task she's midway through: marking, planning, ironing, gardening, vacuuming, cooking. Surely a pleasurable, naked interlude is always welcome.

To be fair, she doesn't always turn me down. When I suggest sex, Tamsin is occasionally amenable, if somewhat unenthusiastic. If I propose something mildly kinky, like bondage or role-play, she'll sometimes agree – maybe once every six months – although not without communicating her reluctance. Even if I suggest anal sex she ... okay, she always turns me down flat with that one, but I can't exactly blame her. When pornography turns to anal, it makes me squirm with discomfort. How do they do that? Surely they're faking it. If my sensitive rear-end received that sort of pounding, I wouldn't be able to sit down for a week.

"Isn't that a condom wrapper?" I say, acting surprised for all I'm worth.

I know it's a condom wrapper and I know how it got there: an hour ago, I found it in my trouser pocket and flushed it down the loo. At least I thought I'd flushed it. I should have checked more carefully.

"I can see that!" Tamsin says, through gritted teeth. "Perhaps now you can enlighten me as to why it's there."

I know why it's there too: I wanted to remove from our house any evidence that I'd recently had sex with another woman. What I don't know is how it got into my trouser pocket in the first place. I have no memory of putting it there, but I'm notorious in our house for leaving things anywhere. My family tell me I don't associate things with places, so my car keys are more likely to be almost anywhere other than on the car-key-hook in the hallway.

Sophia and I have tried to develop good habits after our rendezvous. She tidies away the sex toys and lube, then changes the sheets on the bed and puts the old ones straight into the washing machine, so they're clean by the time she gets home from work. I double bag the condoms and wrappers, and have a shower, ensuring I don't use any scented products. Then I dispose of the trash in a litter bin on the way back to my car. Sophia leaves her house ten minutes after me to make certain we don't arrive back at the office at the same time.

Unfortunately, today something has gone wrong.

*The night after I became an adulterer, as I listened to Tamsin gently snoring beside me, I felt all right. I was fully expecting to be overwhelmed with guilt and remorse, but I wasn't. Sophia and I had had a wonderful time and nobody had been hurt. Tamsin was none the wiser. I'd planned it, carried it out and got away with it. It was easy.*

*When Tamsin arrived home that evening, I was nervous. I thought she'd take one glance at my guilty face and know what I'd done. I thought she'd be able to smell it on me; the stink of sex, guilt, shame, stress, regret. She was oblivious to it all.*

*I forced myself to look her in the eye and maintain an ordinary conversation about routine things, and I tried to act as normal as possible.*

*I wanted to send a message to Sophia to tell her again what a wonderful time I'd had, but there was no way I was going to break rule eight, so I had to contain myself for sixty hours until I could see her again in the flesh.*

Tamsin isn't enjoying getting older, but I reckon she's becoming better looking as she ages. I'm a huge admirer of Tamsin's physique. She hates it. Perhaps she's a bit too skinny and has a few stretch marks, but I can't even glimpse her naked body without becoming aroused. She's a beautiful, classy woman and I could happily admire her disrobed form all day long. Disappointingly, over the last few years, Tamsin has begun to get dressed and undressed away from my view, either by relocating to the bathroom or by waiting until I'm no longer around, so my opportunities for admiring her lovely figure are increasingly limited. On the rare occasions when I do get to see her in all her glory, I try to express my adoration:

"Wow, you've got a gorgeous body!"

"I know you're just trying to be nice, Lee. I'm really fat at the moment."

She isn't.

"You've got amazing legs: toned, shapely and they go on forever. All that work at the gym and on the tennis court is definitely paying dividends."

"What about all my cellulite and these horrible veins?"

I can't see what she's pointing at.

"Your breasts are magnificent. They look better and better as time passes."

"How can you say that? They've never been the same since I breastfed the kids."

They're perfect. The left one is my favourite; it's just slightly bigger.

"You have such a hot, little arse."

"This massive, wobbly thing! You must need your eyes testing. Stop looking at it."

I can't.

Sophia is more voluptuous and probably has a more conventionally attractive figure than Tamsin, but I'm more aware of her flaws: a sprinkling of grey hair, some cellulite, the varicose veins, her wobbly bits starting to head southward.

I simply don't notice Tamsin's imperfections until she points them out. I'm too busy being grateful that she's naked in front of me.

I can't remember the last time Tamsin paid me a compliment about my naked body. Sophia, however, is effusive in her flattery, and I love it. She makes me feel appreciated and admired, but I can't help wishing it was Tamsin doing the admiring, not Sophia.

"It's nothing to do with me!" I say.

It really is though. How do I get out of this?

"Condom wrappers don't just miraculously appear in toilet bowls, Lee. Someone put it there."

I read some good advice recently on the internet: when accused by your partner, rather than getting annoyed or trying to bluff your way out of the situation, it's better to laugh at their suspicions. By getting cross, you're signalling to your loved one that you have a negative response to their accusation, rather than a bewildered one. Also, anger can quickly lead to an argument, and arguments have a tendency to go on for some time and dwell in the back of the mind.

I try to laugh, but to my ear it sounds insincere.

"Perhaps it was John."

"Lee, he's eleven! What would he be doing with a condom and why would he flush it down our loo?"

"Don't they sometimes hand them out at school in sex education classes, so the kids can practice putting them on bananas?"

"At age eleven?" Tamsin says.

"When do you *think* they start having sex? Anyway, I've heard sex education is much more effective these days?"

"Are you sure?"

"Yes. There haven't been any reports of bananas getting people pregnant for over five years."

"This isn't funny, Lee!"

She's not even slightly amused, but I was quite pleased with that one.

"What if it's Charlie?" she asks.

Neither of us is laughing now. I know it's not Charlie, but just the thought of it is alarming. It's only a matter of time until my fourteen-year-old daughter becomes sexually active. If I had my way, she'd have nothing to do with boys until she's thirty.

To save myself, I'm tempted to go along with the theory that the condom wrapper was put there by Charlie. Does that make me a terrible father? Yes. But I'm already a terrible husband.

"You don't think Charlie's having sex?" I say.

"It's possible. A girl in her geography class had a baby last year."

"What! Charlie wouldn't do that, would she?"

"I honestly don't know. Should we talk to her?" Tamsin says.

How do I respond? If I agree to us interrogating Charlie, she will rightfully deny any knowledge of the condom. As will John. Then I'll become the prime suspect. If I disagree, at least there will be some uncertainty about the true culprit, but the shadow of suspicion will be cast over my kids for a long time to come.

*The following Monday, shortly after arriving at work, I popped into Sophia's office. She looked up as I entered and gave me a warm, welcoming smile. It was apparent that she was delighted to see me, and it made me feel special. Sophia was very good at making me feel special: she listened attentively and seemed genuinely interested in whatever I had to say; she maintained eye contact with me for far longer than was really necessary; she paid me compliments; she noticed when I had my hair cut or wore new clothes; and she even laughed at my terrible jokes. It was a huge boost to my self-esteem.*

*I carefully checked we were out of earshot before I spoke.*

*"Friday was awesome, Soph! You're incredibly sexy. That was probably the best hour of my life, ever," I gushed.*

*"Meh!" she replied, shrugging. "It was all right."*

*I was crestfallen. I'd given it my all. Those were my very best moves. From the ecstatic noises she'd made, I had thought I'd done a reasonable job.*

*"I've had better," she said.*

*There was an awkward silence.*

*"Lee, I'm joking! You're so gullible! I loved every minute of it. Nobody has ever given me so much pleasure. Is it just me or are we incredibly sexually compatible?"*

*"We certainly are," I said. "Please, can we do it again soon?"*

*"Hell, yeah! Lunchtime?"*

*"Today? I wish! We'd better stick to Fridays for the time being. Let's see how it goes."*

*"But that's four whole days! Every time I look at you I get aroused. I don't think I can wait that long," Sophia said.*

*"Have you tried masturbating? Get yourself a vibrator."*

*"Lee! What kind of girl do you think I am?"*

*"A libidinous, lecherous, randy, insatiable one?" I suggested.*

*"Yeah. Fair point. But don't blame me if I single-handedly bring about a national battery shortage."*

*"You know you can get rechargeable ones now?" I said.*

*"It's a good thing too."*

*"Friday then?"*

*"Friday. No masturbating for you though, Lee. I want you gagging for it when you get to my house. I've got big plans for you this week."*

*"Intriguing! What plans?"*

*"You'll have to wait and see."*

I read somewhere that having lots of orgasms in middle age significantly reduces a man's chances of getting prostate cancer in later life. So I'm really going for it. I have as many orgasms as I possibly can with Tamsin, my preferred option; then some more with Sophia, my Plan B; and I supplement these with a little self-abuse, usually with the aid of some wholesome pornography.

Some porn I find a real turn-off. If it doesn't seem realistic, I'm just not interested. If it's hours of repetitive pounding,

I'll fast-forward in search of variety. I've got no interest in the man's enjoyment. What I want to see is a beautiful woman faking pleasure so well that I'm actually fooled into believing that she's enjoying the experience. Lesbian porn works well too; just get rid of the man altogether. This also avoids any uncomfortable comparison issues. Do all men have penises that big? How do they stay so hard for so long?

My favourite porn movie of all time features a smoking hot couple: Tamsin and me. For a few years, early on in our relationship, as a birthday treat, Tamsin used to let me film us making love. Even after all these years, and hundreds of viewings, these videos still arouse me more than any professional pornography.

Tamsin maintains that porn doesn't really do anything for her, and yet it often makes her sopping wet; far wetter than I've ever been able to make her. I can't seem to pin her down on her favourite type of porn though. Tamsin would deny it, but lesbian action always seems to get her juices flowing. Under the influence of alcohol, she will occasionally admit to enjoying the sort of porn in which two handsome, strapping young studs simultaneously pleasure one impossibly gorgeous woman, but only with the strict disclaimer that *she* would *never* do anything like that in real life. Unfortunately, I never dare mention how aroused Tamsin becomes by viewing pornography, for fear that she might refuse to watch it ever again:

"You seem to be really enjoying this porn, Tam."

"Not especially. It's all right I suppose."

"But, I've never known you get so moist down there."

"Have you put the bins out? It's recycling collection tomorrow."

"Yes. Is it because there's a woman being pleasured by two men at the same time?"

"I *don't* want to have a threesome, Lee."

"I didn't say you *did*. But do you like *watching* threesomes?"

"We're not going to a swingers party either."

"Absolutely not. Why can't you just admit this is turning you on?"

"Why are men in porn always circumcised?"

"Good question, but I know you're changing the subject. I honestly have no idea. How do you feel about circumcised men?"

She looks away. "I don't know, I've never had the pleasure."

"Would you ever have sex with a woman?"

"For the last time, Lee, we are *not* having a threesome!"

Sophia adores pornography. She watches it a lot; usually on her home computer or cell phone, and she makes notes whenever she comes across something novel that she'd like to try out with me. She doesn't seem to have any preference: girl on girl, gang bangs, interracial, guy on guy, S&M; the kinkier the better for Sophia. It's a breath of fresh air to be in a relationship with someone who has such a positive and embracing attitude towards sex.

"No. I think *you* should talk to Charlie about the condom wrapper," I say.

"Why me?"

"You've got womanly bits." I point in the general direction of Tamsin's nether regions.

"So?"

"Don't you think it would be better coming from you? Besides, there's no way I could have a conversation about sex with my daughter."

"But you will with your son?" Tamsin asks.

"Who says I haven't already?"

"Have you?"

"No. But I probably won't have to. He'll learn everything he needs to know from his mates at school, just like I did, and my father before me."

"Oh no you don't, Mister. If *I've* got to have 'the talk' with Charlie, then *you're* jolly well having it with John. After all, you've got manly bits."

"There's not much to say is there?" I'm really not keen. "Just give it a thorough wash every now and then and always wear a condom."

"Is that it?"

"Well, I'm not exactly going to be giving him foreplay tips am I?"

"Definitely not! He needs to learn that stuff from someone who has some talent in that area."

"Thanks very much!" I fell into that one.

Tamsin laughs and pretends she's joking, but I wonder how much truth there is in that statement.

"What about all the physical changes he's about to go through?" she says.

"Don't they cover it all in biology lessons?"

"I certainly hope so."

Tamsin is thoughtful for a couple of minutes.

I flush the toilet and, with a gurgle and a swirl of water, the condom wrapper vanishes around the U-bend. This time! It's annoying it didn't do that the first time I flushed it.

Tamsin finally comes to a decision.

"I'm going to talk to Charlie."

She looks at me expectantly.

"Fine by me," I say and beat a hasty retreat down the stairs.

*My liaisons with Sophia were undoubtedly the highlight of my week. We usually managed to see each other every Friday lunchtime at Sophia's house. On rare occasions we also met at weekends, while*

*Tamsin was out purchasing new items to cram into her already over-stocked wardrobes, and Joe was away somewhere persistently pursuing a small white ball into and out of eighteen holes, in the hope that he completed the task by swinging his weapon fewer times than ever before.*

*Conveniently, Tamsin often went on long, far-flung shopping trips; sometimes on her own, sometimes with a friend or two. Occasionally, she even spent whole weekends away, with Nilofer or one of her work colleagues. Sophia and I always made the most of these opportunities whenever they arose.*

*The sex with Sophia was wonderful right from the start. I found it inspiring to be with such a passionate, enthusiastic, active lover. We were both big fans of foreplay; preferably long-lasting, teasing, varied foreplay. Tamsin's preference was always to skip any foreplay altogether and just get on with penetrative sex as quickly as possible.*

*Typically, making love with Tamsin involved her going through the same six steps:*

*1. Yield to my persistent requests.*

*2. Get me hard with the absolute minimum of physical involvement.*

*3. Apply lube.*

*4. Climb on.*

*5. Bring me to orgasm as quickly as possible.*

*6. Leap out of bed, dress and get on with something more worthy of her time.*

*More often than not, we didn't even kiss each other and there was rarely any snuggling afterwards.*

*With Sophia, however, no two sessions were ever the same. I never had a clue what to expect, but it might have gone something like this:*

*1. Tease me in advance with excessively naughty text messages and photos.*

2. *Dress in a sexy outfit or costume.*

3. *Snog me until my lips were red and swollen.*

4. *Undress herself as part of a choreographed and rehearsed striptease.*

5. *Undress me.*

6. *Employ several types of foreplay, featuring multiple erogenous zones.*

7. *Provide instructions, suggestions, and requests of things I could do to enhance her pleasure.*

8. *Introduce the latest sex toys she'd purchased.*

9. *Whip up extreme mutual arousal.*

10. *Engage in slow sex, fast sex, hot sex, sweaty sex in various positions.*

11. *Have multiple orgasms.*

12. *Recuperate and snuggle.*

13. *Go back to step six and repeat until satiated.*

*Tamsin would quite happily make love the same way every single time, but Sophia wanted to have sex in every position I'd ever heard of and several others that were entirely new to me, and didn't even feature in the Kama Sutra. Not only that, she'd provide encouragement, make demands, and come up with novel suggestions throughout. Sophia knew exactly what she wanted and she wasn't afraid to ask for it. Explicit communication during sex was a new experience for me, and I liked it a great deal.*

Over the years I've purchased many sex toys for Tamsin: vibrators, dildos, role-play costumes, sexy underwear, butt-plugs, massage oil, flavoured lube; even erotic literature and sex guides. She's never expressed any gratitude for these gifts, but that's understandable because I'm actually buying them for me. I always feel awkward when I suggest we use a sex toy to enhance our love lives. The look she gives me seems to say: "Why do you need these things, you big perv. Can't we just have regular sex like normal people?" However, to be fair to Tamsin, she will occasionally agree to try some of the least outlandish items. Disappointingly, though, most of our sex toys have been used no more than once – highly successfully in my opinion – but then they've found their way into Tamsin's bottom drawer, never to be seen again. Her go-to accessory seems to be an old electric toothbrush which I've never seen her clean her teeth with and yet, suspiciously, it often needs recharging.

In my imagination, Tamsin spends her days off work, as soon as the house is empty, in the hedonistic pursuit of the ultimate orgasm. I picture her laying out all her sex toys on the bed the minute my car has left the drive, and then spending the next few hours pleasuring herself with multiple gadgets, as she fantasises about servicing the whole England Rugby Union team; in high heels. And possibly stockings too. Tamsin does look particularly sexy in heels and stockings.

Sometimes I pretend to forget my lunch, just so I can pop back home and catch her in the act, but I've had no luck so far. Somehow, when I burst in, she always seems to be fully dressed and busy doing menial housework of some sort. What a disappointment! Maybe she genuinely does have little interest in sexual pleasure; she merely goes through the motions to please me. I'm very grateful if that's the case, but I want more.

"Well, that was awkward."

I'm reading my book in bed and Tamsin has just entered our bedroom, looking flushed.

"What was?" I say.

"I've been talking to Charlie for the last twenty minutes. It didn't go well."

I put down my book, accepting that I'm not going to make it to the end of the chapter for the foreseeable future.

"What did she say?"

"Hang on a minute."

Tamsin retrieves her mismatched pyjamas from under the pillow and goes into the bathroom to get changed ready for bed.

I'm not sure what to make of this. She doesn't seem angry with me, which is a good sign.

"Was it hers?" I call through the closed bathroom door.

There's no response. I can hear Tamsin cleaning her teeth with her regular manual toothbrush, not the electric one that's reserved for special occasions. She can probably hear me, but is unable to reply due to having a mouth full of froth.

I'm impatient. There's no point even trying to read my book; I won't be able to concentrate. I want to know what Charlie said.

Eventually, Tamsin comes out, somehow managing to look sexy in her PJs and fluffy pink socks.

"What did Charlie say?"

Tamsin climbs into bed and makes herself comfortable before she speaks.

"Well, initially all I got was a whole load of 'Mu-um! Oh my God! Go away! I don't want to talk about anything.'"

"That sounds like Charlie. How did you bring it up in the first place?"

"I just said, 'Charlie, you know you can always talk to me, don't you?'"

"And that made her defensive?" I said.

"Not at first, no. I was a bit vague, initially. I don't think she realised what I was talking about, but she looked worried."

"Uh huh."

"After a while, I just came out with it and asked her if she knew anything about the condom wrapper in our loo. That's when she started to get anxious."

"Because it was hers?"

"No. I thought at first it was because I was talking about

contraception and she was uncomfortable with that topic, but she was actually just keen to convince me the condom was nothing to do with her."

"Did you believe her?"

"I did. She seemed to be telling the truth, but I could tell she was hiding something. I kept probing and asking awkward questions and, finally, she realised I wasn't going away until she spilt the beans."

"Go on." I'm intrigued.

"Charlie said some of her friends have been coming round to our house after school, before we get home. Not every day, but two or three times a week."

"Just girls?"

"No. Mostly girls, but occasionally some boys too. They hang out in the kitchen and drink tea and coffee, but she said sometimes couples have 'popped upstairs for some privacy.'" She mimes air-quotes.

"Her friends and their boyfriends?" I say.

"It doesn't seem to work that way anymore. They no longer use those labels. I'm afraid we're a bit behind the times, Lee. In plain English, on a few occasions, including this afternoon, one of Charlie's female friends has snuck upstairs with one of her male acquaintances, and she reckons they're having sex. She thought they were using *her* bedroom, but now says it's possible they were using ours, or maybe our bathroom. Anyway, the bottom line is, the condom wrapper almost certainly came from one of them."

"I see," I say, trying not to appear overly relieved.

What are the chances? It looks as if someone else is going to get the blame for my mistake.

"I told Charlie it was okay to have a couple of friends round after school for a hot drink, but it was completely unacceptable for them to be using our house as their personal shag pad."

"Absolutely!" I nodded in agreement.

"I was appalled. Can you imagine the trouble we'd be in

if one of her friends got pregnant in our house?"

"Well, at least they're using condoms," I say.

"That's hardly the point, Lee."

"No. You're right."

"Anyway, I asked Charlie to enquire if one of them had flushed a condom down our loo."

Uh oh!

"Good idea," I say.

"Unfortunately not. She refused point blank. She doesn't want to lose any friends over this. I think we've found our culprits, but we're unlikely to get any confirmation from them."

Never again. From now on I'm going to empty my pockets thoroughly before coming home, and double-check the toilet is completely clear after I flush.

# CHAPTER EIGHT

## *The Dream*

"Hi. Come in. Make yourself at home", Tamsin says to Sophia as she hands her a glass of champagne.

They sit together on the sofa, start making polite conversation and take synchronised sips of their drinks.

Tamsin is wearing a little black dress which was indecently short while she was standing, and has ridden up even higher since she's sat down. On her feet she sports silver, sparkly stiletto shoes and a diamond ankle bracelet. Her long legs are moisturised and shiny; tanned a lovely golden bronze.

Sophia's toned arms and shoulders are bare in the stylish strapless trouser suit that enhances her shapely figure. A simple, pearl choker necklace adorns her throat, and leopard-print dress-pumps complete the outfit.

I've never seen them both looking so attractive.

I pop into the kitchen to check on the food. It's coming along on schedule, and should be ready to eat in about twenty minutes.

When I re-enter the living room, to my absolute amazement, I find them kissing. Tamsin's hand is resting on the back of Sophia's neck, while Sophia's fingers are slowly sliding up the outside of Tamsin's thigh.

I keep quiet and watch.

The kisses are soft and sensuous, but Tamsin and Sophia are both beginning to exhibit signs of arousal; breathing more heavily as their ardour increases.

Tamsin parts her thighs slightly and Sophia's hand moves in between them, slowly making its way higher.

I hear Tamsin gasp with pleasure; a sharp intake of breath as Sophia's fingers reach their goal.

I watch as Tamsin caresses Sophia's flushed neck; her fingertips progressing ever so lightly over Sophia's clavicle, and on downwards towards her enticing breasts.

Sophia spies me out the corner of her eye, and tenses. Their faces turn towards me, then they leap apart to opposite ends of the sofa, and make an effort to compose themselves.

"What are you doing?" I ask, open-mouthed with surprise.

Tamsin looks enquiringly at Sophia who, after a thoughtful pause, nods back in reply.

My eyes are glued to Tamsin's as she taps her hand on the sofa between them.

"Lee, come and sit down. There's something we need to tell you."

*Sophia loved role-play. On several Friday lunchtimes, I arrived at her house to discover that she'd already donned a costume and was playing a character. I'd quickly have to identify and take on the supporting role:*

*Naughty pupil to her strict teacher.*
*Business tycoon to her high-class escort.*
*Sultan to her concubine.*
*Gardener to her duchess.*
*Patient to her nurse.*
*Plumber to her neglected housewife.*
*Rugby player to her physiotherapist.*

*Photographer to her underwear model.*
*Boss to her secretary.*
*Secretary to her boss.*
*Butler to her maid.*
*Abducted human to her alien scientist.*
*Virgin to her experienced lover.*
*Customer to her exotic dancer.*
*Prison warden to her convict.*

*She seemed to have an inexhaustible supply of inspired ideas, and we threw ourselves into our respective parts with gusto. We had some great sex, but we often ended up in fits of giggles, laughing at each other's attempts to remain in character.*

*"Hi."*

"Come in, slave."

"You look amazing, Soph. Where did you get the Egyptian queen costume?"

"Did I say you could speak?"

"Sorry, my queen."

"Speak again, without my permission, and I'll have you beheaded and then castrated. Or possibly the other way round."

A brief intermission ensued to allow me to get over an outburst of chuckling, while Sophia maintained her haughty composure.

"How can I serve you, my queen?" I said, back in character.

"Take off your clothes," she said.

I complied.

"Now come and stand before me."

I did.

"Closer, slave."

Fine by me.

"Now, kiss my neck." She angled her head to the left so I could get better access.

"That's nice. Now the other side." Another tilt of Sophia's regal head.

*"Very nice indeed, slave. Okay, now softly suck on my ear-lobe."*

*Okey dokey.*

*"And the other one."*

*Symmetry is very important during foreplay.*

*"That's excellent. Next I want you to uncover my breasts and lick my nipples."*

*I did as I was commanded, but it was no hardship. I was thoroughly enjoying myself.*

*"Stop."*

*I didn't want to.*

*"I said stop, slave!" She grabbed me by the testicles and squeezed just hard enough to get my attention. "Don't make me hurt you."*

*"Sorry, my queen." I said, in a voice that sounded unusually high.*

*She slowly released the pressure on my scrotum until it felt more like pleasure than pain.*

*"Lie down on your back," Sophia ordered, and I obeyed, making myself comfortable as she untied her shoulder straps and then shimmied to encourage her sheath dress to drop to the floor; still strikingly regal in her crown and jewellery. I was delighted to discover that she wasn't wearing any underwear.*

*"Now, stick out your tongue," she said, as she kneeled astride my head and began to lower herself, tantalisingly slowly, towards my mouth…*

I miss Tamsin when we're at work, and I make an effort to keep in touch with her during the day; mostly by text message, but also email and the occasional phone call. I appreciate that it isn't easy for Tamsin to reply. As an over-worked primary school teacher her role is pretty full-on, and she hardly gets any breaks during the day. Consequently, she rarely replies to my messages, and, if she does, she usually comes across as exasperated and not particularly pleased to hear from me.

Electronic communication with Tamsin has a tendency to dampen my ardour, whereas Sophia's responses are tantalising and arousing. She always replies instantly to my messages, conveying her happiness and gratitude to be in communication with me.

Sophia and I had begun to text each other a lot; thirty to fifty times per day was not uncommon. The vast majority of these messages were affair-related: risqué photos, kinky sex suggestions – conceived to relieve our mutual concupiscence – and erotic fantasies.

I'd love to discover what Tamsin fantasises about. Behind those twinkly innocent eyes, there must be a few lewd thoughts occurring. When we make love, is she in the moment with me or, in the dark behind her firmly closed eyes, is she thinking about someone else? Does she imagine she's screwing the Head Teacher of her school? He's a few years younger than her, and rather fit if I say so myself. I've noticed him checking her out when he thinks she's not looking. Does she pretend she's with a beautiful woman, like in the pornographic movies she enjoys so much, but claims not to? Does she simply alter her location and picture the two of us making love in the surf on a tropical sandy beach?

I have no idea.

I've asked Tamsin many times about her fantasies, but she won't provide me with any details. She claims she *never* fantasises but, just occasionally, when she's close to passing-out-drunk, she might acknowledge that she does sometimes let her imagination roam free. However, to my disappointment, her reveries always feature some faceless man with whom she's doing something vanilla.

That's what she *says*.

I don't believe her.

I wake up with a start and an impressive erection.

"Tell me, Tam!" I'm confused and rather disorientated.

"Tell you what?" she says. I get the impression she's been awake for quite a while.

"Nothing," I mumble. "I was having a strange dream."

"I could tell. You were making weird noises in your sleep just then," Tamsin says while I'm turning off my alarm.

"Really? What sort of noises?"

"Sighing and moaning. It sounded like you were having a lovely time."

"I don't remember *that*," I say.

"You don't remember having a sex dream? I thought I was going to have to throw a bucket of cold water over you."

"I don't think I was, Tam."

"Are you telling me you *haven't* got a massive erection down there?"

"Put your hand down and find out," I say, hopefully.

"I'm all right thanks," Tamsin replies and gets out of bed. "So you don't remember your dream at all?"

"Bits of it. It was the one I have quite often where my front teeth come loose and fall out while I'm on my way to an exam that I haven't revised for, having forgotten to get dressed."

"Bizarre!" she says. "So how come you kept mumbling someone's name?"

❖ ❖ ❖

*Sometimes, while we were getting our breath back, Sophia and I would actually talk. We spoke about many things: work, family, current affairs, television programmes, our likes and dislikes; but the one topic we studiously avoided was our spouses. Obviously, we kept each other informed if our respective other half was going to be absent for a suitably long period, but otherwise, I never men-*

tioned Tamsin and she never mentioned Joe. Except on one occasion.

About five weeks into our physical relationship, as we both lay panting and sweaty on the floor in a tangle of bedsheets, I brought up a text message that Sophia had sent me back when she'd had the flat tyre.

"What other things is Joe useless at?"

"Huh?"

"You said he's useless at mechanical stuff and many other things. What things?"

She frowned. "I did, didn't I?" She reached up to the bedside cabinet and grabbed her cup of tea, which must have been stone cold by then.

"So, what things?" I asked again.

"Where do I start? DIY, gardening, housework, getting me pregnant. The only thing he is any good at is holding down the sofa when the golf's on TV."

"Are you trying to start a family?" I said.

Her face dropped.

"We were. We tried for several years, but I never got pregnant. Every month the disappointment became more and more upsetting. In the end, we just stopped making the effort."

"I'm sorry," I said. "Did you try IVF?"

"No. Joe said we couldn't afford it. To be honest, he wasn't that bothered. It was me that was desperate to have a baby."

"I see."

"Once we stopped trying to conceive, there didn't seem to be any point having sex anymore, and it gradually petered out altogether. In fact, we haven't made love for at least eighteen months."

"Oh dear," I said.

"It's quite sad. Once the intimacy stopped, so did the affection. God, this is depressing! Anyway, now I've got you to satisfy my every desire, so let's not waste any more time talking. I'm sure I can come up with a better use for that tongue of yours."

Ding, ding! Round two.

◆ ◆ ◆

It's not just fantasies and pornographic videos that Tamsin refuses to get excited about, she doesn't like erotic photographs either.

Sometimes, when the mood strikes me, I use one of my password-protected phone apps to browse erotic photos on the internet. Occasionally I find a good one; by which I mean, one featuring impossibly perfect specimens of humanity, at least one of whom is a beautiful, classy female, with little or no body hair; plus real or well-faked ecstatic pleasure writ large on her face; and good lighting to boot. If the subjects are participating in an atypical or kinky sex act, that's even better. Once I've found one I like the look of, I'll send it to Sophia with a message such as, "I want to do this with you!!!"

She loves it. She always responds quickly and enthusiastically, with an encouraging reply. "Ooh! Yes, please. When?"

The next time we meet at her house, we'll try to re-enact the photos. Sometimes this is successful, but more often than not, we simply aren't flexible enough to get into the required positions. It doesn't matter though. We still have great fun experimenting.

I've tried sending sexy photos to Tamsin a few times, with the same request: "I want to do this with you!!!" Her replies are tardy and indifferent. A couple of hours later she might reply, "Ok. Can you pick up some milk on the way home?" or, "If you like. Maybe next weekend."

When the following weekend comes around, there'll be no mention of it and, unless I bring it up again, it'll be forgotten.

Tamsin has never said, "No. I don't want to do that." She simply ignores my requests and suggestions until they've slipped so far into the past that we've moved on to different issues.

I attempt my laughing technique again.

"Really?" Chortle, chortle. "Whose name was I mumbling? It wasn't that hot newsreader was it?"

"The Asian one? I knew you fancied her," Tamsin says.

"It'd be hard not to. She's a real stunner."

"Don't you think her eyes are too far apart?"

"No idea. I'm always too distracted by her décolletage to notice," I say.

"You mean her boobs, don't you?"

"Yeah. It's her boobs." My eyes go out of focus as I contemplate her ample bosom for a few seconds.

"Was it *her* name I was mumbling?"

"No, Lee, it wasn't her."

"You know dreams don't actually *mean* anything, don't you, Tam? They're just random electrical impulses in our brains that generate arbitrary images and thoughts from our memories. Absolute nonsense most of the time, but our brains try to make sense of them."

"Thanks, Professor."

"Well, what do *you* dream about?" I ask.

Tamsin considers the question.

"Mostly just rainbows, puppies and sunsets."

"Yeah, right! You never dream about your family, colleagues from work, people you meet?"

"Possibly," she says. "I don't have dreams very often, but even when I do, I've usually forgotten them by the morning."

"Do you fancy a cup of tea?" I say as I start to get out of bed, hoping to distance myself from this conversation before it gets any worse.

"Hang on a sec, Lee. We haven't finished talking about your sex dream."

"I told you, it wasn't a sex dream, it was just a mixed-up jumble of nonsense," I say.

"Then, who is Soph?"

*One afternoon, I was sitting at my desk, pretending to be hard at work, when a text message arrived on my phone.*

*"I think I'm pregnant! Any ideas for baby names?"*

*I could see Sophia spying on me from next to the coffee machine, her phone in her hand and a cheeky smile on her face.*

*"New phone. Who is this?" I replied.*

*"How many women are you shagging?!!" was her typed response as she feigned a shocked expression.*

*"It's hard to keep track. I reckon it's 7 blondes, 5 brunettes, 2 redheads and 1 lady with alopecia totalis of indeterminate hair colour."*

*"Does that list include me?" I can see her pouting across the office.*

*"No. Plus you. So about 16 women in total! Obviously, you're my favourite. X"*

*"Thanks, babe. You're so sweet. How come I'm your favourite?"*

*"It's that thing you do with your little finger!!!"*

*"Er ... That's not me. You must be thinking of someone else!"*

*"My mistake! That must be blonde number 4. Her name's Olga or Inga or something Scandinavian."*

*"Speaking of names. Any ideas for our baby?"*

*"I've always liked Gertrude, after my grandmother, or possibly Smokie, my old pet dog."*

*"Smokie Bolton?! Hmm!! I don't think you're taking this seriously. I'm tempted to bring up little Millenia Jane on my own!"*

*"I love it! Milly ... or MJ for short?"*

*"If you like. And for a boy?"*

*"Thelonious?"*

*Sophia shakes her head at me. Frowning and looking genuinely annoyed, she heads back to her office.*

Tamsin has become something of an expert at turning me down gently, whether I request lovemaking verbally or electronically. Over the years, she's developed a subtle way of letting me know that I'm not going to get lucky any time soon. An hour or two before bed, she'll casually drop into the conversation an issue of some sort. This is to make it clear that if I bring up the possibility of sex in the near future, the response will be a definite no, so don't even bother asking. A few examples:

"Well, that was a stressful day at work."

"I hope I can shift this headache soon."

"What's the time? I feel really sleepy already."

"My throat's a bit tickly. I hope I'm not coming down with something."

"Bloody kids!"

"Your mother phoned earlier…"

"I really must shave my legs at the weekend."

I've become quite an expert at interpreting these hints, and I now realise that, on these occasions, it's just never going to happen, so it's best if I find something else to do for ten minutes in bed that evening. Maybe read some more of my book.

Once she's given me the secret sign, Tamsin can't be persuaded or cajoled into having sex for love nor money. I know; I've tried a couple of times. In the past, my persistence, or nagging as Tamsin refers to it, has led to days, if not weeks, of the cold shoulder. It's better by far for me to just suck it up and wait patiently for a more conducive moment.

"Isn't Sophia one of your colleagues from the office?" Tamsin asks.

"Er ... yes, I think you're right. But I don't call her Soph," I say. "There was a Sophie in my Year 4 class at school. Perhaps it was her."

"Why are you having sex dreams about an eight-year-old girl?"

"She's not eight anymore. She must be forty-five now, like me."

"Was she attractive?" Tamsin says.

"No. She was eight! And I was into trains and super-heroes back then. Not girls."

"So you probably weren't dreaming about her then. It must have been Sophia from work."

"I'm telling you, Tam. I honestly can't remember my dream."

I'm trying to keep calm, not wishing this to escalate into a full-blown argument.

"Could I have said sofa, as in 'Ooh, what a lovely comfy sofa'?"

"No. It was more like 'Ooh, Soph, that feels so good.'"

"Did I say that?"

"No, but that was the gist of it."

"You're just teasing me, aren't you?" I say.

"Partly, but you definitely sounded like you were thoroughly enjoying yourself in your dream, and I don't think it was with me or with the Asian newsreader with the impressive breasts."

"Tam, you know in real life I worship the ground you walk on. I'm a one-woman man. *You* are my dream girl."

"Apparently not!" Tamsin says.

"You've been making quite a few accusations lately. I'm starting to think you don't trust me anymore," I say, trying to sound light-hearted.

"I trust you when you're awake, but who knows what you get up to when we're both asleep."

"Does it count as infidelity if it's in a dream?" I say.

"What do you think, Lee? You're the one who had the dream?"

"Actually, I read an article about this very subject."

"I'm not surprised," Tamsin sighs. "You seem to be reading a lot of articles lately."

"Apparently, the experts reckon that cheating dreams are usually about insecurity, low self-esteem, and fear of abandonment."

"So, you're having sex dreams about other women, because you're worried I might leave you, due to your tiny penis?"

"What? Is it *really* tiny?"

"You see!" Tamsin says, triumphantly. "You're so insecure."

"I'm not. I'm totally secure and confident in my manly prowess."

I pause.

She waits.

"But, be honest, Tam. It's not really tiny, is it?"

"What do you think?"

She's so mean sometimes.

"I think it's perfectly adequate. Now reassure me, or I'm going to keep having sex dreams about other women."

"Okay, Lee. Calm down. It's perfectly adequate."

"Is that it? I was hoping for more."

"So was I," she laughs. "But we can't always have what we want. What would you like me to say?"

"I'd like you to say: Lee, you're a sex god with the most magnificent love truncheon there's ever been. You satisfy all my desires and nobody else could ever compare to you."

"Lee, my darling, you're a sex god with the most magnificent love truncheon there's ever been. You satisfy all my desires and nobody else could ever compare to you."

She pats my cheek, patronisingly.

"Thank you. Was that so hard?" I say.

"Not recently. Maybe it's time you considered using those little blue pills."

She snorts in her effort to keep from bursting into hysterical laughter.

"Oh, come on! What's with all the insults?"

"I'm sorry, Lee. You know I don't mean it."

"I'm not so sure. Tonight I, and my mighty love truncheon, shall be dreaming about the new reception teacher at your school. Now, do you want a cup of tea or not?"

# CHAPTER NINE

*The Email*

It's the day after my bizarre dream. Tamsin is out playing tennis and I'm at home in my office, unpleasant thoughts running through my mind. Intellectually, I know dreams don't actually mean anything significant, and mine didn't contain any sort of revelation or hidden message, but the memory of it is fresh enough that I've still got a lingering feeling that Tamsin and Sophia cheated on me, with each other. Clearly, that never happened, but I still find myself walking into Tamsin's office and switching on her laptop computer, with the intention of reading her emails and browsing her search history. Just to be sure.

I start with the search history. It's not particularly enlightening:

Clothes shops.
Holiday accommodation.
Celebrity gossip.
Tennis equipment.
Local news.
More clothes shops.
Personalised greetings cards.
Food shops.

Slimming tips.
Hotel and spa special offers.
Cheap flights.

Apparently not security conscious at all, Tamsin doesn't bother to keep her phone password-protected or to secure her laptop. She has even less security on her email account, which is permanently signed-in. Why would she need to log-out when her laptop is safely at home? After all, *she* has nothing to hide. Unlike me.

*Sophia and I have been exchanging emails for years, as is common for people who work closely together in an office environment. Our first emails were dedicated entirely to work issues; businesslike, relevant and concise:*

"Can you forward me the invoices before the end of the week?"

*As we got to know and like each other better, they became less formal, but still fairly innocuous:*

"That's a really nice skirt, is it new?"
"Great haircut, it suits you."
"You look refreshed after your holiday."

*Over time they became a bit less anodyne:*

"You look good today."
"That jumper brings out the colour in your eyes."
"Is it coffee time? I miss you."

*Then increasingly personal:*

"Your knees are distracting me this morning!"

*"You smell lovely! New aftershave?"*
*"I prefer work when you wear high heels!"*

*Before long they were rather rude:*

*"Is it my imagination or are you wearing stockings and suspenders under that skirt?!!"*
*"I saw you bending over the photocopier provocatively!! You're such a tease!"*
*"Nice cleavage!!"*

*Then crude:*

*"Is it cold today? Your nipples are looking rather perky!!!"*
*"I can't stop looking at the bulge in your trousers!!! What have you got in there?!!"*
*"I'm imagining you naked right now!!!"*

*By the time our affair was in full swing, they had become practically pornographic:*

*"Thinking about you deep inside me makes me want to go to the bathroom to masturbate!!!!"*
*"Babe, I love how your breasts bounce when you're riding me hard!!!!"*
*"Send me a photo of your rock hard cock!!!!"*

*Fearing that our emails might be less than secure, and concerned that we might use up the world's supply of exclamation marks, we both agreed it would be sensible if we used work email for business-related communication only, and we switched to texting for the naughty messages. And the pictures!*

I've not been sleeping well lately.

As soon as my head hits the pillow, the guilty thoughts begin. I'm an adulterer. I'm having sex with another woman. While I'm lying awake, the family I adore are sleeping peacefully nearby, oblivious to the fact that I'm a fraud. They have no idea that my selfish actions might tear apart their happy lives.

Even if I do manage to fall asleep, I often wake up with a start, in a hot sweat, imagining that I've been found out and I'm being confronted by the people I love and admire the most. On these occasions, it's almost impossible to get back to sleep. My mind is too busy trying to come up with justifications for my unjustifiable behaviour, and I have imaginary conversations with my accusers for hours; until finally I hear the garden birds singing the dawn chorus, and I get up for work, feeling shattered.

Audiobooks help sometimes. I've discovered that if I put in my headphones and concentrate hard on a good story, my mind will eventually stop torturing me, and I can slip back into the arms of Morpheus, only to wake, too soon, with the story still playing in my ears.

Perhaps I should end the affair. Sophia and I have been lucky so far, but we've nearly been caught a few times. Why not finish it while nobody knows? I could go back to my previous, stress-free life, when I used to be able to sleep soundly throughout the night.

Why don't I stop committing adultery?

Because I'm enjoying it too much.

It's the most exciting thing that's happened to me for many years.

"Spying on Mum's emails, are you, Dad?"

I didn't hear Charlie approaching, and she's guessed correctly that I'm doing exactly that.

"No. They just happened to be on the screen," I reply

nonchalantly, minimising that particular window, opening another and searching for the latest football results.

"Why aren't you using the computer in your office?" she says.

"Flat battery. I thought it would be quicker just to use Mum's."

"Can't you find the football scores on your phone?"

"I could do, but it's charging upstairs."

"I see." I don't think she believes me. "If you're looking for Mum's email messages to all her secret lovers, I doubt you'll have any luck. Everyone uses the drafts trick these days."

"What's the drafts trick? I've never heard of it."

"Come on, Dad. You must know this one. If you type something in drafts, such as the top-secret nuclear launch codes, but don't *send* the message, someone else – maybe your Russian handler – can use your password to log-on to your email account from anywhere else in the world – say Russia for example – read the message and then delete it. The message never gets sent or received, so it doesn't appear in your in-box or your sent messages folder. It's not a completely untraceable email, but it's much harder to find."

"That's really clever," I say. "Is it something lots of people do?"

"No. I don't think so. But it's quite a useful method of communication if you're trying to keep your emails secure from prying parents."

"Just to put my mind at rest, Charlie, can you tell me something?"

"Sure."

"Are you an undercover Russian spy?"

"Nyet," she innocently replies with a shake of her head and strolls out of the room.

"Good talk, comrade!" I call after her.

*One Friday, I arrived at Sophia's house, entered the usual way, and walked straight up the stairs to the spare bedroom. On opening the door, I found Sophia seductively reclining on the bed. She'd changed out of her smart office clothes and into a tiny, figure-hugging, red dress, red stockings and suspenders, red high heels, and a red bow in her hair.*

*"Happy Valentine's Day, babe," she said, as she stood, sauntered over to me, and started to undo my belt …*

*Afterwards, immediately before I left her house with my obligatory bag of used condoms and wrappers, Sophia handed me a red envelope and looked at me, expectantly. I tore open the envelope, and inside it was a cute Valentine's Day card featuring, on the front, a picture of two teddy bears in a loving embrace. Inside the card, Sophia had hand written, "You are the love of my life! Will you be my Valentine? XXX"*

*"Aww, thanks, babe," I said. "That's really sweet, but didn't we decide we weren't going to exchange cards or presents? Remember rule seven: No gifts or mementoes."*

*"This isn't a gift or a memento. It's just a card. I thought you'd like it." Sophia pouts.*

*"I do. It's really thoughtful. But now I've got two problems: I didn't give you anything for Valentine's Day, and where I am going to put this lovely card? I can't take it home or put it on my desk at work."*

*"You've given me plenty already," she said, and winked at me. "If I'm not mistaken, there are three condoms in that bag. You've made me very happy indeed."*

*"Not bad for an old man," I said, feeling rather proud of myself.*

*"You've still got it, stud. But I don't see why you can't have the card on your desk at work. You could pretend it's from Tamsin. It's not signed, so nobody will realise it's actually from me."*

*"What if someone mentions it to her? 'That's a very romantic card you bought for your husband, Tamsin.' Then I'd be in huge trouble."*

*"Fair enough. But at least you could keep it in your office drawer. Then it'd be hidden from prying eyes, and you could take it out whenever you want to be reminded of how crazy I am about you." She smiled up at me, adoringly.*

*I looked back at her, feeling uncomfortable.*

*"Am I really the love of your life? I thought we were going to make sure we didn't fall in love with each other. Rule fourteen, remember? Be honest, Soph. Are you falling in love with me?"*

*She paused, for just a fraction of a second, before she burst out laughing.*

*"You wish!"*

*She spun me around by the shoulders, pointed me towards the open door and gave me a resounding slap on the backside.*

*"See you back at work, babe."*

Would it be weird if a man collected data for four consecutive years – and put it in a secret spreadsheet – to keep a record of every single activity of his connubial sex life? Maybe the spreadsheet would record who initiated the sex, the number of orgasms he and his wife had, the type of foreplay, the duration, the length of time since their previous sexual encounter, the day of the week, a score out of ten, and, most importantly, the position, chosen from the following options:

Missionary
Cowgirl
Reverse cowgirl
Rear entry
Spooning
Doggy-style
69
Anal
Sitting
Standing

Cunnilingus
Fellatio
Hand job

Would that be weird?

After I hear Charlie go upstairs and close her bedroom door, I return my attention to Tamsin's laptop, and re-open the email window. First, I scour the in-box for anything suspicious. Predominantly the emails are work-related; also there are lots of adverts from clothes and shoe shops, plus the usual unsolicited promotions that have made it past the spam filter. After scanning back through six months of anodyne emails, I find a handful of slightly flirty ones to Tamsin from her worryingly handsome head-teacher:

"Don't forget your appraisal meeting in my office after school tomorrow. If you haven't achieved your performance management targets, I may have to punish you!" This is followed by a winking face emoji.

"Can we meet up sometime to discuss my feedback of your lesson observation? Your place or mine?!"

"Due to budget constraints, I'm afraid I won't be able to replace your interactive whiteboard, however, I am open to bribery!"

It's the exclamation marks that push these messages over the top, from mildly flirty and humorous, to slightly creepy and inappropriate.

After a while, I give up searching through Tamsin's in-box and switch to the sent messages folder. This is even less enlightening. It's entirely routine work communication, plus a few villa inquiries for our next summer vacation. Tamsin doesn't appear to have sent any emails to her boss in reply to his potential overtures, which is something of a relief.

Next, I check the deleted items folder and find it empty. Tamsin has always been very good at tidying up after herself.

My email account is a mess. There are hundreds of unread messages, some of which are over six months old. My sent messages folder is bloated even though my employers insist that we delete all our sent emails on a regular basis, for data protection reasons.

Finally, I open Tamsin's drafts folder. It contains one email, with the subject line: 'Stuff!'

I open it.

I barely have time to register that it's about ten lines long, when it disappears from the screen, to be replaced with the words: "No Mail."

I can still see an afterimage of the outline of the email, but all the detail is gone.

A small number one has appeared next to the trash folder, but, as I watch, that too disappears.

*One Thursday, at the end of the working day, as people were heading home, Sophia dropped by my desk to say goodbye, wearing a long black coat. Being hard at work, I didn't notice her at first. She stood close to me, with her back to our colleagues, and quietly cleared her throat to get my attention. When I looked up and smiled, she didn't say anything, just smiled back and then, slowly and seductively, began to undo the buttons on her coat. After the first two buttons, it became apparent that she was no longer wearing the blouse she'd had on earlier in the day. The widening gap in her coat revealed a tantalising glimpse of a black, push-up bra and a magnificent cleavage. She didn't stop there. As Sophia continued to unfasten the buttons, I realised that she'd also misplaced her skirt. When the last button was freed, she simply stood there, an angelic expression on*

*her face, as I tried not to drool. There was a six-inch gap between the two sides of her coat, and that gap framed a gorgeous view. Beneath the coat, she was wearing a highly effective bra, and ... absolutely nothing else. My eyes instinctively sank to the tiny incongruous patch of immaculately coiffed body hair. I shifted in my seat, pleasantly uncomfortable, and Sophia smiled her knowing smile. She was fully aware of the effect she was having on me.*

*"I want you to think about me on your drive home," she purred. "This is what I'm going to be wearing tomorrow lunchtime."*

*She opened her coat wide, just for an instant, raised her eyebrows and smiled, then closed the coat, re-fastened all the buttons, turned and walked away, calling over her shoulder, "See you tomorrow, Lee."*

I like my pornstars to have little or no body hair. It seems cleaner and more aesthetically pleasing. A large, overwhelming bush just distracts from the action. Nobody wants to see adult movie performers hacking their way through dense undergrowth in order to get to the good stuff.

Sophia maintains an immaculate lady garden. She has a trim little landing strip, but otherwise, there's never a pube to be found. I don't know if she's had laser treatment down there, or if she undergoes frequent and regular depilation, but she certainly deserves full marks for maintaining high standards of unwanted pubic hair removal.

Tamsin occasionally has her bikini line waxed, but I can't make head nor tail of her timing. She'll always have it done immediately before we go on our summer vacation, which makes perfect sense if it's bikini weather, but there are other apparently random times throughout the year when she'll undertake a bit of a muff refurbishment: sometimes before a party, or a shopping trip, or for no obvious reason whatsoever.

I suppose it's not unlike me getting a haircut. If there's a social event imminent, I might have a trim, but if not, I let my hair grow until it looks too long, and then I visit my local barber. I guess that would appear random too.

I also do a bit of grooming and manscaping. Just some light personal trimming; certainly nothing involving lasers, waxing or chemicals.

I wonder what the disappearing email said.

Perhaps Tamsin had just finished composing it and sent it at that moment, possibly between games in her tennis match. But then it should have moved to her sent folder, not to the trash. She must have decided that she no longer wanted to send it, so she deleted the draft and emptied the trash as a matter of routine. It was about ten lines of writing, though. How strange that Tamsin would spend so long composing an email, only to delete it without sending.

It probably wasn't that interesting. I guess I'll never find out. I can't exactly ask her.

"Hey, Tam. I was snooping through your emails earlier and I nearly managed to read one in your drafts folder, but it disappeared too quickly. What was it about?"

An unsettling idea pops into my mind.

Should I be worried that Tamsin might be having an affair with her Head Teacher?

I burst out laughing and shake my head.

That's totally impossible. I'm not convinced that Tamsin even enjoys having sex, so it's highly unlikely that she'd go looking elsewhere for any extra.

*In late April, the weather turned summery, and we had several*

*consecutive unseasonably hot and sunny days. I was rather sweaty after the drive to Sophia's house, as my car had heated up while left in the shadeless staff car park. I opened the back gate, expecting to enter the house as usual, only to discover Sophia, reclined on a lounger, sunbathing stark naked in her garden.*

*She looked incredible. Other than sunglasses, she was as bare as the day she was born. There was sweat running down her chest and in between her beautiful breasts, before pooling in her navel. Her right hand was between her thighs as she touched herself brazenly and provocatively.*

*"Hi, babe," she said, her voice husky. "Get your kit off and join me."*

*"What about your neighbours?" I said in a whisper.*

*"Don't worry. I chose a spot that isn't overlooked by anybody."*

*"Are you sure?" I said, gazing around at the buildings nearby.*

*"Absolutely. Now, are you going to take your clothes off, or do I have to do it for you?"*

*Her fingers were moving faster. I could tell she was highly aroused.*

*I was too. Alfresco, hot and sweaty sex was something I'd always wanted to try.*

*I stripped naked in seconds, not even pausing to arrange my discarded clothes into a neat pile, and I dived headfirst between Sophia's parting thighs.*

*That afternoon, I arrived back at the office looking dishevelled and overheated, but I had a big, contented grin on my face for the rest of the day.*

As the years have passed, Tamsin has refused to let herself go physically, unlike many women of her age. I feel sorry for some men: those men who fall helplessly in love with lithe, attractive girls in their prime, who subsequently give up all exercise and stop watching their weight the moment they've hooked themselves a husband. Before long these poor guys find themselves committed, legally and emotionally, to an overweight, unfit, uncomely wife – whose physical decline has merely begun – with no options other than divorce, an affair, or remaining in a marriage with a partner who they're no longer physically attracted to; until death. How depressing!

I'm fortunate. Tamsin's gym workouts and tennis matches have helped her to maintain a slim, toned physique into her forties. However, despite still having a great body, she's begun to wear less sexy clothes when she goes out on the town. She always makes an effort to appear attractive and stylish, but she no longer dresses in the unashamedly sexy way she used to in her twenties. I think that Tamsin is still attractive enough to wear more daring outfits, and to allow herself to be lusted after for the way she looks, but she disagrees. She clearly doesn't want to be seen as a sex object. That's fair enough. She doesn't want to be thought of as mutton dressed as lamb. But, in my opinion, it's way too soon for her to start dressing her age; she's more like lamb dressed as mutton.

I regularly tell Tamsin how attractive she looks; that she has a better body than many women half her age, and she ought to be more confident about her appearance and flaunt it. I think she's extremely sexy, but when I tell her so, I always receive a negative response:

"How can you find me sexy after you've seen me giving birth?"

"You know I suffer from haemorrhoids and varicose veins, unlike girls in their twenties."

"I'm too old to wear a skirt that short. People would laugh at me."

While Tamsin's skirts are getting longer, her hair is getting shorter, and I don't like it. Before my eyes, she's turning into her mother. It won't be long until I'm married to an old woman.

Sophia, however, is quite happy to dress like a slut at every opportunity. Bless her! In fact she thrives on it. She doesn't care what people think or say. The disapproving looks she receives from a handful of prudish women are a small price to pay if she manages to turn the heads, and brighten the days, of a few red-blooded men.

# CHAPTER TEN

## *The Argument*

"Wruut?" *said the text message from Sophia.*

*This had become an alternative greeting we used occasionally instead of "Hi." It was just a quick way of saying "What are you up to?"*

*Over the course of our affair, Sophia had begun to keep closer tabs on my movements. It was quite endearing really. She just liked to know where I was and what I was doing when we were apart.*

*"I'm at the gym," I replied. "About to bench press 200kg!"*

*"Is that a lot?"*

*"I don't like to boast, but the gym owner has invited a local news crew to film it!"*

*"Really?"*

*"No! I could never lift that much."*

*"I bet you could do it if you put your mind to it. I think you're very strong. X"*

*"If only! My record is 120kg, and that was six years ago. Back when I was young!"*

*"You're still my hero! Xxx"*

*"Thanks, babe. I need to work on my fitness so I can keep up with you in bed!!!"*

*"You're already amazing in bed!!! X"*

*"You're not so bad yourself! xx"*

*"Thanks. Any requests for next Friday?!!"*

*"Actually, there's one thing I've always wanted to try!"*

*"Name it. I'd do anything for you! X"*

*"You're wonderful! Can you get hold of a sheep costume in your size?!"*

*"Ha ha! Or should that be baa baa!"*

*"No. I'm serious. I've always wanted to try bestiality!!"*

*"Ok. I'm up for it! X"*

*"What kind of perv do you think I am?!!"*

*"The regular kind! Any serious requests?"*

If I *was* the sort of weirdo who kept a spreadsheet for four years, recording every detail of my sex life with my wife, it would probably say that I initiate sex roughly ten times more often than she does; a ratio of 10:1.

Okay, I admit it. I did this and I'm not proud of it.

The ratio was probably 1:1 when we first got together at university, 3:1 by the time we got married, 5:1 after Charlie was born, 7:1 after John came along, 8:1 when Tamsin hit thirty-five and 10:1 now.

There's nothing I can do to make Tamsin initiate sex more often than she does, and I expect this ratio to worsen considerably as we get older.

It isn't fair. Tamsin can make me initiate sex whenever she wants. I don't think she's even aware of it, but all she has to do is one of the following things:

Let me glimpse her naked body.
Wear short dresses or skirts.
Tell me one of her fantasies.
Bend over and pick up something from the floor.
Lick her lips.
Undo one extra button on her blouse.
Eat a banana.

Go away for a few days.
Moan in her sleep.
Snuggle.
Say the word 'moist'.
Give me a massage.
Ask for a massage.
Wear stockings.
Suck her finger.
Flirt with another man.
Put her hand on my thigh.
Walk around after a shower wearing nothing but a towel.
Kiss my neck.
Try on clothes in front of me.
Hug me for slightly longer than I'm expecting.
Brush one of her breasts against my arm.
Lie naked on our bed with her legs wide open while reading erotic literature and touching herself.

She's never tried the last one, but I suspect it would be successful.

Now that I'm considering it, perhaps I've been doing Tamsin an injustice. Maybe, she's been initiating sex a lot more than I've been giving her credit for, but she's done it subtly; in a way that makes me believe it was my idea.

Sometimes I wonder what our sex life would be like if one of us stopped initiating sex altogether. To be honest, if she stopped, I don't think either of us would notice the difference; but if I stopped, we could go months on end without making love.

I actually tried this once – when I was particularly frustrated with Tamsin's lack of effort in the bedroom – but after three or four weeks of no action whatsoever, I became so horny that I cracked and begged for a resumption of my conjugal rights until she succumbed, and put me out of my misery. I don't think she was even aware that we'd gone so long without any physical intimacy.

Tamsin isn't very affectionate these days either. If I take her hand when we're out walking, she'll continue to hold mine for a while, until she needs to adjust her hair or do something on her phone. She's never the instigator of handholding. If I hug her, she hugs me back warmly, if briefly, but she rarely originates a hug herself. There are times when it seems as if she feels guilty for not initiating sex very often, because, after two or three months of apathy, she actually begins to bestow sporadic hugs upon me. It's as if she's giving me a consolation prize. "No. I can't be bothered to initiate sex with you, Lee, but here's a ten-second hug instead. I hope it'll suffice." A hug hiatus always follows any occasion when Tamsin originates sex or plays a more active role in our sex lives. "We had sex with the lights on last night, and today you want a hug too!"

*Sophia strode back into the bedroom, stark naked. She truly was a fine looking woman. Her hair was tousled from just having had rampant sex, and her make-up was smeared, but she still looked gorgeous. She could tell I was admiring her, and she smiled content-edly. Picking up her phone from beside the bed, she walked back to the doorway, giving me a lovely view of her pert bottom, then turned and prepared to take a photo of me.*

*"What are you doing?" I said.*

*"You look so good lying there. Tangled up in my bedsheets. Looking up at me adoringly. I want to capture the moment."*

*"That's sweet, Soph. But you know you can't keep it."*

*She took the picture.*

*Then she took a few more, moving around the bed to catch me from different angles, as I laughed at her pretence that she was a professional photographer, working with a reluctant model.*

*"Come on, sweet cheeks, give me some emotion. Make love to the camera. That's it. More pouting. Perfect. Now show me some more skin."*

*"What kind of guy do you take me for?" I said, covering my-*

self up with the sheet.

Sophia joined me on the bed.

"Let's take a couple of selfies too," she said.

Before I could object, she was pointing her phone at the two of us and taking multiple photos.

We pressed our heads together and smiled cheesily at the camera.

Then Sophia took a few further pictures as she kissed my cheek and neck, and more still of us gazing at each other lovingly.

"Let's have a look," she said, and scrolled through the pictures.

We looked at them together. Some were awful. I'd been caught mid-blink in several, and in others my mouth was a funny shape, but there were one or two really nice photos.

"Damn, we make a mighty fine looking couple," Sophia said, smiling to herself.

"We really do," I replied. "Especially you. You're so photogenic."

She kissed me.

"You say the sweetest things, babe."

"It's true." I caressed her cheek. "Now delete them."

"Oh, please, babe. Let me keep this one. We look so good."

"Absolutely not. You know the deal."

She pouted. Sophia naked and pouting is a sight to behold.

"What if I lock it away, in a secret folder, in my already password-protected phone, where nobody could get access to it?"

"No. Even if nobody sees it, I don't want there to be any evidence of our affair in existence."

"Well, what am I supposed to gaze at adoringly when I'm pining for you?" she said.

"There's always my photo in the company brochure. I look pretty hot in that."

"You think?" Sophia looked doubtful.

"Don't you?"

"Meh! This one's better." She looked again at the best photo. We really do look good together."

*"Delete it."*

*"Whatever you say, sir."*

*I watched Sophia painstakingly remove all the pictures, one by one.*

*"There. All gone," she said.*

*"Now empty the deleted photos folder."*

*"You really don't trust me, do you?" She frowned and shook her head, but I don't think she was cross; just a bit disappointed.*

*When the evidence was gone forever, I took the phone away from Sophia and put it on the bedside table. Then I rolled on top of her and gave her my I'm-up-for-another-go-if-you-are face.*

*"Let's have some memorable sex that we can both think about when we're pining for each other."*

*"Now you're talking," she said.*

Summer has finally arrived.

This is my favourite time of the year, especially when we go away for our family vacation. These are the two weeks when my sex life with Tamsin changes beyond recognition. It goes from second gear to fuel-injected turbo boost. The ratio of initiation goes from 10:1 to 1:1.

The one problem with my summer holiday is Sophia. She's decidedly unhappy about the prospect of two whole weeks without seeing me, or even being able to communicate with me. We had a long conversation about this in bed on the Friday before the vacation. So long, in fact, that we only managed to have sex once, and then had a bit of an argument.

*"That was lovely, babe. How am I going to cope without having you to satisfy my womanly urges for such a long time?" Sophia said, snuggling closer.*

*"I'm sure you'll manage." I kissed her on the forehead. "It's only for a couple of weeks. You've always got your huge sex-toy*

collection."

"That's not what I mean and you know it. I need you, babe. Aren't you going to miss me too?"

She looked up at me, studying my face closely.

"Definitely. I love our time together."

She frowned. I got the impression that wasn't the reply she was hoping for.

"So do I. But do you miss me when we're apart?"

"You know I do."

"Well, you never say it."

"I miss you, Soph. I think about you all the time." I said.

"You mean you think of different kinky ways we can have sex together, but do you actually think about me?"

"Yes. Of course."

"You will message me when you're away, won't you?"

I paused. I really didn't want to. I'd rather have a lovely family holiday; spend some quality time with my wife and kids, and have a couple of weeks off from feeling like an anxious, guilty adulterer. Is that too much to ask?

"I won't be able to, babe. I usually switch my phone off the whole time I'm on vacation."

"I don't believe you. You use your phone all the time: you look at the news, make restaurant reservations, check social media and the weather forecast. There's no way it'll be off all the time," she said.

"Okay, I hardly ever use it. I certainly don't have it on the beach or by the pool. Most of the time it'll be switched off in a drawer somewhere. Honestly."

"Couldn't you at least send me one message a day? Just so I know you're all right and you haven't forgotten about me."

"I'd really rather not, Soph. It's only two weeks. I promise I'll make it up to you when I get back."

She didn't reply.

She didn't seem happy at all.

I was just about to break the awkward silence when she blurted out, "You're not going to have sex with her, are you?"

◆ ◆ ◆

I'm really quite proud of myself for doing such a good job of concealing my affair. It hasn't been easy, but I think I've managed to avoid all the potential pitfalls and, when things haven't quite gone to plan, I've successfully improvised my way out of trouble. I'm pretty sure that Tamsin doesn't suspect a thing; but even if she does, she doesn't have any evidence to support her suspicions.

Sophia and I have got away with our adultery by adhering to the fifteen rules that I painstakingly put together.

I do a mental audit of the rules:

1. Neither of us has told anyone about our affair (apart from me telling Jake, but I had to, and I can trust him.)

2, 3 and 8. We've stopped exchanging personal emails and we've been carefully deleting all text messages, photos and search histories. All of our text messages have been sent when we're not with our families and they always begin with an innocuous greeting: 'Hi' or 'Wruut' (apart from my foolish mistake in the car and Sophia's drunken Christmas Day faux pas.)

4. Nobody has accused us of being inappropriately intimate, so we've had nothing to deny.

5. Admittedly, we've stopped changing our cell phone passcodes on a weekly basis, as it just seemed unnecessarily cautious, but we still do it regularly.

6 and 7. We've used cash to pay for condoms, purchased in faraway pharmacies, and carefully disposed of the receipts. Apart from one Valentine's Day card, we haven't shared any gifts or mementoes. (Sophia thinks I'm keeping the card in my locked desk drawer at work, but actually, I shredded it the day

she gave it to me.)

9. In private, we haven't been able to keep our hands off each other, but in public, we've studiously avoided any inappropriate or even questionable physical contact.

10. We've used condoms every time we've had sex. (On a couple of occasions, in the heat of passion, Sophia has encouraged me not to bother, but so far I've been strong, and managed to maintain my one hundred percent record.)

11 and 12. We've relaxed the rule about cosmetics and body lotions because I always shower after our rendezvous, but even so, there have been a couple of Friday afternoons when I've detected a pleasant trace of vanilla and apricot emanating from inside my shirt.

13. We've never been together while under the influence of drugs or alcohol (apart from the office Christmas party and that time at the hotel when Sophia had a few glasses of champagne.)

14. While I love spending time with Sophia, I haven't fallen *in love* with her. I'm crazy about Tamsin, and I can honestly say that I still love her with all my heart. My feelings for Sophia have intensified, and I'm definitely fond of her, but that's it.

Sophia is effusively appreciative of all the sex we've been having, but I'm pretty sure she hasn't fallen in love with me either. However, I'm a little concerned about this. Sometimes I catch her looking at me in the same way that I look at Tamsin. When this happens I always check:

"Soph, you're definitely not falling in love with me, are you?"

She chuckles and shakes her head. "Oh, Lee. You really make me laugh."

"I'm sorry. I do try not to be too adorable, but it's hard. It

129

can't be easy for you."

"It isn't. But I'll cope."

15. Neither of us want to end our affair yet. We're having too much fun. Despite the lack of sleep, I feel ten years younger, and I haven't experienced such a joie de vivre since I first got together with Tamsin at university. Maybe soon the novelty will start to wear off, but for now I'm keen to continue and I think that Sophia is too.

Okay. I'm a realist. I'll acknowledge that my audit has identified a few slip ups, but we've always managed to survive unscathed and undiscovered.

So far.

*"She's my wife, Soph. Of course we're going to have sex if she wants to."*

*Sophia looked as if she was about to burst out crying.*

*"Why are you being so horrible to me?" she said.*

*"What do you mean? This is just an affair, remember? It's supposed to be in addition to our marriage, not instead of it. Don't forget, this was your idea."*

*Her eyes were brimming with tears, but she was trying to compose herself.*

*"Don't I make you happy?"*

*"Definitely," I said.*

*"I thought you enjoyed making love to me."*

*"I do. I love it. It's the best sex I've ever had in my life."*

*"Then why do you need to keep sleeping with her? Aren't I enough for you?" Sophia said.*

*"One day a week doesn't exactly satisfy all my needs."*

*"Are you saying you want us to see each other more often?" she said, brightening a little.*

*"No. I'm saying, I'm a married man who will occasionally*

*have sex with his wife too. And you have to just deal with that."*

*"But wouldn't you prefer it if we could spend more time together?"*

*"In a perfect world, I guess that'd be nice, but for now, we're both married and just having a really enjoyable affair."*

*"I can't believe that skinny bitch is any good in bed. Does she satisfy you the way I do?"*

*"Whoa! First of all, don't call Tamsin a bitch. And secondly... no, actually she doesn't satisfy me the way you do, but that's not the point," I said.*

*"I'm sorry, babe. I guess I'm just feeling a bit jealous. But I really don't see why you have to keep sleeping with her. If once a week isn't enough, tell me. I'm sure we can find a way to meet up at other times and in other places."*

*"No. It's too risky. Our current arrangement is fine, Soph."*

*"It might be fine for you, but it isn't for me," she said.*

*"We need to get back to work. Have you seen the time?" I glanced at my wristwatch.*

*"So, you'll message me while you're away?"*

*I paused, considering how I should reply. This was becoming a problem. I really didn't want my affair to interfere with my family life, but I didn't want to hurt Sophia either. She was a big part of my life too, and I was fond of her, but my family was my priority.*

*"No."*

*Sophia looked crestfallen, but I took a deep breath and continued.*

*"This is time with my family. Rule eight, remember? Let's take this two-week break as an opportunity to take stock of our relationship and decide where we go from here."*

*"What does that mean?" she said, raising her voice. "You're not breaking up with me are you?"*

*"No, no, no! Absolutely not. I just feel like a couple of weeks apart will give us a chance to think about 'us' and decide if we're both benefiting sufficiently from our affair; if we're being careful enough; if there's anything we can do to improve it; where we go from here..."*

" ... *new fantasies to act out; any positions we haven't tried yet*," Sophia said, perking up.

"*I'm starting to think you've got a one-track mind*," I said, relieved that her mood was improving. "*I need to jump in the shower.*"

I leapt out of bed and headed to the bathroom.

"*Wait a minute.*"

Sophia untangled herself from the sheets and jumped inelegantly out of bed, breasts jiggling all over the place, to my delight.

She ran to me, embraced me and squeezed me in a bare bear hug.

"*Hold me,*" she said, her voice muffled by my neck. "*We're okay, aren't we, Lee?*"

I put my hand under her chin and gently tilted her head up, so I could look her straight in the eye.

"*Of course we are. You know I'm crazy about you.*"

She smiled up at me, and I kissed her.

# PART TWO

# CHAPTER ELEVEN

*The Holiday*

I love our summer vacations.

Tamsin does all the research. She chooses the location – somewhere with guaranteed sunny weather – finds a charming villa with a swimming pool, books the cheapest flights, and researches the best eateries nearby. The inexpensive flights mean that we often arrive and depart at unsociable hours, but we use the money we save to treat ourselves to some delicious evening meals at the local restaurants.

These meals allow me to experience quality family time with the three people I care about most in the world.

For me, there are two main highlights of our vacations.

The first is the dining. There are few greater pleasures than exotic food, shared with the family, outdoors, on a sultry evening, at a highly regarded restaurant. We all dress smartly and look our best; Tamsin and Charlie sporting golden tans, John and me rather pink and tender, after failing to apply sufficient sun cream.

After a couple of drinks the banter is great fun. These are the moments when Tamsin and I get to rediscover our children. Unable to leave the table, we're actually able to have conversations with them. Without wi-fi, they quickly lose interest in their gadgets, and have to resort to face-to-face communication with each other and with their parents. We learn all sorts of interesting tidbits about Charlie and John that we'd never discover if we were still at home.

The second highlight is the sex. I admit that this is something of an obsession for me, but I can have no complaints whatsoever when we're on our summer vacation. Tamsin becomes a different person. Away from her job and housework, she has time to relax and wind down. It takes a while, but after a few days our sex life really picks up. Maybe it's the humid heat. Maybe it's the alcohol, which we often start to imbibe before lunchtime. Maybe it's pasty white skin turning bronze and healthy-looking. Whatever it is, I'm very grateful. Tamsin can't get enough of me. Sometimes she wakes me up in the morning to have sex. Sometimes she summons me to our bedroom for a siesta that doesn't include any napping. Sometimes, when we're out, she'll make it crystal clear that she's keen to get me back to the villa for a damn good rogering. She's even made love to me in the swimming pool after the kids have retired for the evening, but only in the shallow end. Tamsin isn't a confident swimmer.

Sometimes we just have quickies, like at home, but more often than not, we enjoy long, slow lovemaking sessions and multiple orgasms. It's heavenly!

For two weeks every year, I have the sex life that I've always wanted with the woman I adore. For the other fifty weeks, I know what I'm missing, and I cheat on my wife to supplement the shortfall. Sophia is merely a stand-in; a surrogate; a pale imitation of the real thing. Often, I imagine I'm making love to Tamsin when I'm having sex with Sophia, but I so wish it could be Tamsin all the time.

"Phew! Turn up the A/C," Tamsin says as she rolls off me and lies on her side of the bed, arms and legs extended like a starfish. "I'm sweating buckets."

She always looks incredible straight after sex: a rosy glow on her cheeks, a twinkle in her eyes, and a mottled flush across her sweaty chest. Today, her long brown limbs and the bright white patches where her bikini has been, make her appear even more exotic than usual.

I comply and adjust the air conditioning.

"That was wonderful. I don't know what's got into you today, but I love it," I say.

"Nothing's got into me. Can't a girl just want to make love with her husband?"

"Absolutely. But you were so turned on. How come?"

"No reason."

"You can tell me, Tam. Was it an erotic scene in the book you're reading? Or were you just lying there enjoying a hot fantasy about that handsome waiter who kept flirting with you last night?"

"Ha ha! I'm pretty sure he was gay. He seemed keener on you."

"Aren't you going to tell me?" I say.

"It was nothing. I simply felt like having sex. If you keep going on about it, I won't bother next time."

"Sorry. I just like to know what turns you on. I love it when you're horny."

"Why did you call me 'babe'?" she says. "You've never called me that before?"

Oops!

"Did I?"

"Yeah. Right before you finished."

"I don't know. The heat of passion, I guess. Maybe something I saw on TV."

"More likely to be from all that porn you watch."

"How dare you! I've never watched pornography in my life!" I lie, insincerely.

"Yeah, right!"

"Did you like it?" I say.

"What?"

"Me calling you 'babe'?"

"Not especially. It just took me by surprise. I prefer it when you call me 'Tam' or 'Tamsin'. Or even 'Shnookeylumps.'" Deadpan.

"I don't think I've ever called you 'Shnookeylumps.'"

"My mistake. That must have been someone else."

She giggles at me as she steps back into her bikini bottoms.

She really is a different person on holiday. I wish she could be like this all year round.

Sophia likes to talk dirty. During sex she uses the most obscene words I've ever heard for body parts and physical actions. Some terms are so explicit, they cause me to blush with discomfort. I can't even bring myself to say them, let alone write them:

> Oh, ****! That's so ****** good.
> Lick my ****** **** faster!
> **** all over my ****!
> That's so ****** deep in my *****!
> Your **** feels so ****** amazing up my ****!
> Don't ****** stop. I'm going to ****** ****!
> **** me harder, you *****!
> Treat me like a ****** *****!
> Your huge ****** **** is going to make me ***** so hard!
> ***** my **** while I **** your *****!

Tamsin prefers no communication whatsoever during sex. Occasionally she'll shift her position slightly in order to move one of my body parts into a more enjoyable location. Very rarely she'll adjust my hand by moving it herself. But she never actually says anything.

Up a bit.
Just a tad slower.
Now put your hand here.
Deeper, please.
Roll over.
Don't stroke me there, it tickles.
Just keep doing exactly that.
Change position.
Okay, I'm warmed up enough for you to go down on me now.

These are all things that Tamsin tries to communicate non-verbally, but often I'm left in the dark, quite literally, having to guess what she actually wants me to do. "You should just know what I want!" she says.

If she absolutely has to describe a body part, she'll always use the correct biological term.

Penis instead of cock, prick or knob.
Testicles instead of balls, nuts or bollocks.
Breasts instead of tits, boobs or knockers.
Bottom instead of arse, bum or butt.
Vagina instead of cunt, pussy or fanny.

Tamsin would certainly never say anything remotely vulgar.

"Oh my God!" Tamsin purrs, her body still shuddering and spasming with pleasure.

"Did you like that?"

"Hang on a minute." She sighs and stretches contentedly.

I wait patiently as she basks in the afterglow of what appears to be a particularly enjoyable orgasm. She lies there, eyes closed and a contented smile on her face.

"Okay, Lee. You can speak now."

"Nice orgasm?"

"Delightful! Where did you learn how to do that?"

Uh-oh!

Sophia taught me. Then she made me practise, over and over again, until I got better at it. Apparently, I'm pretty good now.

"I think I read about it in a magazine article," I say.

"Lovemaking Weekly?"

"That's the one."

"I must remember to write to the editor and thank him. You have my permission to do that to me again whenever you like."

"Excellent."

"Now, what can I do for you?" Tamsin says.

I really love our summer vacation.

We're on the eighth day of our holiday and it's going well. Everyone's having a pleasant time; enjoying the sun, sea, pool, food and drink. John has had a bout of diarrhoea, but he's on the mend now. Tamsin and I are getting on famously, better than we have for months: enjoying each other's company; catching up with each other's lives; reading and discussing the same books; and having lots of awesome sex. It's a reminder of how good we can be together.

Charlie and John are splashing about in the pool, laughing and playing a game which seems to have complicated and easy to misinterpret rules.

Tamsin is reading her book in the shade of an olive tree and taking occasional sips from a glass of something long and cool.

I pop inside the villa to use the bathroom, and I grab my phone out of the bedside drawer to take with me. I switch it on for the first time in several days to find several notifications. Most of them are uninteresting: items of breaking news, a couple of messages from Jake checking up on us, and unimportant emails which can be responded to at a later date.

There's also one text message from Sophia.

"Hi."

Just that.

This wasn't supposed to happen. I thought we'd agreed to no communication during my vacation, so I'm a little peeved about this. After some consideration, I decide the best option is simply to not reply.

I switch my phone off, replace it in the drawer and head back to the pool.

Tamsin swallows.

"Do you want some water?" I say.

"Yes, please."

I pass her the bottle from beside the bed and she gulps down half of it.

"That was incredible, Tam. God, you're so hot!" She hands back the water, and I have a swig myself to replenish my body fluids. All this sweaty sex is dehydrating.

"That's weird," Tamsin says, getting up from the floor and joining me on the bed. "That's exactly what Dave said when he sent me that prank message."

Get some new material, Lee!

"Really? That *is* weird. I guess it must have just stuck in my head."

"Maybe," she said, unconvinced.

I change the subject. "Have I ever told you how much I enjoy it when you do that?"

"Only every single time I've done it."

So, what's that, about seven times since we've been married? Sophia's sucked me off more times than that in the last three months! It's probably best if I don't say this out loud though.

"I can't help it. It's awesome! In fact, I think I can safely say, it's my favourite thing in the world."

"Really?"

"Really."

Well, that should definitely inspire Tamsin to up the frequency. Who am I kidding?

I love oral sex; both fellatio and cunnilingus. To be honest, I'd struggle to pick a favourite. Obviously, receiving it is heavenly, but I thoroughly enjoy performing it too; having the power to give someone the exquisite delight of simply lying back and experiencing pleasure. I'm reluctant to ask Tamsin to go down on me because it always feels like I'm adding to her never-ending list of chores, but I don't have the same qualms when it comes to Sophia. She engages in it so enthusiastically, it feels as if I'm doing her a favour by allowing her to suck my cock. Tamsin would never ask to receive oral sex, unless she was particularly drunk and horny, but never sober. It doesn't matter how many times I tell her that I really enjoy it, she's convinced I'm pretending and, without the dutch courage provided by alcohol, she's too inhibited to say what she wants. Sophia, on the other hand, expects cunnilingus every time we have sex. She's just in it for the pleasure and has a total lack of self-consciousness about her body and her desires. There's something extremely sexy about a woman who has the confidence to demand whatever she wants, whenever she wants it.

"Are you awake?" Tamsin whispers. Her hand softly stroking my inner thigh and gradually inching its way higher.

I am now.

I glance at the clock. It's 2:45 a.m. We only had sex two hours ago. Tamsin is insatiable at the moment. It's wonderful.

"Yes," I whisper back. "What can I do for you?"

"I'm still horny." She giggles as she kisses her way down my chest and abdomen, towards my erection.

I think she's still a bit tipsy too.

The following day, while everyone else is relaxing post-lunch by the pool, I take my phone to the bathroom, lock myself in and switch it on.

There's another message from Sophia.

"Hi. Again!"

Followed by another one a few hours later.

"Advance warning: I shall be sending you another message at 12:00 BST tomorrow 3rd August."

I see.

Sophia isn't going to let me get away with simply not replying. She's letting me know that her next text message is not going to be a bland greeting. It's going to be something for my eyes only, that I wouldn't want anyone else in my family to see.

I appreciate that she's missing me and, to be honest, I feel a bit guilty that I've hardly thought about her while I've been away. However, this seems like a threat. "You're going to message me, or else..." is the implication.

My initial plan is to reply straight away and instruct Sophia to allow me to enjoy my family holiday in peace. If I tell her I'll be switching my phone off for the remainder of the vacation, then she won't be able to contact me. Problem solved.

But, after some consideration, I realise that I can postpone responding until just before noon tomorrow, thereby buying myself nearly twenty-four hours of text-free uninterrupted vacation, before I eventually reply with a polite version of, "leave me alone for a bit."

I put my phone on charge, as the battery is low, change the passcode, because it's been the same for three weeks running, and then turn it off.

I'm a leg man. Tamsin reckons I'm obsessed with breasts, but my preference is long, shapely legs. Legs like Tamsin's: some curvaceous muscle on the thighs and toned calves that look great in high heels. A golden brown tan helps too. Tamsin's legs are always at their best on our summer vacation; the result of a few months of outdoor tennis and a couple of days sunbathing. I can't keep my eyes or my hands off them. When we're making love, I imagine I'm watching us from a dark corner of the room or peering in through the window like a voyeur. Before me, I can see my cute, little white bottom, pounding away in between Tamsin's lovely brown legs, spread wide open just for me, or wrapped around my waist or neck. What a view! I'm a lucky guy, and the best part is, I don't have to imagine it when we're on vacation, because it actually happens.

The next day, when the kids finally surface at around eleven o'clock, Charlie requests a full-English breakfast at a beachside cafe. Tamsin and John think this a wonderful idea, but it rather interferes with my plans for midday.

"I might give it a miss if nobody minds," I say, surprising everyone, as I'm normally the first person to suggest a hearty fried breakfast.

"Are you feeling okay?" Tamsin asks, mildly concerned.

"Yeah. I think so. I've been having a few strange tummy rumblings, so I'd rather not be too far from a loo, just in case I need to go in a hurry."

"TMI, Dad!" John says, making a face at me.

"It's probably nothing, but I'd rather not risk it. You guys go without me," I say.

"Are you sure, Dad?"

"Yeah. It'll give me a chance to read my book in peace for a while, without you two squealing in the pool and distracting me."

"Okey-dokey. Get ready then, kids. We're leaving in fifteen minutes," Tamsin says.

It was more like forty minutes, but they've finally left and I've retrieved my phone, switched it on and found some welcome shade under the olive tree. It's scorching hot today. There's not a cloud in the sky, but a slight sea breeze is making the weather more bearable.

My stomach is properly rumbling now. I feel fine, but the thought of a big plate of fried eggs, bacon, sausages, baked beans, fried bread, black pudding and hash browns is making me extremely hungry.

It's just before noon, and I'm composing my text message to Sophia to request that she leaves me in peace for the remainder of my family vacation. I'm struggling to find the appropriate tone. I don't want to be too harsh because I'm flattered that she's missing me so much, but then again, I need to be firm about the boundaries that should be in place when we're with our families. Rule eight is there for a reason.

After a few fruitless minutes, I give up trying and determine to just wait for Sophia's message, and see what she's got to say for herself.

At 12:00 on the dot, my phone buzzes.

It's Sophia.

"Hi, babe. I miss you so much. Xxx"

That's not too bad. I type my reply. "I thought we agreed to have a two-week communication break."

"I'm going crazy here all alone. How are you?"

"I'm on my family vacation! You have to stop sending me messages."

"I'm really missing you, babe. Are you missing me too?"

"You said that already. I need you to stop this. We'll talk when I get home."

"Is she with you now?"

"No. I'm on my own, but I have to go."

"Have you got time for phone sex? I could call you!!!"

"You're not listening to me."

"Would you like me to send a very naughty photo of me in my new see-through lingerie?!!"

That's enough. I switch on caps lock.

"READ THE NEXT BIT CAREFULLY: I'm on holiday with my family. After I've sent this FINAL message, I'll be turning off my phone and leaving it off until I step off the plane back in England. DO NOT CONTACT ME ANYMORE. Have another look at the rules. We'll talk at work."

I send it.

Before I have the chance to turn off my phone, I get an incoming message from Sophia. It's a photo. She's sprawled provocatively on a bed, wearing only some sheer sexy underwear I've never seen before. She looks absolutely ravishing, and I can already feel a stirring in my loins. The accompanying message says, "This is what you're missing! Xxxxx"

I sigh, delete the photo and all the messages, switch off my phone and go and find something to eat.

On the last full day of our vacation, it becomes apparent that Tamsin is leaving holiday mode and moving back towards mother, housewife and teacher mode. She becomes irritated by the smallest thing, and I can see her shoulder muscles tightening as she gets more and more stressed, especially after I tell her to relax. She pauses scrubbing the toilet bowl and takes a few minutes to let me know all the things that are on her mind: packing, cleaning the villa, getting to the airport on time, stocking the fridge at home, all the washing and ironing we've accumulated over the past two weeks, school work, buying new uniforms and P.E. kit for the kids, getting a wax at the beautician's ... The list goes on, but I tune out and focus instead on the sunlight reflecting off the waves in the bay. I'm going to miss it here. The views, the tranquility, the lovemaking.

Conversation is stilted at our final meal, and Tamsin has barely touched her cocktail. The kids are still in good form, but the banter isn't what it was.

When we get back to the villa, we all head straight to bed for an early night as we need to wake up at an ungodly hour to catch our flight home.

Tamsin is looking at herself in the bathroom mirror while she brushes her teeth. I go and stand behind her, put my hands on her hips and start to kiss her neck, employing my infallible seduction technique.

I slowly slide my hands upwards and cup her breasts.

Tamsin tolerates it for as long as it takes her to clean her teeth, rinse and spit, then she wipes her mouth on the nearest towel.

"Right. Let's get some sleep," she says.

She forces her way out of my arms, takes a couple of painkillers out of her toiletries bag and washes them down with water.

She stretches and fakes a yawn.

"I'm so sleepy," she says and climbs into bed.

So that's it.

No more hot sex with my wife for the next fifty weeks.

My thoughts turn to Sophia.

# CHAPTER TWELVE

*The Reconciliation*

I t's not until we're in the car, driving home from the airport, that I switch on my phone.

It was a terrible journey. After a restless night at the villa, with not enough sleep for any of us, and a headache-inducing early start with two grumpy kids, we arrived at the airport in plenty of time for our flight, only to discover that it had been delayed by three hours. Unable to sleep at the airport or in the tiny seats on the plane, we arrived in the U.K. feeling tired and miserable. The overcast skies and heavy drizzle as we made our way from the plane to the terminal building didn't help lift our moods. John's suitcase was the last one to appear on the luggage belt, so we were the last people off our flight to pass through customs. Then we found ourselves at the back of the queue to collect our car from the long-stay car park. By the time we'd battled through the wind and rain back to our car, we were all fed up, and Tamsin and I were considering never going on holiday abroad again. Having had slightly more sleep than me, Tamsin kindly volunteered to drive the first part of the long journey home.

With trepidation, I see my phone come to life.

I don't know what to expect from Sophia. It could be anything: a tirade of abuse, a heartfelt apology, a sexual fantasy, a series of naked photos, a warm welcome back to the country.

There's nothing.

I can't help feeling disappointed.

Nothing.

Now we're back in the country, and Tamsin is reverting to her usual ice-queen self, I was beginning to look forward to spending some alone-time with Sophia. Don't get me wrong; Tamsin is now, and will always be, my favourite person in the world to make love to, but Sophia is an outstanding surrogate.

But there's nothing.

Does Sophia hate me now?

Is it all over?

If it is over, is that a good thing or a bad thing?

I guess I'll find out at work on Monday.

I try not to have favourites. I like everything equally. At least, that's what I always say.

Tamsin will try on several outfits before a party and ask me which one I prefer. I always say I like them all equally. It doesn't go down well, but I've come to realise that my opinion doesn't actually matter. She knows which one she prefers, and that's the one she's going to wear, whatever I say. If I chose the frumpiest outfit, she'd accuse me of thinking she was old; if I chose the most revealing outfit, we'd probably have a row about how I always want her to dress like a slut. My sexy is her slutty. It's best if I express enthusiasm for them all equally. Even if Tamsin presents me with five dowdy dresses, the sort her mother would wear, I still have to fake equal enthusiasm for them all, if only to avoid conflict. If we have a disagreement before a party, it significantly reduces my chances of getting any action afterwards.

I once told my mum that my favourite meal was gammon and chips. Big mistake. Ever since, whenever we visit her and Greg, she always prepares a replica meal of gammon and chips. Every time! Where's the variety? Where's the effort?

Sometimes Sophia asks me what my favourite position is for having sex. This is something Tamsin would never do, as it would require us to have a conversation about lovemaking, which she avoids at all costs. When Sophia asks, as she does regularly, I'll always say that I like them all equally. Simply seeking information, she doesn't mind which one I choose, but it's become my habit to not commit to a preference. Hopefully, Sophia will keep coming up with new and creative options until we find the ultimate sexual position.

Provided she's still talking to me.

At work on Monday, Sophia is playing it cool. She arrived early for the staff meeting, contributed more than usual, exuded professionalism, and didn't look at me once.

I don't like it.

At my first opportunity, I enter her office.

"Morning," I say, breezily.

She looks up from her computer screen, her face inscrutable.

"Oh, hi, Lee. Good holiday?"

"Yes, thanks. How are you?"

"Really well, thanks. How can I help you?"

So, this is how she's going to play it. Well, two can play that game.

"I was just wondering if I'd missed anything important while I was away."

"No. I don't think so," she says. "You should have been copied-in to all the relevant emails."

"Okay. Thanks. See ya."

I walk back to my desk.

Let the passive aggression commence.

Tuesday continues in a similar way: mutual polite profession-alism.

I tried to initiate lovemaking with Tamsin last night, but she thought she might have a migraine coming on, so no luck there.

By Wednesday afternoon, it's getting a bit close to Friday, and I still haven't had any action at home. I was hoping that Sophia would cave first and be the one to instigate a reconciliation between us, but she continues to treat me as merely another colleague.

I try a tentative text message.

"Hi."

No reply.

I try again. "You ok?"

No reply for twenty minutes. She's getting her revenge.

Finally, a reply comes. "Hello, stranger. I'm fine thanks. How are you?"

"Sad. I miss you. X"

"Aww! I miss you too."

"Are we still on for Friday?"

"What do you mean?"

"Are we meeting at your place on Friday?"

"Why?"

"You know why."

"Tell me."

"I want you!!! X"

"What for?"

"You know. Why are you being so obtuse?"

"Tell me."

"I want to make love with you! Xxx"

"Was that so hard?"

"I'll tell you what *is* so hard!!"

"I thought you were only having sex with your wife now!"

"Don't be like that. We were on holiday. What was I supposed to do?"

"You were supposed to message me and tell me how much you missed me. Every day!"

"I'm sorry. I messed up. Xxx."

"Yes. You did."

"Please forgive me. Xxx"

"Why should I?"

"Because I'm adorable and a total stud?"

"Hmm. I'm not so sure anymore. What's in it for me?"

"Unfettered access to my smoking hot bod and incredible sexual prowess?!"

"Not enough. What else?"

"My stamp collection?!!"

"I'm tempted! What else?"

"What do you want?"

"I want you to stop having sex with Tamsin altogether and just make love with me. X"

This is totally out of the question. The whole point of this affair is to have some extra sex to supplement the meagre ration I receive from my wife. There aren't supposed to be ultimatums. If I say this, however, Sophia might never have sex with me again. But if I agree to her demand, I'll have to stop making love to my favourite person in the world.

It's a tricky situation.

"Agreed. X" I lie.

"What's agreed? Be specific."

"I agree to stop having sex with Tamsin and only make love with you."

I cross my fingers and hit send.

This is what Sophia wants to hear. I don't have to abide by it. After all, she won't know if I continue making love with Tamsin. It's only a little white lie.

"Really?"

"I promise. X"

"Oh, Lee. That makes me so happy! Xxx"

"Good. So, Friday...?"

"Definitely! I'm going to blow your mind!!! Xxx"

"Just my mind?!!"

"Wait and see!!! Xxx"

On Thursday morning, my phone beeps twice as two text messages arrive almost simultaneously. I can't help experiencing a frisson of excitement about receiving two coincident messages from the two gorgeous women that I'm having sex with. I bet there's nobody else in the office as lucky as me.

Naturally, I open the one from Tamsin first.

"Jake has two tickets to the football on Saturday. He wants to know if you want to go with him or maybe John?"

"Do you think John would be interested?" I reply.

"Yes. He and his mates seem to be getting more into football lately, and it would be good for his street cred if he went to this match. It's a big game."

"Fine by me. Tell Jake thanks and let him know that John would love to go with him."

"Will do."

"Fancy some rumpy later?! X"

No reply. She must have gone back to her classroom.

I open the message from Sophia.

"Hi."

"Hi, babe. What's up?"

Sophia responds with four messages in quick succession.

"Lee, please can you enter my orifice?"

"Oops! I meant 'come in my orifice'."

"OMG! I meant 'office'!"

"Or did I?!!!"

I chuckle. Sophia's messages are definitely more entertaining than Tamsin's.

"You're very funny! And very naughty!! I can't wait to be alone with you tomorrow. X"

"Me too. Although you realise I'm going to have to punish you!!!"

"Gulp! What for?"

"For not keeping in touch with me while you were on vacation."

"Sorry (again!) What's the punishment going to be?!"

"I think you deserve a damn good spanking!!!"

"Eek! My poor bottom. You won't leave any marks will you?!"

"I'll try not to. I reckon 10 hard smacks should suffice. However, because I'm nice, I'll take off 1 smack for every time you make me climax!"

"Excellent plan! What if I make you climax 12 times?"

"Then you'll owe me 2 smacks!!!"

"Ooh, I love maths! Challenge accepted! x"

Now, this is something of a dilemma. I love making Sophia climax. It's not quite as much fun as making Tamsin climax, but it comes close. However, I've also discovered that I rather enjoy being spanked. It's something I'd never experienced before, having never dared bring it up with Tamsin. I can imagine her response if I did:

"You want me to do *what*?!"

"Take my trousers down, put me over your knee and smack my bare bottom until it goes bright red."

"Seriously?"

"Yes. And at the same time, can you tell me I've been a very naughty boy."

"You want *me* to say *that*?"

"Yes. Preferably in a deep, throaty, sexy voice."

"How hard should I spank you?"

"Nice and hard, please. I want to hear a loud smacking noise."

"With my bare hand, or should I use a paddle or a whip?"

"Your hand should be fine. Hard enough to leave handprints if you'd be so kind."

"Isn't that going to hurt me as much as it hurts you?"

"Of course. Newton's third law of motion states that for every action there's an equal and opposite reaction."

"But *I* don't *like* pain."

"Hmm. I suppose you could use a paddle. That way it shouldn't hurt you at all."

"But we haven't got a paddle."

"You'll have to improvise."

"How about a rolling pin?"

"Are you mad, woman? I'm not convinced you're taking this seriously."

"A table tennis bat?"

"Now you're getting it. That would do nicely. It should generate a nice resounding thwack."

"Okay. What's my line again?"

"You've been a very naughty boy."

"You've been a very naughty boy."

"Not bad, but slower, deeper and more alluring."

"You've been a very naughty boy."

"Perfect. Now, if you could give me three smacks each time you say it. One on 'very', one on 'naughty' and the final one on 'boy'."

"Okay."

"Preferably with each smack getting slightly harder."

"It's complicated, isn't it? There's a lot to remember."

"Do you want me to write it down?"

"No. It's fine. I think I've got it."

"Ready to go then?"

"Not quite. I've got a couple more questions. What if I actually hurt you?"

"Ah! Now that's a good question. We should have a safe word."

"What's that?"

"Well, if it's really painful and I'm not enjoying it, then I'll say an agreed word and that'll tell you to stop."

"What word?"

"It could be anything. Banana? Serendipitous? Cerise?"

"Why can't you just say 'stop'?"

"Well, I might say 'stop', but not really mean it, because I'm acting."

"Huh?"

"You see, I'm playing the role of a naughty schoolboy who doesn't want to be spanked, so he's saying 'stop' to the sexy headmistress who's administering a thoroughly deserved punishment."

"Am I the sexy headmistress?"

"You certainly are."

"Do I have any other lines? What's my backstory?"

"Listen. All you've got to say is, 'You've been a very (smack) naughty (Smack) boy (SMACK)."

"In a slow, deep, alluring way?"

"Correct."

"So you don't want to be spanked?"

"No. (Sigh.) The schoolboy doesn't want to be spanked, but I do. So I'll be saying 'stop' in my role as the schoolboy, but the actual me *wants* to be spanked. Therefore, I can't have 'stop' as my safe word, because when I say 'stop' as the schoolboy, I actually mean 'keep going' as me. Do you see?"

"I think so. The safe word has to be something a schoolboy wouldn't normally say while he was being spanked."

"Now you've got it."

"But what if the schoolboy wants to say 'Wouldn't it be serendipitous if someone stuck a cerise banana up my arse'?"

"Ooh! Good point. He might say that. Why don't *you*

pick a safe word?"

"Wouldn't it be easier to have a safe sentence?"

"Like what?"

"How about, 'Tamsin, stop doing that, it bloody hurts'? I think it's quite unlikely a schoolboy would say that to his sexy headmistress."

"You're a genius, Tam. Let's go with that."

"Okey-dokey."

"All ready now?"

"Nearly. Just one more question."

"Fire away."

"WHY...?!!"

After a modicum of thought, I realise there's no dilemma at all. It's win-win for me. Either I make Sophia climax many times, which I love doing, or I get soundly spanked, which I love being.

Sophia really is exceptional at coming up with stimulating scenarios. Long may it continue.

# CHAPTER THIRTEEN

## *The Kitchen*

I'm standing in Sophia's kitchen, looking down at the top of her head as it oscillates backwards and forwards with a steadily increasing rhythm. My arousal is on the verge of reaching its zenith when the landline telephone rings. Sophia stops what she's doing, much to my disappointment, gets unsteadily to her feet, walks over to the breakfast bar and answers the phone.

I can only make out one side of the conversation.

"Hello?"

Faint, but unintelligible noise.

"Hi, Joe. What's up?"

Longer faint, but unintelligible noise.

"Sorry. You know I put my cell phone on silent when I'm at work."

She doesn't.

More faint, but unintelligible noise.

"You're coming home now?!" I can hear the panic in her voice. Hopefully, Joe can't.

More faint, but unintelligible noise.

Sophia draws aside the curtain and looks out the window.

"I see. Well, actually I'm at home at the moment too." She starts waving her free arm wildly, gesticulating frantically to get me to move. "I popped home to get some lunch."

She covers the mouthpiece and hisses in my direction, "It's Joe. He's nearly home. Hide!"

What do I do? Where do I go?

"I can see you now," Sophia says, feigning serenity and looking out the window again. "I'll put the kettle on."

She hangs up the phone and shouts at me, "He's coming down the road. Get out of sight, now!"

"Where? What's he doing here? Will he go upstairs?"

I'm horrified. Is Joe the violent sort, who'll murder his wife's lover with his bare hands and bury him in the garden, or the reasonable type, who'll invite him to partake in a friendly cup of tea while the situation is discussed calmly and rationally? Probably somewhere in between those two extremes, but hopefully nearer the latter.

"I don't know. Hurry! He's coming up the drive. Get down!"

She points behind the breakfast bar and I duck down just in time as the front door is already opening.

I lie on the floor beneath the breakfast bar, trying not to make a sound. I'm barely breathing and already feeling uncomfortable. My right hip is pressing against the unforgiving floor tiles and causing my leg to go numb; my bottom is still smarting from the spanking that it recently received; and I haven't even been able to tidy myself away and zip up for fear of making a sound and being detected. It occurs to me that my phone could ring or ping at any moment, but I'm too petrified to reach into my pocket to switch it off.

Sophia and Joe are about ten feet away, the other side of the breakfast bar, and I can hear every word they say.

"Hi, babe. What a pleasant surprise. I didn't expect to

find you here," Joe says, his voice deep and intimidating.

I hear them kiss.

"Forgot my lunch, so I thought I'd nip home and grab a quick bite," Sophia says.

"Lucky me. You look gorgeous today. Do you always look this good in your work clothes?"

"I certainly do."

"I hardly ever see you dressed for the office. By the time I get home, you've usually changed into something more comfortable. I like it."

Joe drops his car keys onto the breakfast bar, directly above my head.

"I'm glad you approve."

"Oh, it's more than approval. It's arousal. Got time for a quickie?"

I wasn't expecting this. Twenty minutes ago Sophia and I were in bed together upstairs. Five minutes ago I was in her mouth.

"It'll have to be *very* quick. I need to be back at work soon," she says.

To my surprise, she doesn't sound unenthusiastic.

"Awesome! I'm sure I can manage 'very quick.'"

From my hiding place, in the silence, I can hear kissing, and the rustling of clothes being removed and falling to the floor.

Then there's a noise that I'm very familiar with. Sophia is moaning with pleasure.

"Oh, babe!"

I don't know precisely what's going on, but I've got a pretty good idea, and Sophia is definitely enjoying it.

I hear the metallic jingle of Joe's belt being undone, then the unmistakable sound of a zip being unfastened.

A heavy thump tells me that Sophia has been lifted onto the breakfast bar.

This situation couldn't get much worse.

Sophia and Joe are having frenetic, noisy sex on the breakfast bar, six inches above my head.

From the sounds they're making, it's going really well. Sophia is giving Joe plenty of encouragement as their pace increases. She's either a brilliant actress, or she's thoroughly enjoying herself.

I can't hold back the notion that the thrill and danger of making love with her husband, while her lover is listening just inches away, is a huge turn-on for her.

I feel humiliated.

Sophia told me that she hadn't had sex with Joe for over eighteen months, but that's not the impression I'm getting from the noises I can hear. Neither of them is gasping, "This is so good. Why haven't we done it for over eighteen months?" They sound like a couple who have regular sex. It seems as if Sophia has been lying to me.

How did I get into this situation? Flaccid cock out, hiding on the floor under a breakfast bar. I normally find the noises of sex arousing, but the fear of imminent death and/or genital mutilation is having the opposite effect.

For a second, it occurs to me that Joe might be able to see me in the reflection of the cooker, but then I realise, with relief, that his view is blocked by my jacket hanging on the back of a kitchen stool.

My jacket is hanging on the back of a kitchen stool!!!

Nothing arouses me more than the acoustics of sex. The irrepressible moans, sighs and sharp intakes of breath are a huge turn-on. Then there's the purred encouragement:

"God, yes!"
"Oh, that's so good!"
(Sigh!)

"Slower."

"Deeper."

"Right there. That's it!"

(Gasp!)

"Oh my God!"

"Don't stop!"

"I'm so close!"

"You're amazing!"

"Mmmmmmmmmm!"

"Yes, yes, yes, yes, yes."

"Oh, Lee!"

I hope I never go deaf.

Sophia and Joe climax loudly at the same time. Or she fakes it. I honestly don't know anymore.

They're both panting heavily as they try to regain their composure.

"Oh my God, babe! I'm going to have to come home at lunchtime more often," Joe says, in between gasps.

"Yes, please. That was wonderful," Sophia says.

"I love you so much, Soph."

"I love you too, babe."

I can hear them retrieving items of discarded clothing from the floor, and getting dressed.

"Did you finish?" Joe asks.

"Couldn't you tell?"

"Is that a 'yes'?"

"Hell, yes! You always make me come, but that was particularly hot. We should have breakfast-bar-sex more often. How was it for you?"

"Awesome! Have you seen my other sock?"

"By the kettle. I'll get it."

"Ta. Sorry to love you and leave you, but I've got to get

back on the road. I'll just grab my file from the living room."

I hear retreating footsteps as Joe moves from the tiled kitchen floor onto the carpet of the hallway.

"Stay there!" Sophia whispers.

I take the opportunity to tuck away my floppy appendage and zip up, but I don't reply.

The click of a handbag and swishing sounds tell me that Sophia is brushing her hair.

She picks up two jangling sets of keys from the breakfast bar as Joe re-enters the room.

"Got it. Right, I'll see you later, babe. Probably around eight-ish?"

They kiss.

"Okay. I'll walk out with you."

Two sets of footsteps get quieter as they make their way to the front door. I hear it open and then slam shut. In the distance, two car engines start and slowly fade as the vehicles move off down the drive.

Silence.

I'm in Sophia's house on my own.

I don't move for five long minutes.

I just listen.

I can hear the hum of distant traffic on the main road, a blackbird singing in the back garden, a clock ticking somewhere in the kitchen, and the deep rumble of the washing machine in the utility room as it removes the guilty stains from the soiled sheets.

I raise my head above the breakfast bar and scan the room.

The kitchen is deserted.

I stand and walk cautiously to the window.

The drive is empty of cars.

I'm already late back for work, but I can't resist the opportunity to have a snoop around Sophia's house while I've got the chance.

I head upstairs.

My primary interest is Sophia and Joe's bedroom. I've never been in it before, having only been invited to use the spare room and the bathroom. It's large, tastefully decorated and dominated by a huge double bed. I'm surprised they still sleep together. That certainly isn't the impression Sophia gives when she describes their relationship, but I can't remember her explicitly saying that they no longer share a bed.

The first place I explore is the nearest bedside cabinet. Inside I find two books; one's a spy thriller and the other a self-help guide for boosting self-confidence. There's also a phone charger, Joe's passport, some earplugs, a half-empty bottle of over-the-counter painkillers, a golf magazine, some headphones and a packet of tissues.

Well, I've learnt something new about Sophia: she sleeps on the left side of the bed.

In *her* bedside cabinet – which is much fuller than her husband's, and more cluttered – there's a romance novel, lip salve, a rabbit vibrator, a diary, moisturising cream, cotton buds, massage oil, lubricant, nail varnish remover, some batteries, thrush ointment, a glass dildo, a purse containing £3.71 in coins, several miscellaneous chargers and leads, an old cell phone, a pack of playing cards with a different sex position on each one, an out-of-date packet of condoms, a very out-of-date packet of contraceptive pills, a hairbrush, a bar of chocolate, an eReader that won't switch on, a digital camera, some toy handcuffs, a pocket vibrator, a well-thumbed book of erotic short stories, a few photos of Sophia and Joe on a beach somewhere sunny, and a large, sharp kitchen knife.

I leaf through the diary.

At first glance, it doesn't seem particularly interesting. Sophia has recorded a few events retrospectively; films she's seen at the cinema, medical and dental appointments, phone calls she's made or received, and outfits she's worn to social functions. There are also quite a few apparently random letters, squiggles and dots.

Flicking back and forth through the diary, and doing a quick mental calculation, I suspect that 'P' on five or six consecutive days, roughly four weeks apart, is likely to be something to do with Sophia's monthly cycle.

But what do the other hieroglyphics mean?

Some dates have tiny dots in the corner. Last Friday has two; so does the previous Friday, and the one before it has three. There's also a Saturday a few months ago with three dots. It doesn't take much thought to realise that these dates correspond with the days when Sophia and I have had our liaisons. I guess the dots represent the number of times we had sex, or possibly the number of orgasms Sophia had.

On the days with the dots, there are also letters and numbers in tiny writing. I try to figure out what they could stand for.

M.
Missionary position?

C.
Cowgirl? Cunnilingus?

O.
Oral sex?

O with a dot in the middle.
Oral sex the other way round? Cunnilingus versus fellatio?

4.

A score out of ten? A percentage?!

Q.
Absolutely no idea. It can't be 'quickie'. We don't have those.

V.
Vibrator?

P.
Period? Porn? Penis? Penetration?

R.
Role-play? Reverse cowgirl?

F.
This one comes up a lot. Almost every time we've had sex. Fellatio? Fornication? Fantasy? Fisting? Fantastic?

D.
Dildo?

9.
Length of my penis? In inches? I wish! Definitely not in centi-metres.

A.
Anal?

X.
Xylophone? Is that a sex thing? X-ray? I've got nothing.

S.
Sixty-nine? Standing up? Shower? Sausage insertion?!

I realise I'm simply guessing and I could have many of these completely wrong, but when I think back to what we got up to on these dates, it's probable that at least some of my guesses are accurate.

What on earth is Sophia doing keeping a record of our sex life? If *I* can find her diary and figure out what the symbols mean, surely Joe can too.

On the one hand, this is alarming. It contains evidence of our affair; the very thing I'm trying to eliminate. It's the complete opposite of rule one: delete everything. She's actually recording everything.

On the other hand, it's a relief to realise that I'm not quite as abnormal as I'd thought for keeping a record of my sex life.

On the bedroom wall, near Joe's side of the bed, there are eighteen framed photographs of Sophia; on the beach, in her car, at restaurants, in their garden, at a wedding, amidst mountains, near a river or a famous landmark. They have one thing in common: Sophia looks beautiful in all of them. It's obvious that Joe has chosen his favourite photos of his wife and displayed them on the wall by his bed as a kind of shrine to the woman he loves.

I try not to think about how much it would hurt Joe if he was to become aware that his cherished wife and I have turned him into a cuckold. This snooping hasn't helped ease my conscience. I pause for a few minutes, looking at the photos and feeling guilty for what I'm doing to this poor deluded man.

It's an unarguable reason why Sophia and I should just end our affair.

Before I leave, I can't resist having a sneaky peek through Sophia's underwear drawer and, I'm embarrassed to say, having a quick sniff of some of her knickers. Why am I doing this? Is it anything to do with my ape ancestors sniffing the bottoms of potential mates? I certainly hope so, otherwise I'm a pervy knicker-sniffer as well as an adulterer.

It's not been a good day so far. My self-esteem has reached an all-time low.

Now I'm really late back for work. I jog downstairs, pick up my jacket and put it on. Checking the pocket for the bag containing one used condom and its wrapper, I exit the house through the back door as usual, only then realising that I'm unable to lock it. Sophia usually does this from inside the house after she's kissed me goodbye. It can't be helped. There's no way I'm going to leave through the front door. That would look too suspicious to anyone who saw both homeowners departing, followed ten minutes later by me, skulking guiltily away.

As I'm walking to the car, my phone vibrates. It's a text message from Sophia.

"I'm so sorry about that. I had no idea he was coming home. Xxx"

I don't reply.

Two minutes later, "Are you there?"

I don't reply.

One minute after that, "I feel terrible. Are you ok?"

I reply.

"I couldn't lock your back door."

"Don't worry about that. I'm really sorry, babe. Xxx"

"Don't call me babe. We need to talk, but not now. Driving."

"Please don't be cross. I'm crazy about you. Xxx"

I don't reply.

# CHAPTER FOURTEEN

*The Car*

I arrive back at work at least forty-five minutes late and head straight to my desk, carefully avoiding looking in Sophia's direction.

My phone buzzes every few minutes to signify incoming messages, but I ignore it and try to focus on my task.

After an hour or so, Sophia leaves her office and comes over to talk to me.

"Lee ..."

"I'm sorry, Soph," I interrupt. "I'm swamped at the moment. Can you come back later?"

I smile insincerely.

"Sure. No problem," she says breezily as she pivots and returns to her office.

I can't resist admiring her retreating backside. She swaggers with the confidence of a woman who's had two cocks inside her during one lunch break.

I recommence my task, pausing only to switch my phone to silent mode in order to stop the onslaught of pings and vibrations that have just resumed.

As soon as the first person in the office packs up to leave, I do the same, calling "See ya!" and "Have a good weekend!" to a few nearby colleagues.

I don't say goodbye to Sophia, however. I know I'm being passive-aggressive, but I'm still feeling angry and humiliated, and I just want to go home and unwind.

As I'm getting into my car, I hear someone calling my name in the distance, but I ignore it and begin driving.

I'm about halfway home when, in my rearview mirror, I see headlights flashing far behind me. Within thirty seconds there's a car right on my rear bumper, lights flashing and horn honking.

It's Sophia.

In the mirror, I can see her gesticulating towards the side of the road. It's obvious that she wants me to pull over.

I keep driving.

She keeps flashing, honking and pointing.

Surely she's not going to follow me all the way home.

It looks like she is.

I keep driving.

It still looks like she is.

I pull over.

She comes to a stop behind me, gets out of her car and runs towards mine, not even pausing to close her car door. She yanks open my passenger-side door and takes possession of the seat beside me.

"What was *that*?" I shout.

"I'm so sorry, Lee."

"You said he *never* comes home at lunchtime."

"He doesn't. That was the first time he ever has. I swear," Sophia says, tears welling.

"Do you realise what could have happened?"

"I do. Please don't shout at me."

Sophia starts to cry. Big fat tears are rolling down her cheeks, combining on her chin and dripping onto her blouse.

"What if he'd found me?" I say, my voice still raised.

"He didn't. We're okay."

"But what if he *had*? He might have literally murdered me. Or worse: he might have cut off my balls. Or worse still: he might have told Tamsin about us."

"But he didn't, Lee. He doesn't know anything about us. Nobody knows. Everything's fine."

"I was terrified! I thought I was going to wet myself."

"I can only tell you how sorry I am. Please don't be cross with me. I don't like it."

She looks at me pleadingly, making eye contact for the first time since getting into the car.

I'm not ready to stop ranting yet.

"It's all right for you. *You* were having a great time."

"I wasn't."

"I could hear you. You were loving it."

"I was just trying to distract him."

"You're kidding! I've never heard you come so loud."

"No. I was pretending. I love you, Lee. I was trying to keep you safe. I did it for you."

"What!"

"It worked, didn't it? He was so focused on me, he didn't even notice your jacket on the back of the chair. I distracted him and he left. All's well that ends well. Can't we just move on?"

She puts her hand on my thigh and looks at me imploringly.

"You had sex right above my head!" I shout even louder.

"He's my husband. What was I supposed to do?"

"You told me you hadn't had sex for eighteen months. That's not what it sounded like to me."

"I don't think I said that. I might have said we've *hardly* had sex for eighteen months."

"No, no, no. You definitely said you hadn't slept together for at least eighteen months."

"You must have misheard or misunderstood. Anyway, what does it matter? The bottom line is, we hardly ever have sex, and I'd far rather be with you."

"Did you have to orgasm so enthusiastically?"

"I was faking it. Couldn't you tell?" She's starting to sound exasperated.

"No, I bloody couldn't! It sounded genuine to me. Have you been faking it with me too?"

"Of course not. You always satisfy me. You know that."

"I don't think I know anything anymore."

My shoulders slump.

I've run out of steam.

"Look, I've got to get home," I say.

"I'm not leaving it like this."

"You haven't got a choice. I'm going home. Out you get." I gesticulate with my thumb.

"No. I'm not leaving until we make up. I have to convince you how much I love you."

"Don't you mean how much you love having sex with me?" I say, unable to keep the bitterness out of my voice.

"No. I don't mean that. Lee, I fell in love with you ages ago. Long before we started sleeping together. You must have realised."

"What?"

"I'd already been in love with you for months before you fondled my bottom. I was so happy that day. I didn't realise, until that moment, that you saw me in *that* way. Why do you think I suggested we have an affair?"

"For sex?"

"True. But I wanted to have sex with you because I was in love with you. I thought it would bring us closer together."

"Why didn't you tell me back then? I would *never* have agreed to an affair if I'd known you already had feelings for me."

"I didn't want to scare you off. I guess I was right not to say anything."

"So, what was your plan? Seduce me, make me fall in love with you ... then what?"

Sophia sighs, but says nothing.

We sit in silence for a while.

I'm wondering about the best way to get out of this mess that I've got myself into. Our affair is no longer what I thought it was. Sophia isn't just in it for the sex, like I am. She's in love with me. How many other lies has she told me? She's obviously still sleeping with Joe. From what I heard and saw at their house earlier, Joe loves his wife very much. I'm feeling overwhelmed with guilt. Guilt for cheating on Tamsin, guilt for what I'm doing to Joe, guilt for upsetting Sophia. My life has become way too conscience-stricken.

After a few uncomfortable minutes, Sophia turns on my car radio and tunes it to a station playing classical music.

"Do you mind?" she says. "This silence is unbearable. Please say something, Lee."

I take a deep breath.

"I think we should end it."

"No!" Sophia screams. "We can't end it. I love you."

"We can end it. Rule fourteen: no falling in love, and rule fifteen: either of us can end it at any time."

"Forget your stupid rules, Lee! We're so good together. We can't throw it all away."

"It's too stressful. Let's just call it a day."

"Leave her!" Sophia blurts out.

"What?"

"Leave Tamsin."

"Why?"

"If you leave her and I leave Joe, we could be together, like we talked about."

"I don't remember talking about any such thing," I say.

"Imagine what it'd be like. We'd be together all the time. We could spend every evening curled up in front of the telly. We could go out in public together, to restaurants and the cinema. We could have sex whenever we wanted. Every day of the week."

"There's more to life than sex, Soph." Did I really say

that? I'm such a hypocrite.

"I know," she says. "But we're so compatible in the bedroom. Surely that's a sign we're made to be with each other."

"What are you saying?"

"Who's better in bed; me or Tamsin?"

"You, but ..."

"Tell me our sex life's not awesome."

"It's really good, but ..."

"You have to admit that Tamsin doesn't satisfy you the way I do. You say it all the time."

"That's not the point. Just hang on a minute ...," I say as she tries to interrupt me again.

"Soph, I'm in love with my wife. I always have been. I always will be. Admittedly our sex life could be better, but that doesn't change the way I feel about her. The rest of our marriage is great. We have the odd row, but we work through it and move on. There's no way I'd leave Tamsin or my kids."

"But I'm certain I could make you really happy. Happier than you are with her. She doesn't deserve you. She doesn't love you as much as I do. Give me a chance to prove it. We could start again and make a new family of our own."

I can't help considering what Sophia has said, if only briefly.

It actually is possible that she loves me more than Tamsin does.

And the sex is incredible.

And we get on really well and make each other laugh all the time.

Could I honestly be happier with Sophia?

It's just the briefest aberration.

Tamsin is the love of my life.

My kids mean the world to me.

That's all there is to it.

"Soph, we can never be together the way you want. I made that clear from the start. I'm really fond of you and I love spending time with you, but I'll never leave my wife and family."

Sophia starts to cry again.

I continue, speaking softly. "I'm so sorry. I never meant to hurt you. I thought we both understood the limits of our relationship."

"Please, Lee. Now you know I love you, please give me a chance to convince you that we should be together," Sophia splutters, between sobs.

"It's never going to happen. I don't mean to sound cruel, Soph, but I have to be honest with you. We need to stop seeing each other. We should just concentrate on re-building our marriages. It's the right thing to do."

This doesn't help cheer her up. The tears continue to fall and the sobbing increases to the point where Sophia can no longer speak. I have no choice but to wait until she composes herself.

Eventually, the crying subsides.

Her tears have left a large damp patch on Sophia's blouse, through which I can clearly see her lacy, black bra. I feel awful for being aroused by sexy underwear at a moment like this. What kind of heartless monster have I become?

"Are you okay?" I ask.

"Not really." She looks at me, holding my gaze with her red-rimmed eyes.

"I hate seeing you so upset."

"It's not your fault," she says.

"I should be getting home."

"I know." She puts her hand on my knee. "I don't want it to be over, Lee. Please, at least think about it before you decide definitely. Sleep on it over the weekend."

I'm convinced that my mind is already made up, but I can't say that. I don't want Sophia to start crying again.

"Okay. I'll do that. But don't get your hopes up. We both know that ending our affair is the right thing to do."

"Thanks," Sophia says and leans forward to kiss me.

"Don't." I raise my hand between us and lean away from her. "Look, I'll see you on Monday."

There's nothing more to say. Just one word.

"Bye." She offers me a wan smile, opens the door, stands and walks forlornly back to her car.

I watch, miserable and guilt-ridden, as Sophia makes a U-turn and drives off towards her house, and when she's out of sight, I start my engine and head home.

The first thing I do on arrival is go upstairs and lock myself in the bathroom in order to read and delete my recent messages and call log.

There are twenty-three messages from Sophia:

"Hi."

"I'm really sorry. Xxx"

"Please can we talk in my office? X"

"I'm so sorry. Xxx"

"Please say something. X"

"Why won't you reply? X"

"Come to my office. I need to talk to you. Xxx"

"There's something I want to tell you."

"It's important."

"If you don't reply to my messages, I'm going to come and speak to you in person."

"Why are you being so mean to me?"

"I just want to explain."

"I love you, Lee. Xxx"

"I'm in love with you. Xxx"

"Say something."

"I had no idea Joe was coming home."

"He's never come home before."

"What do you want me to say?"

"Please don't be like this. X"

"I'm so sorry I had sex with him. I really didn't want to. Xxx"

"I love you so much! Xxxxx"

"I'm going to continue to send messages until you reply."

"Please come and see me before you go home. X"

I delete them all.

      The affair is over.

      I can relax.

# CHAPTER FIFTEEN

*The Letter*

T he next day, shortly after Tamsin politely but firmly re-
buffs my suggestion of Saturday morning sex, I offer to
give her a lift to the train station. She's spending the day shopping with Nilofer. As she lowers herself into the passenger seat
of my car, and turns to smile at me, I have to admire her. She
looks stunning today. Her hair and make-up are perfect, and
she's wearing a very elegant new outfit. I've definitely made
the correct choice. Tamsin is the woman I want to spend the
rest of my life with.

I start the engine and the radio springs to life as I begin
to drive.

"Classical music!" she says. "I didn't realise you were
into this old stuff."

"Oh, yes. I'm a big fan. There are probably all sorts of
things you don't know about me."

"Like what?"

"Er … like I'm considering taking up tennis so I can
spend more time with you."

"That's wonderful," Tamsin says, the same way she says
it when I go down on her. I have my doubts that she really
means it.

"And you've started to chew gum? I didn't know that either." Tamsin points to the wad of gum in my cup-holder.

"I have indeed. Why do you think my breath is always so fresh?"

This is a trick I learnt during my internet research into having affairs: always keep some chewing gum in the car. That minty smell disguises all sorts of suspicious aromas. Buying gum is one more thing I won't have to do anymore.

We arrive at the station and Tamsin climbs out of the car.

"Thanks for the lift. See you later," she says.

"Hey! Haven't you forgotten something?"

"What's that?" she leans back into the car.

"My goodbye kiss," I say and pucker my lips.

She puts one knee on the passenger seat and leans across to peck me on the cheek.

As she reverses back out the door, she spots something on the headrest of the passenger seat.

"What's this?" she says, holding a long hair between her thumb and forefinger. "Why is there a blonde hair in your car?"

Good grief! I thought the days of concealing my affair were behind me.

"Oh, that's probably from the prostitute I picked up last night for a quick blow job."

"That's not funny, Lee. Any serious excuses?"

"No idea, Tam. Maybe something to do with one of the kids' friends?"

"Maybe." She drops it on the ground, seemingly convinced.

"I'd better go. I think that's my train pulling in."

With that, she scurries towards the station entrance, without a backward glance.

I've considered using prostitutes a few times. Surely, if I'm not getting enough intimacy at home, it would be acceptable to pay a sex worker to reconcile my carnal imbalance? To be honest, I don't think Tamsin would even mind, as long as I didn't bring home any sexually transmitted diseases. At least it would take the pressure off her, and she wouldn't have to endure my constant pawing and requests quite so often.

The appeal of taking advantage of sex workers would be that I could actually ask for what I truly desired, as licentious as it may be, and hand over proportionate financial compensation to the unfortunate facilitator. There'd be no need to feel embarrassed or perverted. It would simply be a business arrangement with a complete stranger who I'd never see again. Wouldn't it be nice to just be able to say:

"How much would you charge to do this, that and the other to me; and to let me do this, that and the other to you?"

"Really? That seems ever so reasonable. How long would I get for that much money?"

"Hmm! Very tempting. And you honestly wouldn't object to doing *that* because there's no way my wife would. Not even on my birthday."

"I see. I must say, that's extremely accommodating of you."

"Yes, I suppose it *is* your job. Presumably, you take cash?"

"Would you want it up front or afterwards?"

"That's fine. Listen, are you *sure* you wouldn't mind doing *that*...?"

I have a couple of problems with the concept of paying someone for sex.

My first problem is, I suspect there's a substantial number of sex workers who're forced to do it against their will, and there's no way of knowing which of them see it as a job – a necessary evil which has to be endured in order to put food on the table; which are being illegally compelled to do it by a third party; or which have to do it in order to pay for an addiction. Is it their choice or are they being exploited?

Presumably, there are high-class escorts who earn far more money than me for having sex with sports figures, politicians and movie stars. They live in expensive apartments, wear nice clothes and can pick and choose who they sleep with. They might even enjoy some aspects of their job for a while, but it's not exactly a lifelong career. I contemplate splashing out on a high-end sex worker:

"How much would you charge to do this, that and the other to me; and to let me do this, that and the other to you?"

"Bloody hell! Do people actually pay that much?"

"I see. And you definitely wouldn't do *that* for any amount of money?"

"Fair enough. It *is* pretty gross. Well, you certainly are an exquisite woman."

"You're welcome. Sorry to have wasted your time."

My second problem is, I don't want to have sex with someone who I'm not attracted to. I've never knowingly met a prostitute in real life, but the way they're portrayed on television is particularly unattractive. The ones in my price bracket are usually either scrawny, spotty, greasy drug addicts or obese, spotty, greasy drug addicts. They certainly don't look like they spend much time at the gym or the beauty salon.

I guess, if I was ever to employ the services of a sex worker, it would be at a massage parlour. A nice, relaxing rubdown, culminating in a happy ending, my eyes firmly closed the whole time, imagining that it's Tamsin's soft hands all over my body. It could be just what I need now that I've ended my affair.

The best thing about my relationship with Sophia was, I could ask her to do anything, and she'd willingly and enthusiastically comply. In fact, she actively encouraged me to tell her my deepest, darkest, kinkiest desires. She was my very own, free, non-judgemental, devoted sex worker.

I'm going to miss her.

It's Monday morning, and Sophia has already made a point of walking past my desk several times. She's clearly made an effort to look her best today and is receiving admiring and lustful glances from most of the men and some of the women around the office. Unwilling to endure another onslaught of text messages, I go to see Sophia in her office at the start of my lunch break. I'm keen to confirm my decision to terminate our affair, clear the air, and resume a professional, friendly relationship with my former lover.

"Hi," I say from the doorway.

"Hi. Come in. Have a seat." Sophia gets up from behind her desk and closes the door, confining me within her territory.

"How are you doing?" I say.

"That depends on what your decision is."

She looks at me, searchingly, trying to read the expression on my face.

Now I can see her up close, it's apparent that she's not in great shape at all. Beneath the thick make-up her face looks puffy, and there are red veins visible in the whites of her eyes. I suspect that she's not had much sleep this weekend. Hopefully Joe hasn't spotted anything amiss.

"Please sit down, Lee. You look ridiculous standing there."

I comply.

I want this over as quickly as possible, so I get straight to the point.

"Soph, I haven't changed my mind. These past months have been wonderful. I've really enjoyed our time together, and I hope you have too, but I honestly believe it's for the best if we stop seeing each other now."

Any remaining vestiges of hope leave Sophia's face, and

she crumples in her chair.

She doesn't say anything, but at least she's not crying.

"You're an important part of my life," I continue. "I really hope we can still be friends. Good friends."

Still she doesn't speak. She gazes down at her hands, resting interlocked on her lap, and looks devastated.

"We've been fortunate to get away with it for so long," I say. "It's best if we don't push our luck, and just end it while our marriages are still intact."

She raises her head and looks at me.

"But I don't want our marriages to be intact. I want to be with you, not with Joe." I shake my head, but she continues before I can speak. "What I told you on Friday is the truth, Lee. I'm in love with you and I want to be with you. Nothing is going to change that. I can't simply switch off the way I feel."

"I'm sorry, Soph. This was never supposed to happen. We both agreed it was about sex, not love."

"I'm afraid it was always about love for me."

"You lied to me." I say it softly, not wanting this conversation to turn into an argument at the office.

"I had to. You were so adamant our affair was just for the sex that I didn't want to scare you off by revealing my true feelings. I hoped, after spending time together, you'd fall in love with me too. And I thought you had."

"What made you think that? I certainly never said it."

"You didn't have to say it. I could tell by the way you looked at me when we made love."

I sigh.

"I'm really sorry. I do love looking at you when we have sex… when we *had* sex. I'm really fond of you, Soph, but I'm not in love with you. I'm in love with Tamsin and that isn't going to change."

I pause, expecting Sophia to speak, but she says nothing, so I try to bring this dialogue to a conclusion.

"Our affair is over. It should never have happened in the first place. I'm so sorry if I've hurt you, Soph, but we must do the right thing now. We need to move on, as friends and colleagues who care a lot about each other, but that's it. No more sex. No more inappropriate messages. It's probably best if we try to not be alone together, at least for a while, until we get back into a routine of behaving appropriately."

She holds my gaze for a long time. An uncomfortably long time. She looks sad and broken.

"That's not what I want," she says.

"But I'm afraid that's how it's going to have to be," I reply, slowly getting to my feet and edging towards the door. "Bye, Soph."

I open the door and head to the kitchen to make myself a cup of coffee I don't think I'll be able to drink.

Have I done the right thing? Sophia has convinced me that she's genuinely in love with me. I feel flattered by that and terrified at the same time. It's uplifting to have an attractive woman fall in love with you, but the revelation that I'm responsible for Sophia's happiness is making me very uncomfortable.

She claimed she was already in love with me before we even started having sex. I know from my earlier research that 51 percent of men and 63 percent of women consider emotional affairs to be actual infidelity. Does that let me off the hook at all? Most people, especially women, would consider Sophia to have been unfaithful to her husband before I even grabbed her bottom, merely due to her feelings for me. It wasn't *my* fault she fell in love with me. She'd already been unfaithful in her heart before I even had sex with her.

I find it bizarre how men and women differ so much when it comes to emotional infidelity.

Most men say, they'd be more upset if their partner was having a sexual relationship, but hadn't fallen in love.

Most women say, they'd be more upset if their partner

had fallen in love, but hadn't had sex with that person.

I don't think I'd be too upset if Tamsin fell in love with another man, but didn't have sex with him. That would demonstrate that she loved me and was committed to our marriage. I'd be devastated, however, if Tamsin secretly had sex with another man, whether she loved him or not. Interestingly, there's something rather titillating about the notion of Tamsin having sex with another man – one she didn't love – and letting me watch. I believe it's a common male fantasy to imagine your wife having sex with another man, and I can see the appeal. There's no way I'd let Tamsin do it in real life, of course, but it's a pleasant thought experiment, nevertheless.

The article I read said, 45 percent of men and 35 percent of women admit to having an emotional affair. I guess Sophia considers herself to be part of that 35 percent. In my mind, I didn't commit adultery until the actual moment I put my penis inside Sophia, and I never fell in love with her. But, somehow, I don't think Tamsin would be reassured by that.

The next few days are better than I was expecting. Although she doesn't look happy, Sophia is keeping herself busy and maintaining an appropriately professional relationship with me whenever we bump into each other around the office and in meetings. If our eyes meet, she smiles tenderly and sympathetically at me. It actually feels as if she's the one who's trying to cheer *me* up. She's made no attempt to resume our break-up conversation, much to my relief.

The first post-affair Friday lunchtime is particularly tough. I see Sophia leave her office, on her own, at the usual time, glancing in my direction on her way out of the building. I suspect she's going home in the hope that I'll follow five minutes later and join her, but I ignore the Pavlovian response going on inside my boxer shorts, and continue to work at my desk. I'm hoping that keeping my mind active will distract me from the sexy woman who's currently anticipating that I'll turn up at her house and make love to her.

Sophia looks so sad as she leaves work this evening. I realise I'm the one responsible and I feel terrible, but hopefully, it's only a matter of time until she gets over me and perks up.

I'm walking across the car park towards my car when I notice that someone has tucked an envelope under my front windscreen wiper.

I pick it up.

It doesn't look like an advert or a flyer. It's just a regular white envelope.

I open it.

Inside there's just a single piece of paper, with two words and some excessive punctuation typed upon it:

"I know!!!"

What does that mean?

'I know' what?

I know you're having an affair?

I know you cheat on your expense claim form?

I know you reversed into my car?

And what's the significance of all the exclamation marks?

Maybe it's a case of mistaken identity and it's not even meant for me.

But maybe it is.

My guilty conscience is telling me that I'm the intended recipient, and that someone knows about my affair, but if I'm right, what's their motive for leaving me the letter? To shame me into doing the right thing? To get some sort of sadistic pleasure from my discomfort? Blackmail?

Things aren't great at home. It's the second weekend in a row with no sex.

On Saturday, Tamsin gets up early to go shopping in some remote mall, not returning until late, laden with several carrier bags from high-end clothes shops. Sometimes, after one of these shopping trips, I'm able to persuade Tamsin to perform a highly entertaining and stimulating fashion show, just for me, in which she models her new purchases and parades around the bedroom; but not this time. She claims to be too tired after spending all day on her feet.

On Sunday, I wake up in a grumpy mood, weary of feeling ignored and neglected by my wife. Tamsin manages to push enough of my buttons to provoke a row about nothing, and now we're barely speaking to each other. I can't help thinking that she's done this deliberately in order to avoid lovemaking for a few more days. Or possibly I'm just horny, tired and paranoid.

Sophia's cousin, Claire, was diagnosed with breast cancer yesterday. She's an emotional wreck at work today and I feel I ought to say something to her. Perhaps I can offer some words of comfort. Isn't that what friends are for?

The minute I enter Sophia's office, she gets up from behind her desk and enfolds me in a spontaneous hug. There's nothing sexual about it. She simply wants me to hold her while she sobs. So I comply. This is clearly a violation of rule nine, but I guess the rules no longer apply now that our affair is over. It just feels like the right thing to do. We're spotted, however, by several people walking past Sophia's office, and it must look curious for two colleagues to be hugging while one of them weeps. I grow increasingly uncomfortable as the embrace continues, and I visualise how we must appear to our colleagues. As soon as I'm able, I disentangle myself from Sophia's arms and take a seat adjacent to her desk. While Sophia shares her worries and fears for her much loved cousin, I contribute a few appropriate platitudes until gradually she cheers up a bit. As soon as I think I can reasonably depart, I make my excuses and leave.

When I return to my desk, I'm aware of conflicting reactions. On the one hand, I want to be a caring and sympathetic person, supportive of my family and friends; but on the other, that was definitely a backward step as far as physically distancing myself from Sophia is concerned. Fortunately, I don't have a third hand, because, if I did, it would be slapping me around the face and saying, "Yes, it did feel wonderful to hold Sophia in your arms again, but you can't have sex with her anymore, so just pull yourself together and stick to your principles."

On Friday morning, I receive a text message from Sophia. It's the first one we've exchanged since I ended our affair.

"Hi."

"Hi, Soph. You ok?"

"Not really. I'm so upset about Claire."

"I understand. It's terrible news. Please let me know if there's anything I can do to help. Anytime. I'm always here for you."

"Thanks, Lee. That's extremely kind. Actually, there is something you can do. I really want someone I can talk to. There's so much going on in my head. I just want to say it out loud. Do you know any good listeners?"

"Me! I'm a good listener." What am I doing? Trying to be a good friend? "Your office? At lunchtime?"

"That would be great, but I'm worried I might blub, and I don't want to make a fool of myself at work. Any chance we could meet at my house at lunchtime instead? Just for a bit of privacy."

Ah!

I thought I'd already made my final visit to Sophia's house. It was that memorable time when I hid beneath the breakfast bar while Sophia and her husband had passionate sex on top of it. Just thinking about it brings me out in a cold sweat. But this would be different, wouldn't it? Our affair is over now.

Before I can reply, Sophia sends another message.

"Just to talk, I promise."

What can I say? She's clearly upset and in need of a confidant. I've claimed that I want us to remain friends, and her reasoning is sound: it would be better to talk away from the office. I can't say no.

"Sure. No problem."

"Thanks, Lee. You're so kind. See you soon. X"

What could possibly go wrong?

Before leaving the office to drive to Sophia's house, I pop into the staff bathroom to freshen up and apply deodorant and aftershave, for no reason.

# CHAPTER SIXTEEN

*The Mistake*

I approach Sophia's house through the back garden as usual. The only slight change to my routine is that I knock before entering the kitchen. Sophia opens the door and invites me inside.

"Hi, Lee. Thanks so much for coming. I really appreciate it."

"That's what friends are for," I say as I make myself comfortable on a kitchen stool.

"Coffee?" Sophia hands me a steaming mug.

"Thanks."

All is good so far. We're being polite and well behaved. Normally, I wouldn't have time to drink anything at Sophia's house; we'd just sprint upstairs to the spare bedroom and start shagging. It feels as if we've turned a corner.

As we sip our coffee, Sophia tells me the latest news about her cousin. Apparently, Claire's prognosis is better than her family were expecting, but she's going to have to undergo several sessions of chemotherapy over the coming months. When she tells me about Claire's young children, Sophia's voice breaks. Her bottom lip starts to quiver, and suddenly the dam breaks and she bursts into tears.

Sophia strides towards me and 1 stand and meet her

halfway. She puts her arms around me, presses her torso against mine and holds me tight. I have no option other than to reciprocate as her whole body quivers with unleashed emotion.

What else can I do?

For a while, she sobs into my neck and I murmur a few kindly platitudes such as, "Everything will be all right", "That's it, just let it all out", and "She'll be fine, survival rates are really good these days." But mostly, I just hold her securely and caress her back.

Unfortunately, the proximity of a vibrant, attractive woman, in combination with my recent dearth of physical intimacy at home, is causing an unmistakable stirring in my loins. A significant stirring. One of which Sophia cannot be unaware. If I didn't know any better, I'd suspect that she's actually pressing herself into my erection and making it worse. I'm acutely aware of Sophia's soft warm breasts pressing into my midriff, which is only exacerbating the problem. However, neither of us comments on my awkward and untimely arousal.

The sobbing gradually subsides, but the hug continues. The crying is replaced by occasional sniffs. I can't be sure if Sophia's nose is running, or she's simply enjoying the smell of my aftershave, but the reason soon becomes clear when she releases me from our embrace and excuses herself to fetch some tissues from upstairs.

I spend the few minutes when Sophia is absent trying to come up with particularly unpleasant or distracting thoughts in order to diminish my arousal:

The Holocaust.
37.2 multiplied by 54.
The current Arsenal squad in order of shirt number.

The most agonising pain I've ever experienced: childbirth.

My mortgage.

The time my mum caught me masturbating in the bath.

Being force-fed shell fish.

Those big hairy spiders that live in the loft and venture into my bedroom when I'm asleep to lay their eggs in my ear-hole.

The knowledge that I'm just an insignificant animal, on an average-sized planet, in a nondescript solar system, going around a typical galaxy, in an unexceptional universe, in a multiverse that will exist for all eternity.

Cancer.

When Sophia steps back into the room, I'm relieved to see that she's stopped crying and has fixed her hair and make-up. She looks much chirpier.

She's also completely naked.

Well, this is awkward. I'm fully dressed, and all alone, in a kitchen containing a very sexy, naked lady. My resurgent erection is reminding me that I haven't had sex for going on three weeks, and this situation looks promising in terms of ending the drought.

Sophia just stands there and looks at me. Her weight is all on one leg while the other leg is bent slightly inwards at the knee. Her hands are resting on her hips, her shoulders pulled back and her chest thrust provocatively forward. Her chin is slightly elevated and her facial expression is neutral. She doesn't say anything. She doesn't need to say anything. Actions speak louder than words, and Sophia's actions are bellowing, "I really want to make love with you, Lee. Do you have the willpower to turn me down?"

Do I?

I know what I *should* do.

I should say, "I'm really sorry, Soph, but our affair is over. It's best if I just leave now." Then walk straight out the door and never look back.

I know what I *could* do.

I could say, "God, I've missed you so much, Soph!" and take her upstairs for a damn good shagging.

This is one of the moments that will gauge my current moral rectitude. It's an opportunity for me to demonstrate that I'm a better man than I used to be and I've learnt from my mistakes. I can take the high road or the low road. Am I the kind of man who takes advantage of a fragile and emotional friend in order to gratify his physical desires? I know what I want to do, but I also know the right thing to do. Do I have the willpower to turn her down?

No.

That would be ridiculous. I'm horny and she's sexy, willing and naked. End of story.

I slowly walk towards her, enjoying the magnificent view the whole way. Sophia looks anxious, but keeps her eyes locked on mine. I stop two feet in front of her.

"Are you sure about this?" I say.

"Yes," Sophia whispers in reply.

I bend down and pick her up in a fireman's lift, then carry her over my shoulder up the stairs as she giggles all the way.

We have sex like never before. It's passionate, intense and borderline violent. Our hands are all over each other, but not gently and sensually like every time before. This time it's rough and aggressive. We manhandle each other all around the bedroom, frequently changing position and asserting dominance over each other. I've never felt so uninhibited and out of control.

When it's over, and we're lying entangled on the

floor, breathing heavily and sweating profusely, Sophia says, "Bloody hell!"

"Indeed," I reply, still shell-shocked.

"That was intense!"

"It really was."

"You make me so happy, Lee." She kisses me on the cheek. Her face is radiant, and she exudes joy and contentment.

Is now a good time to mention that what we've just done was a terrible mistake? Should I take this opportunity to tell Sophia that it should never have happened and we can never do it again?

No. It can wait.

I decide to bask in the postcoital glow for a few minutes more before I break the bad news to Sophia.

I change the subject. "I saw your diary."

"Huh?"

"The last time I was here; after you left. I had a nose around in your bedroom and found your diary."

"What! You shouldn't have done that! You had no right to go through my personal belongings." Her words sound severe, but she's trying to remain calm to extend the pleasant ambience of our lovemaking.

"No. I realise that now, but I was so upset and angry after hearing you screw your husband, I did it without thinking."

"There's nothing interesting in my diary. I barely write anything in it," she says.

"No, but you do record our sex life, don't you?"

"What do you mean?"

"The dots, the symbols, the letters. It's a record of what we've done together each time we've met."

After a long pause, Sophia comes clean. "Yes, you're right. But there's no way Joe would know that."

"How could you do it, Soph? We agreed to delete everything. What if Joe had found it and scrutinised it?"

"He wouldn't have understood what it all meant. It's

just a load of code symbols."

"They weren't exactly hard to decipher. It took me about five minutes to figure out what most of the symbols mean. What's X by the way?"

"That sideways thing we do, when our bodies sort of make a cross shape."

"Oh, yeah. What about S?"

"Sixty-nine."

"I thought so. Q?"

"Quick."

"We don't have quickies."

"No. Quick, not quickies. You finished too quickly for me."

"You never said anything at the time," I say, as my self-esteem shrivels, mirroring my spent penis.

"I didn't want to upset you," she says.

"Very thoughtful of you. F?"

"It doesn't matter."

"P?"

"Look, the important thing is, Joe never looks at my diary, and even if he did, he'd have no idea what the letters and dots mean."

"You've got to destroy it, Soph. It's evidence of our affair."

"Seriously?"

"Absolutely."

"I don't see why it matters. It's just for my own personal use."

"I don't care. Promise me you'll destroy it."

Sophia looks bemused by my insistence.

"Okay, Lee. If that's what you want."

"It is. Thank you." I lean forward and kiss her tenderly on the lips.

"Fancy another go?" Sophia says with a mischievous glint in her eye.

"You're kidding! I'm completely drained. And we need

to be getting back to work."

"Spoilsport!" Sophia smacks me on the bottom as I get to my feet.

"I'm just going to jump in the shower."

"Want some company?" she calls after me.

"You're insatiable, woman!" I shout over my shoulder and lock the bathroom door behind me.

This doesn't feel like the right time to break the bad news to Sophia that, despite evidence to the contrary, we're still irrevocably broken up. Perhaps I'll do it by text message this afternoon. That might be safer and easier.

I spend most of the afternoon pretending to work at my desk, but in reality I'm trying to compose a suitable text message; one that will be precise, contrite, gentle, irrefutable, reasonable and final, all at the same time. It isn't easy.

The timing is crucial as well. I want to send it very close to the end of the workday, so I can then escape to the safety of my home, but I should also leave sufficient time to answer any queries Sophia may have.

Unfortunately, five minutes before the allocated time, Sophia pre-empts me and sends a text message of her own.

"Thank you, sweetie. That was heavenly. I'm so glad we're back together. I've already started planning some fun activities for next Friday!!! Xxxxx"

Ah!

This just got a lot harder.

My first instinct is to accept the status quo. It was an exceptionally enjoyable way to spend a Friday lunchtime, and the prospect of a repeat performance in a week's time is very tempting indeed. Also, I wouldn't have to deal with the histrionics that would inevitably follow if I was to tell Sophia that our affair definitely is over, and that today was simply a mistake on my part. However, I know it can't continue. The sex is lovely, but the price is too high. Sophia is becoming emotionally dependent on me and the likelihood of being found out is rising as she ceases to fully adhere to the rules of our affair. This isn't what we agreed, and I feel justified in calling a halt to the whole business. It's regrettable that I slipped up today, but Sophia was *naked* for goodness' sake.

I carefully edit my response.

"I'm so sorry, Soph. I was weak today. That should never have happened. It was my fault for coming to your house. It's obviously not safe for us to be alone together. Our affair has to stop. That was the last time. It was indeed heavenly. Let's leave it at that, with one last wonderful time together. Still friends?"

I wait anxiously for a reply, half expecting to hear a scream of anguish coming from Sophia's office.

When the reply arrives, it's not what I'm expecting.

"You're wrong, I'm afraid. I won't rest until I've convinced you of what I already know: WE BELONG TO-GETHER!!!"

This is new. I compose a quick reply; I want to go home.

"I fear you'll be wasting your time and energy. As far as I'm concerned, our affair has ended amicably and we're now just good friends."

"And as far as I'm concerned, we are still in a sexual relationship and we're very much in love with each other. I simply need to convince you of that fact. Xxx"

"I think we might have to agree to disagree then, but I won't be coming round to your house anymore or sending you inappropriate messages."

"We'll see! Have a good weekend. I'll be in touch, sweetie. Xxx"

# CHAPTER SEVENTEEN

*The Final Straw*

"**O**h my God! What's happened to your back?"

It's the morning after my relapse and I've just stepped out of the shower.

"Nothing." I try to inspect myself over my shoulder in the bathroom mirror, but the steam and the uncomfortable angle make it impossible to see anything on my back.

I grab a shaving mirror and go into the bedroom to look at a reflection of my reflection in the wardrobe mirror.

Now I see what Tamsin has already spotted. There are several red, raised weals on my back. To me, it looks exactly like the marks that would be left after someone with sharp fingernails scratched someone else's back during unrestrained, no holds barred fornication. I have no recollection of Sophia being quite so aggressive, but in the heat of unbridled rough sex, I probably just didn't notice it happening.

"Crikey! That looks nasty," I say.

"I agree. How did you do it?"

"Er ... When I was out running after work yesterday I tripped and fell over. It didn't seem too bad at the time."

"You fell over while running and landed on your *back*?"

Tamsin says, incredulous.

"Yeah. I guess I must have stumbled over a tree root or something and I sort of twisted in midair and came down heavily on my back."

"That must have really hurt."

"Not that much actually. My pace was pretty good, and I thought I might be close to a record run, so I just rolled up onto my feet and kept going. I'd completely forgotten about it until now."

"You need to be more careful, Lee. You're no spring chicken anymore."

"You're right. I'll definitely be more careful in future."

I will. No more adultery. That was the last time I'm ever going to be unfaithful to my wife. There'll be no more suspicious scratch marks, text messages or phone calls from now on.

Tamsin takes the dirty washing out of the laundry basket and sniffs the shirt I was wearing yesterday.

"Mmm! Your shirt smells nice. Are you wearing new aftershave?"

"No. Just my usual stuff," I say.

"I like it. It's quite a feminine smell. Vanilla possibly?" She sniffs it again and hands it to me for confirmation. She's right. Tamsin is something of an expert when it comes to vanilla.

"How strange. Perhaps all the ice-cream I've been eating has affected my sweat glands."

"Yeah. Two things, genius: it doesn't work like that and you don't even *like* ice-cream."

"Good point."

It's puzzling that my shirt smells like it does, because that's undeniably the fragrance of Sophia's body lotion. She was wearing it yesterday, presumably ignoring rule seven as she wasn't expecting to be getting quite so intimate and physical with me. However, when I showered afterwards, all trace of the smell should have been eliminated, and yet there's a noticeable vanilla aroma emanating from my shirt.

"I reckon you've been sampling ladies perfume at the shopping centre. If you want me to buy you a less manly aftershave, you only need to ask." She smiles, unable to resist teasing me at every opportunity.

"Thanks, Tam. I'll think about it."

In the evening, I'm watching television with Tamsin when she pauses the movie and turns to me.

"I saw one of your colleagues in town today."

"Oh yeah." My heart speeds up in anticipation of another potential crisis. "Who was it?"

"Sophie? Sophia? Something like that. I met her at your Christmas party. The chubby one."

"Ah. Did you chat?" I'm beginning to sweat.

"We did actually. She came over and said hello and then started asking about our holiday. She spoke to me as if we were lifelong friends. It was bizarre."

"I didn't realise you knew each other that well."

"We don't. It made me rather uncomfortable, to be honest."

"What did she say?"

"Nothing really. She said you'd told her all about our summer holiday, and she was thinking of going to the same region with her husband. I can't remember his name. John is it?"

"I'm pretty sure it's Joe," I say.

"That's it. She was mostly trying to get my advice about the local restaurants, as far as I could tell."

"I see."

"Maybe I've made a new friend." Tamsin looks at me wryly.

"Maybe you have. Shall we carry on with the movie?"

"Yeah." She presses play and we say no more about it.

I'm struggling to concentrate on the plot, however, as deafening alarm bells are ringing regarding Sophia's recent erratic behaviour.

Did she deliberately cause those marks on my back in order to make Tamsin suspicious? Did she tamper with my shirt while I was in the shower to make it smell questionable? Did she approach Tamsin in town as some sort of warning to me?

I'm worried that Sophia is no longer trying to conceal our affair. On the contrary, she seems to be trying to point Tamsin towards it by giving her obvious clues. Perhaps she's decided that if I won't leave Tamsin to be with her, then she'll force Tamsin to leave me.

After an anxious night, with little sleep, I was too stressed to even try to initiate sex with Tamsin this morning, but she didn't appear to notice. There have been no more Sophia incidents and I'm beginning to relax as we all sit down for Sunday lunch. Tamsin and John have cooked us a delicious looking roast dinner, but I can't say I'm particularly hungry.

Five minutes into the meal my phone vibrates in my pocket.

I ignore it. I hate it when people use their cell phone during mealtimes. We should be conversing with each other, not looking at our gadgets.

It vibrates again twice more in quick succession.

I ignore it and ask Charlie to pass me the roast potatoes.

During a lull in the conversation, we all hear my phone buzz three more times.

"Someone's very popular today," Tamsin says, looking annoyed.

"Sorry. It's probably just notifications about the goals in

a football match."

"I don't think anyone's playing at the moment, Dad," John contributes, helpfully.

Four more evenly spaced vibrations. They're coming roughly every thirty seconds now.

"I'll turn it off," I say.

I take the phone out of my pocket and have a sly glance at the screen below the level of the table, so nobody else can see it.

"It's only Jake. I'll give him a call after lunch."

I switch off my phone and replace it in my pocket.

Tamsin looks suspicious.

I wonder what she'd say if she'd seen the message that I'd just glanced at.

It contained a photo of something I recognised immediately.

Sophia had decided that Sunday lunchtime was the appropriate moment to send me a photo of her vagina.

It's not until evening, while Tamsin is having her Sunday night bath, that I switch on my phone again and look at the messages.

The first few are graphic photos of body parts: vagina, breasts, legs, anus, lips, ear, fingers, buttocks. None of the snapshots enable the viewer to identify the owner of these erogenous zones, but I'm well acquainted with all of them. Together they make up a deconstructed collage of my favourite parts of Sophia.

Then the messages begin.

"Hi!!!!!!!!!!!! Xxx"

"I hope you like my photos, sweetie. Xxx."

"They're all parts of my body that you know intimately! X"

"I had a lovely time on Friday. I hope you did too. Xxx"

"I can't wait to do it again next Friday. Xxx"

"And the following Friday! Xxx"

"Soon we'll be able to do it every day!!! X"

"I hope you realise how much I'm in love with you. Xxx"

"This ..........."

Twelve minutes elapsed until the subsequent message arrived.

"........... much! Xxx"

"I had a lovely chat with Tamsin yesterday."

"How strange that I should just happen to bump into her in town!"

"I really don't understand what you see in that shrew. She's so scrawny!"

"I bet she doesn't make you come as hard as I do!!! Xxx"

"I'd better go. Things to do. Plans are afoot! X"

"I can't wait to see you tomorrow, sweetie! Xxx"

"No need to reply. I know you're probably busy having your lunch! Xxx"

I'm going to have to have serious words with Sophia tomorrow. She's completely out of order.

While I remember, I quickly send a text message to Jake.

"Hi, mate. If Tamsin asks, you sent me a load of messages today at about 13:15."

"WTF???" came his speedy reply.

"It's not my fault. I did the right thing and split up with the woman from work, but she's having trouble accepting it's over. She sent me a bunch of messages today during Sunday lunch! I told Tamsin they were from you, so if she asks, you know what to say."

"All right, mate. I've got your back. But let's make this the last time, yeah?"

"Agreed. Thanks again for taking John to the football. He had a great time."

"No problem. It was good fun."

"See you soon."

"Will do. And be careful, mate. This Sophia sounds a bit unstable."

"No worries, mate. It's all under control."

My memory must be deteriorating as I get older. Jake and I have only communicated a couple of times regarding Sophia, and I've absolutely no recollection of telling him her name.

I spend another uncomfortable night thinking about what to say to Sophia when I see her next. What's the best way to convince her that our affair is over and that we both have to get over it and move on with our lives?

The following morning, I start my car engine and begin to reverse down the drive. The back windscreen is filthy, so I switch on the rear wiper to clear away the worst of the grime. That's when I spot it.

Stuck under the wiper, there's another envelope. It looks identical to the one I found the other day at work. Not wishing to draw attention to it, in case anyone is watching me from the house, I drive along the road and out of sight before stopping the car and retrieving the letter.

I tear it open to find another type-written message on a single piece of paper.

"If you don't tell your wife, then I will."

That's all.

It's got to be from Sophia. But this time she left it at my house. At my house! How dare she? What if Tamsin or one of the kids had found it? It had no name on the front so anyone might have opened it. I would have struggled to explain it away if anyone else had found the letter and asked me about its meaning.

This has got to stop.

Now!

I drive to work, getting angrier by the minute. The stress is starting to get to me. I want to go back to my nice, easy, relaxed life, when all I had to worry about was my expanding waistline, hair loss and the kids taking drugs or getting pregnant.

On my arrival at work, I march straight into Sophia's office and have a go at her.

"What do you think you're playing at? Your behaviour is completely out of order!"

She can tell that I'm furious and she tries to placate me.

"Calm down, Lee. This isn't the time or the place for this conversation."

"I don't care! I want to resolve it now. Once and for all."

"Not here. Keep your voice down. People are starting to stare at us."

"Where and when, then?"

"My house? Lunchtime?"

"Oh, no! I'm not falling for that one again. As soon as you get me there, you'll probably try to seduce me."

"You didn't seem particularly unwilling last time."

"You lured me there and lead me astray in a moment of weakness."

"Are you saying you didn't want to have sex with me last Friday, because you *seemed* to be really enjoying it?"

"No. I honestly didn't."

"So you had sex against your will?"

"Absolutely."

"Lee, are you accusing me of rape?" she says, raising her voice slightly.

"Shhh! No. Of course not. Look, perhaps this isn't the

best place for this conversation."

"I agree."

"What about in the car park at lunchtime?" I say.

"Don't you think it'll seem suspicious if we start having a heated conversation in the car park?"

"I guess so."

"I really think my house is the best and the safest place to meet. I promise I won't rape you this time."

"Or cry on me? Or take off any of your clothes?"

"Agreed," she says, believing that she's convinced me.

She hasn't. I begin to decline her invitation. "I'm not sure …"

"For goodness' sake, Lee! We need to talk in private. There's something important I have to tell you. I think it'll make you extremely happy."

"I doubt that very much. Unless you're going to tell me you've come to your senses and you want to apologise for your nutty behaviour."

"You'll find out at lunchtime."

"Okay." Without another word, I head back to my desk, resolving to behave flawlessly this time.

When I arrive at Sophia's house, I barge through the back door without knocking. I want this over with as soon as possible, and I'm single-minded in my resolution to behave exactly as a married man should.

Sophia looks radiant and greets me warmly; a contented smile on her face.

"Your coffee, sweetie." She starts to hand me a mug, but I wave it away.

"Forget the coffee. Let's just have our conversation, resolve this mess and get back to work."

"If that's what you want. But if you fancy making love to me, upstairs or in the garden, then I'm also up for that." She actually winks at me.

"That'll never happen again, Soph."

"Oh, I think it will. I've been…"

I interrupt. "Listen! Have you been leaving clues for Tamsin, so she'll start figuring out we had an affair?"

"What do you mean?" Sophia looks a picture of innocence.

"You must realise how badly you scratched me on Friday. I had big red gouges all over my back from your fingernails digging into me. When Tamsin noticed she was suspicious straight away. Luckily, I made up a convincing story, but it was a close shave."

"Lee, you can't blame me for my behaviour in the heat of passion. Sometimes you get me so turned on I lose control. You should see those scratches as a compliment to your superb lovemaking skills."

She isn't taking this seriously at all.

"I can't help suspecting you did it deliberately." I scrutinise her face, looking for signs of culpability.

"That's crazy!" she says.

I need to maintain my momentum before she changes the subject or starts removing items of her clothing.

"And what about my shirt? Did you put body lotion on it when I was in the shower?"

"What! Why would I do that?"

"So Tamsin would smell it and think I was having an affair."

"Of course not. That's ridiculous."

"Then why did my shirt stink of your body lotion the next morning?"

"I honestly have no idea, Lee."

"I suppose you're going to deny sending me all those photos and messages yesterday too."

"No. That was definitely me." She smiles. "Did you like the photos?"

"They arrived in the middle of our Sunday lunch!"

"Yes, but did you like them?"

"I was with my family!" I sound more and more exasperated.

"That's good. I hoped you would be."

"Why?"

"I thought it'd be a thrill for you to receive naughty photos from your mistress in the middle of your family lunch."

Is she psychotic?

I sigh. The anger is fading, to be replaced with despair. I lower my voice.

"And what about the letters on my car windscreen? They must have been from you."

She doesn't reply, so I continue.

"'I know.' You're the only person who knows about us apart from me. And again this morning, 'If you don't tell your wife, then I will.' They must have been from you. All these stupid games you're playing have made it pretty clear that your goal is for Tamsin to find out about us."

"We've already talked about this, Lee. I want you to tell her we're in love and then leave her, so we can be together properly."

"You honestly want me to tell Tamsin about our affair? You're mad! You must realise there's no way I would *ever* do that."

"As I said in my letter, if you don't tell her, then I will."

"She won't believe you. I'll just deny it. It'll be your word against mine."

"What if I show her some proof?"

"You're bluffing. There isn't any proof. We deleted or destroyed any evidence. Rule two, remember?"

"You might have. I didn't."

"What do you mean?" I say.

"I might have kept all sorts of evidence, just so I could convince Tamsin when the time was right."

"Like what?"

"Emails, text messages, photos, receipts …"

"Those can all be faked. Anyone can produce an imitation email or text message. I don't believe you've got any compromising photos of us either, but if you did, they can be tampered with too. I'll just paint a picture of you as my crazy stalker and deny all your faked evidence."

I sound more confident than I'm feeling.

"How do you know I'm not recording this conversation right now?" she says. "In the last five minutes, you've admitted we've made love in the past, you've described how my fingernails gouged your back on Friday, you've revealed that you had a shower in my house, and you've mentioned 'us' and 'our affair'. How would you explain away a recording in which you freely admit all of those things?"

"You're not, are you?" I say, dry mouthed with fear.

"Not what?"

"Recording this conversation."

"I might be."

"Where's your phone?"

"Who says I'm using my phone? Maybe I'm wearing a wire, like on TV." She smiles and continues. "Would you like to frisk me or should I take all my clothes off, so you can check?"

"No! Your clothes are fine where they are."

"Look, Lee. It's time you realised: I've been controlling our relationship from the very beginning. I pretended to go along with your silly rules, but actually, I've been following my own rules."

"I don't understand." This can't be right.

"Remember the puncture I had the night we first snogged?" I nod and she continues. "I let the tire down myself."

"I did wonder about that," I say.

"It was *my* suggestion we begin an affair in the first place, but you didn't exactly take much persuading."

"Well, it seemed like a good idea at the time, but I'm regretting it now."

"I haven't even got a cousin."

"What!"

"You heard me."

I can't believe this. "The whole cancer thing was made up? You lied to everyone at the office?" I'm aghast.

"Yes. And it worked too. It got you back into my bed."

"This doesn't make any sense." I shake my head, bemused. "What do you want from me?"

"I thought I'd made that obvious. I want you to leave Tamsin so we can be together."

"But that's not what *I* want."

"Well, you shouldn't have said it was."

"I never said any such thing."

"You must remember, Lee. We'd just made love in the hotel, the second time, and I snuggled up to you and said, 'I wish we could be together like this forever,' and you replied, 'Maybe someday we can,' and then you fell asleep. I had to wake you up for round three if I remember correctly."

"I honestly have no recollection of saying that, Soph."

"Well, you did."

"Look, whether I said it or not, I didn't mean it. It was just … post-sex pillow talk. Without wanting to sound insensitive, I simply don't want to be with you. I want to be with my wife and kids."

"What about *our* kids?"

"Huh?"

"Lee, I'm pregnant with your baby!"

The world stops.

"Don't be ridiculous! You can't be. We always used condoms *and* you're on the pill."

"I can assure you, Lee, I *am* pregnant."

"Then it can't be mine."

"He's definitely yours."

"He?"

"I know it's a boy. I can tell."

"I don't think it works quite like that, but I suppose there's a fifty-fifty chance you're correct."

"I know." She's so calm.

"It must be Joe's."

"It can't be Joe's. On the few occasions we've had sex lately, I always used a diaphragm."

"I thought you were trying to start a family," I say.

"Joe was. I wasn't. At least, not with him. I only wanted *your* baby. You're the love of my life, Lee."

"I heard you and Joe have sex the other day. You certainly didn't stop to put in a diaphragm."

"I was already pregnant by then. I took a test three weeks ago. Several tests, in fact, just to be sure. They all said 'positive'. But I already knew. I could feel it. I just felt ... different somehow."

"This makes no sense. We always used condoms ... Are you saying you made holes in them?"

She opened her mouth to speak, then paused for a beat.

"Lee, I love you, but I'm afraid I haven't been completely honest with you."

"What do you mean?"

Another long pause. And then finally she continues, speaking slowly, choosing her words carefully, as she makes her confession.

"After we made love – while you were in the shower – I opened the rubbish bag and used a turkey-baster to recover your sperm from the used condoms, and re-tied the bag before you came out. Then, as soon as you left, I ... artificially inseminated myself."

She stops talking and looks at me anxiously, fearing my reaction.

I'm open-mouthed with shock.

"It took a few months to succeed, but we finally did it. We're going to have a baby!"

I can't speak.

"Please say something, Lee. Tell me you're happy."

I'm stunned.

My brain is trying to make sense of everything Sophia's

just told me.

"P equals pregnant," I say, my voice monotonic.

"What?"

"In your diary. The P stands for pregnant."

"I know. Isn't it wonderful?"

# CHAPTER EIGHTEEN

*The Plan*

I turn round and walk out of Sophia's house, hopefully for the final time, not even replying to her question. I'm stunned, and the drive back to the office passes in a blur. I realise I'm in no fit state to do my job. I just need time to think. This is a disaster. Is it even possible to get out of this predicament with my marriage still intact?

I pull over to the side of the road, phone the office and inform them that I've come down with a migraine, and I'll be taking the afternoon off. Then I silence my phone, drive to a quiet spot out of town, park the car, and settle down to consider the consequences of Sophia's revelations.

My initial thought is that Sophia could be lying to me. It's evident that she wants me to leave Tamsin to be with her instead. That much is true. But the rest? Surely she's not pregnant. Has she really collected evidence of our affair? Does she have a cousin who has cancer? Was she controlling our relationship from the start? Or is it all lies, intended to trick me into admitting our affair to Tamsin?

I'm overwhelmed. I need to get to grips with what's real and what's fabricated, by thinking about these issues one at a time.

The biggest bombshell Sophia has dropped is the supposed pregnancy. Can she really be pregnant?

Yes. She's of childbearing age and she's sexually active.

If she *is* pregnant, could it be mine?

Before the revelations of today, I would have said no. We always used condoms, and Sophia told me that she was on the contraceptive pill. However, it's possible she was never on the pill at all, but merely claimed so. It's also possible that she retrieved my sperm from our used condoms and squirted it inside herself after I'd left her house. That would also explain why she often arrived back at the office much later than me on the Friday afternoons of our liaisons. I'm no expert, but I guess you could get pregnant that way, especially if you did it many times.

Would she actually do that? Embark on a chronic and covert plan with the sole objective of getting pregnant with my child, against my will?

Again, in the past, I would have said no. But that was before Sophia disclosed that she wants to have a family with me. Perhaps she believes I'll be more likely to leave my wife to be with her if that family is already underway.

Could somebody else have got Sophia pregnant?

If she *is* pregnant, then she obviously hasn't been taking the pill, so it's possible that Joe is the father. I heard them having unprotected sex a couple of weeks ago, while I was uncomfortably ensconced beneath their breakfast bar. Perhaps that's a common occurrence. She claimed she used a diaphragm whenever they made love, but did she always have the time and the opportunity to insert one beforehand without Joe becoming suspicious? Surely Joe is a more likely candidate for father-of-the-foetus than me.

I doubt very much there are any other potential contenders. I know Sophia thoroughly enjoys sex, but I can't imagine she'd sleep with anyone else. Would she?

Could she be lying about being pregnant?

Absolutely. She's already shown herself to be a liar. Either she's been untruthful with me since the beginning of our relationship or she's lying to me now. She claims she's taken several pregnancy tests, but I haven't seen any evidence with my own eyes. She doesn't *look* pregnant, but it's much too soon for her to show. She hasn't mentioned having morning sickness or any other symptoms. I want to believe that Sophia isn't pregnant, but my instinct is telling me that she's being truthful. The joy and conviction on her face as she broke the news seemed totally authentic.

She might be lying currently about being pregnant, but that's not the sort of falsehood that she could maintain for long. At some point, it would become apparent that her abdomen wasn't swelling as it should be. The likely motive for Sophia's pretence at this time, would be to provide her with a short-term emotional blackmail strategy conceived – literally – to convince me to leave Tamsin for her as soon as possible.

My intuition is telling me that Sophia really is expecting a baby, as she claims. And if I'm right, and the child is mine, then what? Would I want her to have a termination?

This is a delicate issue. I've always been pro-life when it comes to abortion; Jake and I have discussed it at length and we agree on this matter: once the parental DNA has been exchanged and recombined to create the blueprint for a unique new human being, who has the right to destroy it? But this time it might be my child potentially having its life prematurely terminated. My moral code says let it live; my evolutionary imperative to pass on my DNA says let it live; but my overriding compulsion is for self-preservation. This insubstantial embryo could destroy my marriage and thereby my whole life. A future trouble-free existence, as selfish as it may be, is my only objective.

If Sophia was to say to me, "I'm having your baby, but I'll bring it up myself and nobody will ever know it's yours," then I might be persuaded to go along with that.

If she was to say, "I'm having your baby and I want us to bring it up together," then that would undoubtedly lead to the end of my marriage, and my preference would be a termination instead, contradicting my previous convictions.

I realise this sounds heartless, but I've already got a family and *they* are my priority.

Of course, there's no way I could force Sophia to have a termination, so it really doesn't matter about my preference.

Looking back over our affair, I realise I don't really know Sophia at all. I suspected she might have faked the puncture, but I didn't mind that at the time. I knew she'd been the one to suggest having an affair in the first place, and I was fine with that too. I thought we were on the same page when it came to planning it, though, and that simply wasn't true. If Sophia is being honest with me now, the whole procedure was designed to get me to leave my wife and family, and begin a new life with her. The rules I'd so carefully constructed meant nothing to Sophia, and she only acquiesced in order to get me into bed. I'm going to have to re-evaluate our whole relationship from a different perspective: knowing that her ultimate goal was not just to have some high-quality extra-marital sex, but, in fact, was to tear asunder two marriages and for us to set up home together.

It terrifies me that Sophia might have spent our whole affair collecting evidence she can present to Tamsin in order to wreck my marriage. If this is the case, what evidence does she have, and is it refutable?

Can I simply deny all of Sophia's accusations and belittle any spurious evidence? Can I portray her as a delusional, psychotic stalker? Would Tamsin believe me if I did? Possibly. But what about Jake? Jake knows the truth. He's the one person to whom I've admitted my affair. He could contradict all my denials.

My one redeeming thought is that, at this moment, Tamsin doesn't know anything about the affair. She's still blissfully ignorant of my infidelity, so my marriage is still intact.

I intend to do anything in my power to keep it this way. Anything.

I can't help deducing that all my problems would go away if Sophia was dead. What an appalling thought! Obviously, I'll try to reason with her first; but what if she won't listen to reason? I'm definitely not going to actually murder her. That would be crazy. But if I was, how would I do it? Make it appear like an accident? There must be a way to kill someone and get away with it. There are probably a few thousand websites designed with that very purpose in mind. To be clear, though, I'm really not going to do it. It's just a thought experiment.

At this stage.

Possible methods for murdering Sophia:

Poison her coffee at work.
Hire a hitman.
Make it appear like a mugging gone wrong.
Sabotage the brakes in her car.
Push her off a tall building.
Buy a sniper's rifle and shoot her from a safe distance.
Fake her suicide.

I can't do it. I'm not that guy. I'm the guy who can commit adultery, not the guy who can commit murder. That's several steps too far.

If Sophia's latest revelation is the truth, she's been manipulating me since before our affair even began, and she now considers herself to be close to achieving her goal: starting a new family with me. I just hope I can convince her to do three things: keep our affair secret, dispose of any evidence she may have of my infidelity, and not tell anyone that I may be the father of her unborn child. That's a lot of convincing. I'm not confident.

I drive home and try to relax, but the knot in my stomach is worsening. I feel physically sick and I can't concentrate on anything other than my predicament. Every time my phone vibrates, I expect to hear more bad news.

The evening goes by relatively peacefully. Tamsin has remarked that I look pale and sweaty and she's convinced I'm going down with the flu. I showered as soon as I got home, and again before bed, but I can't seem to eradicate the stench of fear and despair.

I wake late on Saturday, after another disturbed night, to discover that Tamsin has already gone shopping. There was a time when I'd be resentful that another weekend morning had passed without us having sex, but today I'm just relieved she's not here. If I'm honest, it's highly unlikely that I could have managed an erection anyway.

My phone vibrates and I know, even before I look, that it's going to be a message from Sophia.

"I've been thinking about baby names! Xxx"

I reply straight away.

"Why are you doing this to me?"

"My current favourites are Ben, James, Thomas, Daniel and Mark. What do you think?"

"You have to stop, Soph. This is crazy."

"Very traditional, I know. Biblical too, I guess. But I don't really like more modern names."

"I'm never going to leave Tamsin, so just stop." I run my hand through my hair and notice several strands drop to the carpet.

"I hope he has your nose. You have a particularly regal nose! Xxx"

"Have you even seen a doctor to get the pregnancy confirmed?"

"Welcome to the conversation! No. Not yet. But I took another test this morning and I really am pregnant!!! I'm so happy, Lee! We're going to have a baby!!!"

"If that's true, why don't you and Joe bring it up together and just leave me out of it?"

"Because I'm in love with you, silly! Not Joe."

"But I'm not in love with you. I love my wife."

"I'm certain you'll grow to love me as much as I love you. When little Ben/James/Thomas/Daniel/Mark comes along, we'll be such a perfect family. Xxx"

"You're not listening to me. It's not going to happen."

"Let me tell you what *is* going to happen. I'm going to give you until midnight on Friday to tell Tamsin about us."

"What??? Why midnight on Friday?"

"So we have the rest of the weekend for Joe to pack up and leave home and for you to move in with me. I can't wait! Xxx"

"You're mad!"

"We could start off living at my house and then buy a new place together once the divorces are finalised."

I typed the next message with trepidation.

"What happens if I don't tell Tamsin by midnight on Friday?"

"Then I'll come round to your house next Saturday morning and tell her myself. But I'm sure it would be much better coming from you. X"

"I'll deny everything. She won't believe you."

"She will when I show her my proof."

"You're bluffing. You haven't got any real proof."

"I'm afraid, my love, I have incontrovertible proof, but I'd prefer not to use it."

"Why not?"

"Because I'd rather not cause embarrassment to my future husband. Xxx"

"What is the proof?"

"You'll have to wait and see. It's very good!!! X"

"Please don't do this. Just be sensible."

"I'd better go. I'm planning a delicious, candlelit meal for us next Saturday and I want to find some nice recipes. Xxx"

"I'm not going to tell Tamsin about us and I don't think you will either."

"One of us definitely will. I really don't want to hurt you, Lee. You're the love of my life. But if I can't convince you to be reasonable and just leave Tamsin, then I'll have to resort to more drastic measures!"

"How about if I pay you? How much will it take for you to leave me alone?"

"You're funny! This isn't about blackmail. It's about true love. X"

"I'm serious. I'll give you £15000 cash if you'll leave me and Tamsin alone."

"Ha ha! Hilarious!!! See you on Monday, sweetie. Xxx"

"What can I do to make you stop torturing me?"

No reply.

"I'll do anything you ask."

No reply.

I ring Sophia's cell phone.

She's switched it off.

I spend the remainder of the weekend planning my strategy. I've got about five days to come up with a scheme that will both save my marriage and eliminate any existing evidence that I've committed adultery.

So, here's Plan A:

Meet with Sophia somewhere private.

Insist that she shows me her proof of our affair.

If it's a bluff: walk away, hope Tamsin will accept my denials and get on with my life.

If it's genuine evidence: convince Sophia not to show it to anyone, ever, then walk away and get on with my life.

And if plan A doesn't work, here's Plan B:

Murder Sophia, then walk away and get on with my life.

I'm rooting for Plan A, but Plan B is shorter and simpler.

Of course, I do have another option. I could simply confess everything to Tamsin and throw myself on her mercy. I'm sure that conversation would go well:

"Hi, Tam, can we have a quick chat?"

"Bins?"

"Done."

"Dishwasher?"

"Done."

"Okay. Chat away."

"Right, well, I've done something a bit silly ..."

"Go on."

"I've been having an affair with someone from work"

"Ha ha! Good one, Lee."

"No, genuinely."

"Who?"

"Does it matter?"

"Not especially. Why?"

"Just for some extra sex."

"Fair enough. You haven't been getting much from me lately. Did you contract any sexually transmitted diseases?"

"No. I always used condoms."

"Well done. Is it over now?'

"Definitely. She turned out to be a right psycho!"

"That's okay then. No harm, no foul. What would you like for tea?"

Or possibly not so well:

"Tam, we need to talk."

"That sounds ominous."

"I want you to know that you and the kids are the most important things in my life and I love you all dearly."

"Oh my God, Lee! What have you done?"

"I've been having an affair with someone from work."

"What! Lee, how could you?"

"Please don't cry."

"You've broken my heart."

"I'm so sorry."

"Pack your things. I want you out of my house now."

"Please, Tam. It was a huge mistake. I love you. I promise it'll never happen again."

"Get out of my sight! I can't bear to look at you."

"Please ..."

"I hate you and I'll be filing for divorce as soon as I possibly can. Now fuck off, you piece of shit!"

Or possibly really badly, culminating in some sort of murder-suicide event.

I can't tell Tamsin. I couldn't bear to humiliate myself in front of her. I'm following rule one for as long as possible: never tell anyone. I *had* to tell Jake, to get out of a sticky situation, but I have no intention of ever telling anyone else.

At work on Monday, Sophia is positively blooming. She looks radiant, refreshed and happy. Her co-workers are drawn to her like bees to nectar. Never has she been so popular. She flirts shamelessly with some of the younger men, often looking over in my direction to see if I'm watching. I am, but I'm pretending to be very busy. She takes every opportunity to come and see me and make polite conversation. Nobody would know that she's threatening to turn my life upside down in less than five days' time.

The week passes at a snail's pace. At least twice every day, Sophia asks me, either directly or by text message, if I've told Tamsin yet, and every time I reply in the negative, but whenever I try to extend the conversation, to dissuade Sophia from her mission, she chooses not to respond.

◆ ◆ ◆

On Thursday, while Tamsin is out playing tennis and the kids are nominally tidying their rooms, I put the finishing touches to my argument to convince Sophia to back off, and not inform Tamsin about our affair. Then, when that's finished, I do something I never dreamt I'd do. I actually resort to making a pros and cons list to determine whether or not I should murder Sophia.

Pros:
  All my problems would be solved.
  No more Sophia to tell Tamsin about the affair or show her any evidence of it.
  No more pregnancy.
  No anxiety every time my phone rings or vibrates.

No more constant fear of discovery.

I'd get to keep my family and my home.

I'd maintain the respect of my wife, kids and friends.

I'd have a fresh start; a second chance to try to live an unblemished life of happiness and contentment.

Cons:

No more mind-blowing sex.

I'd be a murderer.

I'd have to live with the guilt of my crime until the day I died.

If hell exists, I'd burn there for all eternity.

I'd probably get caught and spend at least fifteen years in prison, being anally raped on a daily basis, and losing my wife and kids forever as well.

The anal rape thing is the deal-breaker. I'm just too good looking to go to prison. I'm going to have to reason with Sophia and hope for the best. If she chooses to tell my wife and succeeds in convincing her, then I'll have to beg Tamsin to forgive me. Maybe, in time, she could come to trust me again.

# CHAPTER NINETEEN

## *The Canal*

A t work on Friday morning, Sophia approaches me, smiling sweetly, and asks her usual question.

"Have you told Tamsin yet?"

I whisper my response, hoping nobody nearby can overhear our conversation. "No. I need to talk to you first."

"I've said all I have to say, Lee. It's up to you now. You just need to tell her."

"Shh! Not so loud. I really need to talk to you today, Soph."

"I'm not interested." She's refusing to lower her voice. "We can talk once you've told your wife."

She turns on her heels and strides away.

An hour later, I attempt a text message.

"Hi."

No reply.

"Please, can I talk to you?"

No reply.

"For your sake, it's vitally important we talk."

No reply.

At lunchtime, I go to Sophia's office, hoping to at least begin a dialogue with her. There's nobody there.

I wait for about ten minutes and then, assuming she's gone home, I decide to drive to Sophia's house and have it out with her once and for all.

As always, I park several streets away and let myself into her garden through the back gate, but when I try the kitchen door, I'm surprised to find it locked.

I knock on the door, expecting Sophia to appear and let me in, but there's no response from inside the house. I bang louder. Perhaps she hasn't heard me. Still no signs of life from within the building. I walk around the house to the front door and try ringing the bell. I can hear it echoing inside, but still no one comes to let me in. I even shout through the letterbox, but to no avail.

I'm beginning to think something sinister may have happened to Sophia, when I realise there's no sign of her car on the drive or on the street nearby. Where is she?

I take out my phone and call her.

She answers after two rings.

"Hello?"

"Where are you?"

"Oh, hi, sweetie. I'm at the supermarket. Just buying some things for our romantic meal tomorrow night."

"What?"

"Can you hear me okay? I'm at the supermarket."

"Yes. I can hear you fine. I'm at your house. I thought we could talk."

"I told you, we've got nothing to talk about until you've told Tamsin about us."

"Come on. Be reasonable. We need to discuss this."

"We have discussed it. Now you need to get on with *doing* it."

"Look, Soph…"

"How do you like your steak cooked? That's something I really ought to know about you already." She chuckles. "Luckily we've got the rest of our lives to get to know each other better."

"I need to see you," I say.

"It's a simple question. Medium? Medium rare?"

I sigh. "Medium rare. When can we talk?"

"I've got to go, sweetie. I'm nearly at the front of the queue."

"Hang on…"

"See you later. Love you."

"Soph…"

She's hung up.

I make a few further attempts to speak to Sophia in the afternoon, but every time I bring up her ultimatum, she raises her voice to the point where I'm forced to change the subject to something more generic.

At the end of the day, I pack up at the same time as Sophia and, as soon as she leaves – without even saying goodbye to me – I discreetly pursue her to the car park. I watch her walk towards her car and follow, timing my arrival to coincide with her unlocking the driver's door.

"Soph, please can we go somewhere and talk?"

She sidles closer to me and, before I realise what's happening, she embraces me in a spontaneous, overly friendly hug; right in front of at least seven of our co-workers, some of whom are looking in our direction with bemused expressions on their faces.

"What are you doing?" I whisper.

"I've got big plans for you tomorrow night, sweetie," she

says as she reluctantly releases me from her amorous embrace.

She slides into her car, lowers the window and calls out, "See you tomorrow, Lee!" before blowing me a kiss as she drives away; leaving me standing, bewildered and speechless, next to her empty parking space.

One of my male colleagues raises his eyebrows at me, and two female co-workers, who had been heading towards their respective cars, change direction, walk towards each other, and begin a whispered conversation, occasionally glancing in my direction.

I've got to put a stop to this, but I don't know how. I'm not prepared to chase Sophia across town in my car, and I'm reluctant to go to her house at this time of the day in case Joe comes back from work prematurely.

I drive home, racking my brain trying to decide what to do next. I've got less than seven hours until my deadline runs out. What will Sophia do if I haven't told Tamsin by midnight? Will she really come round to my house tomorrow morning and show Tamsin evidence of our affair? I can't bear to even think about what that would be like.

Would they talk calmly and rationally? Would they fight each other the way women are supposed to do, with scratching and hair pulling?

My biggest fear is that Tamsin would just say to Sophia, "You can have him. He's all yours. I don't want him anymore."

The clock is ticking.

Shortly after 7:30 p.m. Tamsin leaves the house to spend the evening at a local pub with some of the girls from her tennis club. Normally, I'd be happy about this because she often returns home horny after one of these nights out. I don't know if it's the alcohol, or the flirting with men at the pub, or the ribald discussions about their sex lives, but something gets Tamsin's juices flowing.

Tonight, however, I'm relieved that I've got some time alone to try to salvage my marriage, while Tamsin remains oblivious to the gathering storm clouds heading her way.

I send a text message to Sophia.

"Hi."

No reply.

"Can you talk?"

No reply.

"I need your help."

No reply.

"I reckon I know what I'm going to say to Tamsin, but I'd really like your advice first."

Sophia replies.

"What are you going to say?"

"It's quite long and complicated. I'd like to tell you in person to get your feedback."

"Why? Can't you just tell her? I'm sure it's fine."

"Your opinion means a great deal to me. I'd really like to hear what you think."

"We don't need to meet up for that. My advice is to say this: 'Tamsin, I've fallen in love with someone else and I'm leaving you.' Nice and simple."

"That's brutal! After all these years of marriage, I owe her more than that."

"Your problem is, you're too nice! X"

"You used to say you'd do anything for me. Well, I'm asking you to meet me now so we can discuss what I'm going to say to Tamsin."

Sophia doesn't respond for several minutes. I'm about to send another message when she replies.

"Ok. Where and when?"

"Thanks, so much, Soph. How about the lay-by where you had your 'puncture'? Half an hour?"

"Make it 45 minutes. I want to make myself look beautiful for you! Xxx"

"See you then. Xxx"

I get to the designated spot thirty minutes later, but I'm disappointed to discover that on this occasion it's not vacant. There's a van selling burgers and hot dogs, and as I'm waiting for Sophia to arrive, I see three cars turn up and park. Their drivers head to the van, order food, eat and leave, but it's a slow process. We're not going to have the lay-by to ourselves this time.

Sophia finally arrives about twenty minutes after the agreed time. She reverses into the space directly behind my car, switches off her engine and comes to join me.

"Hi, sweetie. Sorry I'm a bit late."

"No problem." I want to begin this conversation on the right footing. "I thought we'd be alone here, but people keep coming and going. I'd rather talk to you somewhere more private."

"Do you like my new dress?" she says.

"Yeah. It's very nice. You look lovely." She really does. Why did she have to spoil everything by breaking the rules and going all nutty? "Perhaps we could walk along the canal towpath. Is that okay?"

"Fine by me."

It's a lovely evening; mild weather and no breeze at all. The sun is slowly sinking towards the horizon and the sky ahead of us is a beautiful combination of shades of orange and red. The birds in the trees are singing serenely as if all is well with the world.

Once we're out of sight of the other people in the lay-by, Sophia takes my hand and I choose not to resist.

Under other circumstances, it would be a very pleasant, romantic, evening stroll.

We walk, hand-in-hand as the light fades; neither of us speaking until we reach the canal.

The towpath is deserted. There's no one in sight in either direction. Even the sounds of traffic have faded into the distance. We could be the only two people alive.

Stopping at the water's edge, we turn to face each other. Sophia looks up at me and smiles warmly.

"I'm so happy." I don't know what to say to that. She continues. "I'm really looking forward to our life together, Lee. This is like a fresh start. Just you, me and the baby."

She rests her hand protectively on her stomach.

"I can't tell her, Soph."

"What do you mean?" she looks confused, her smile cooling.

"I can't bring myself to tell Tamsin about the awful thing I've done to her."

"Of course you can. I'm sure she'll understand when you tell her how much we love each other."

"I don't want her to understand. I don't want her to know at all. I want her to be happy that she's married to me. I want her to love me. I want her to be ignorant of my adultery."

"But that can't be. How can we be together if you don't tell her about us?"

"You're not hearing me. I don't want us to be together. I want to be with Tamsin for the rest of my life."

Sophia's face transforms from confused to annoyed.

"Why are you doing this to me? We're going to have a baby? You have to tell her."

"I can't."

"Then I will."

"Please don't, Soph. It would make her so upset."

"This isn't about her. It's about us."

"I don't think she'll believe you. If I deny everything, then you'll just come across as some sort of crazy woman who's developed an unrequited crush."

"Oh, she'll believe me all right."

"What makes you so sure?"

"I told you. I have proof."

"I really don't think she'll be convinced by your fake emails and text messages."

"They're not fake. You know that."

"But I'll deny sending them. I can lie quite convincingly when I have to. I've had a lot of practice in the last few months."

"What about this then?" Sophia takes her phone out of her pocket and after a few presses of the screen, she hands it to me.

I hear it before I see it. It's the sound of two people making love. There's moaning, gasping, slurping, sighing, squelching. It could be me, but it's impossible to tell just from the sound.

Then I see it. It's a good quality recording of me, standing naked in Sophia's spare bedroom. Someone is clearly kneeling in front of me, their back to the camera, wearing only a pair of stockings and high-heeled shoes. They're giving me a blow job.

"What's this?" I can't take my eyes off the screen. My knees have gone weak.

"Don't you remember?"

I stare at her blankly.

"That's the first time we ever had oral sex. Do you think my bum looks too big? I hope it's just the weird camera angle."

I swallow.

"You recorded it?"

"Of course. I filmed us every time we made love. I've got dozens of clips like this. I like to watch them when we're apart."

"But ... you have to delete them. All of them."

"No way!" Sophia takes her phone off me and, after a few more presses and swipes, she hands it back again. "This is one of my favourites."

We're in Sophia's kitchen. She's wearing a classy evening

dress, high-heeled sandals and sparkly jewellery. She's perched elegantly on the work surface with her legs demurely crossed. I appear on screen from the left and walk towards her. "According to my friends, you're the best high-class escort in the city," I hear myself say. I scroll forward fifteen minutes into the video clip. Sophia is now naked and pressed up against the glass kitchen door as I take her from behind.

"Do you remember it? That session was so hot. You made me climax five times before you shot your load all over my breasts. I loved it. We must do that one again soon."

"I don't understand," I say, shaking my head. "Who filmed these?"

"Me. I set up my old phone to start recording before you arrived at my house. I hid it in cupboards or behind plants; wherever I'd decided we'd have sex that day. I thought you'd spotted it once, but you never did."

"You filmed us every time?" I still can't come to terms with this.

"Yes."

"And the recordings are all on your phone?"

"Yes. On this phone and on my old one. I've also backed them up onto my laptop and my work computer. I thought it would be sensible to keep lots of copies. I'd be devastated if I lost them."

An idea pops into my head.

"Just a minute … The F in your diary? Did that mean you filmed us?"

"Now you're getting it."

"I can't believe it." I'm stunned.

"We can watch them whenever we like. I find it a real turn-on. I think you will too. We make a very sexy couple on screen."

"So they're just for your personal use?"

"That was the idea, yes."

"And no one else will ever see them?"

"Well, that rather depends on you?"

"What do you mean?"

"I mean, if you tell Tamsin about us today, then nobody ever has to see them. They'll be our secret. But if you refuse to tell her, then I'll be forced to email a few choice clips to her, and you really don't want that. To be honest, you look a bit foolish in some of them; the ones when I spanked you and when you were pretending to be my slave, for example."

"But ... you don't have Tamsin's email address." I'm grasping at straws.

"I do. There's one on her school's website. You mustn't get too hung up on Tamsin, though. Unless you come clean about our relationship, I'll be sending clips to all our work colleagues as well. Pretty soon they'll be all over the internet. You might even become a pornstar when people see your amazing technique."

"You can't be serious. You're in all these videos too."

"I've never been more serious in my life. Don't worry about me. I can easily edit them so my face doesn't ever appear."

I imagine Tamsin, Charlie, John, my friends, my family, my colleagues all laughing hysterically at videos in which I humiliate myself with my mistress.

All of a sudden a red mist descends.

I lose it.

I raise my hands to Sophia's shoulders and give her a hard shove, dropping her phone in the process.

She stumbles away from me until her heel catches on a tree root and she falls backwards, arms windmilling, towards the setting sun.

"Lee ..." Sophia shouts before there's a spectacular splash, and she disappears beneath the green, frothing water.

My first thought is, she won't be happy about me ruining her new dress.

My second is, I hope she doesn't swallow any of that slimy, foul-smelling canal water.

In a moment of panic, one thought comes to the fore:

she can't swim!

Am I going to have to jump in and rescue her? I don't mind my jeans getting wet, but I'm wearing my favourite shirt. Have I got time to strip off?

Then, to my great relief, she comes coughing and spluttering to the surface. I expect to receive an earful of fully justified abuse, but, to my surprise, after some ineffectual splashing, she disappears beneath the surface again.

The water quickly stills above her.

She genuinely can't swim.

I'm about to jump into the canal and pull her to safety when I stop at the edge of the towpath.

What if I do nothing?

Sophia will die. She won't be able to tell Tamsin anything. She won't be able to show anyone embarrassing videos of me.

I need to think fast.

It's not my fault she tripped over a tree root. It's not my fault she can't swim.

But I brought her here, and I pushed her.

I see bubbles making their way to the surface and gently popping as they release the last of Sophia's precious air. It surprises me that each one doesn't contain a tiny scream.

This is ridiculous! She's drowning and I could save her, but I can't move. I'm paralysed. Surely doing nothing at this point is outside my moral limits.

I've got to jump in, but how long has she been down there now? One minute? Two? That's too long already, surely. She must be dead by now.

There are no more bubbles.

Three minutes?

She's not coming back up.

There's no sign she was ever here.

A few die-hard birds are still singing in the deepening gloom. The surface of the water has become as still and calm as it was before we arrived.

"Evening!" I nearly jump out of my skin.

An elderly man is walking his dog along the towpath.

"Looks like you've dropped something." Without breaking stride he nods in the direction of Sophia's phone, which is still lying on the grass where I dropped it.

"Cheers, mate." I pick up the phone as the man walks on, without a backward glance, acknowledging my thanks with a wave of his hand. The dog snuffles in the long grass and I continue to observe them until they move out of sight.

My brain is in overdrive. That was way too close for comfort. Three minutes earlier and that man would have seen me push Sophia into the canal and then stand by watching as she drowned. As it is, he's a witness to my presence at what may well become a murder scene.

Should I chase after him and murder him too?

No!

Am I sure?

No.

I've never been in a situation anything like this before. I don't know what to do. Ordinarily, when I want to know the steps required to perform a task, I look them up on the internet.

"What should I do if I've just pushed someone into a canal and not made any effort to save them and somebody witnessed the whole thing?"

I suspect a question like that might set a few alarm bells ringing. The internet is not an option. I'm on my own here.

As I see it, initially I have three options to choose between: turn myself in to the police and tell the truth about what happened; turn myself in and lie about what happened; or keep quiet about it and try to cover up my involvement.

I can't turn myself in. I'd have too much explaining to do.

I choose option three.

How do I go about covering it up?

Should I jump into the canal and fish out Sophia's lifeless body, then bury it far away in a deep grave where it will never be found?

Should I just leave her at the bottom of the canal and hope that her corpse is never discovered?

I haven't seen a dead body before. I really don't want to see this one. It's staying there.

I press a few buttons on Sophia's phone, but it's password protected. I try my birthday and it unlocks straight away. A wave of sadness washes over me. Sophia genuinely did love me and yet here I am, thinking of her in the past tense already.

It's quite dark now, too dark for anyone else to be out walking their dog. I use the torch on Sophia's phone to scan the surrounding ground. The compacted soil is hard and dry so neither of us has left any footprints. Some grass is down-trodden, but it will spring back up in a short while. I can see no evidence that anything nefarious took place on this spot only a few minutes ago.

I search through Sophia's phone, looking for anything that might link her to me. The location function is switched off. That's good. I can't find anything suspicious in her search history either. There are records of a few phone calls between us which I quickly delete. I discover a few candid photos she's taken of me and I delete these too. Finally, I locate the videos. Sophia wasn't exaggerating; there are dozens of them. We've definitely had a lot of sex and she's recorded it all. I have a look at a few clips and they bring back poignant memories. She was right, we do make a very sexy couple on screen.

One by one I delete the video files until they're all gone.

Satisfied there's no longer anything that incriminates me on Sophia's phone, I'm about to wipe my fingerprints off and throw it into the canal when an idea occurs to me. If Sophia's body is discovered, the police will be less likely to investigate her private life if it appears she's thrown herself into the canal with the intention of ending her own life.

I open her email app and start to compose a suicide note.

"My darling Joe

If you're reading this, it's because I'm at peace now. I'm so sorry to do this to you, but I've been really unhappy for a long time and I simply don't want to go on living in this world anymore.

Please forgive me.
Sophia"

It's not good, but it's the best I can come up with in my current state. Presumably, the best approach is to keep it short and vague.

Should I send it straight away or leave it in Sophia's drafts folder?

If I send it now, to Joe, it will alert him straight away to the fact that something is amiss. He'll immediately start searching for Sophia and almost certainly inform the police. However, if I leave it in Sophia's drafts folder, unaddressed and unsent, it won't be discovered until someone logs-on to Sophia's email account.

I don't send it.

I give the phone a thorough clean with my handkerchief and then throw it towards the spot where Sophia went under for the final time. It's too dark to see much anymore, but I hear it splash as it enters the water, then the silence resumes.

I'm reluctant to leave this spot. I feel like I ought to say some final words to the woman who loved me so much that she was prepared to leave her husband and embark on a new life with me. It's also possible that she was carrying my child. God, I hope not!

I can't come up with anything to say that doesn't sound trite, so I simply nod in her direction, as a last farewell, and head back to the lay-by.

# CHAPTER TWENTY

*The Aftermath*

My mind is racing as I walk back to my car.
What next?

As I approach the lay-by, my first problem comes into view. It's Sophia's car, parked directly behind mine. Presumably, the keys are in her pocket at the bottom of the canal. The only other vehicle present is the burger van, containing one occupant, who's still open for business, but has no customers at present.

What should I do about Sophia's car?

As I see it, the following things are likely to happen over the coming hours and days, in roughly this order:

Sophia will be reported missing to the police by Joe.

The police won't be too worried initially because people disappear for short periods all the time.

When she fails to turn up or get in touch in a timely manner, there will be a search for Sophia, her car and possibly her phone too.

Sophia's car will be discovered in the lay-by. (I've never been in her car, so I don't need to worry about fingerprints or DNA evidence from that source.)

A detailed search will be carried out in the area around her car.

Divers will search the canal.

Sophia's body will be found.

The police will contemplate the possibility of foul play.

Joe will be the initial prime suspect because it's usually the husband who did it.

Sophia's 'suicide note' will be discovered.

A cursory investigation will find nothing suspicious.

The police won't find any evidence incriminating Joe or anyone else.

In the absence of evidence to the contrary, Sophia's death will be recorded as an open verdict – a suspicious death, but probably suicide.

That would suit me just fine.

Would there be any benefit if I was to drive Sophia's car somewhere else, assuming I could somehow retrieve her keys?

It would probably trigger a fruitless search away from the actual crime scene, but presumably Sophia's cell phone service provider would inform the police where her phone was last used, so there would still be a search near the canal, with a high likelihood of her body being located.

I leave Sophia's car parked where it is and walk towards mine, keeping my face averted so the man in the burger van can only see the back of my head in the darkness. There's no way he'd be able to identify me. I'm also confident that there are no security cameras around here, away from any major buildings, which is a small comfort.

Lowering myself into the driver's seat, I start my engine and drive away cautiously.

Should I try to establish some sort of alibi?

If the police come to the conclusion that Sophia was murdered, and they can establish the time of death with any accuracy, it will be useful if I can supply witnesses who saw me, or thought they saw me, elsewhere at that time. Her cell phone service provider should be able to provide a fairly accurate record of Sophia's final movements and the time when her phone ceased working. I need to generate evidence that I was at some other location when it, and she, gave up the ghost.

I decide to go to the pub nearest to my home. God knows, I could use a drink. I drive there by the most direct route that avoids potential CCTV cameras, enter and look around for any familiar faces. Fortunately, this pub is busy on Friday nights and there are several people I recognise by sight, acquaintances rather than friends.

My plan is two-fold. I want to be remembered and I want to generate the impression that I've been here far longer than I have in reality. To this end, I approach several clusters of people that I recognise, force my way into their conversations, mention something I said to someone else in the pub earlier in the evening, claim that I've come straight from work to the pub and spent the whole night here, and then repeat the process. Hopefully, if asked, someone will think they saw me long before I actually arrived.

"Hi, Tom, fancy seeing you here. I've not been in this pub for ages, especially not so early. Can you believe I've been here since six-thirty …?"

" … yes, Richard, I said exactly the same thing to Harry over there a couple of hours ago …"

"It's certainly filling up in here now. The place was empty when I arrived …"

I stay until last orders, moderating my alcohol consumption because I want to keep my wits about me, before finally driving the short distance home, as cautiously as possible.

I'm in bed, feigning sleep, by the time Tamsin arrives and slips under the covers silently beside me, blissfully unaware that she's sleeping with a murderer.

As I lie in bed, unable to sleep, I think back, over and over again, to the moment of the accident. Yes, I'm calling it an accident now. What actually happened is unclear. I have two opposing memories that contradict each other in a few details. I can picture both vividly in my mind's eye. In one, Sophia provokes me and I push her gently backwards, she trips and falls into the canal. In the other, I merely take a step towards her and she moves backwards voluntarily, trips and falls in. They can't both have happened. I know what really took place, but perhaps, if I focus on the second one and try to forget the first, then, in time, I'll come to accept the false memory as reality, and I won't have to feel so guilty about my role in Sophia's inadvertent death.

At some point before dawn, it occurs to me that it might be a good idea to destroy the clothes and shoes I'd been wearing yesterday evening. It wouldn't look good if a police investigation found Sophia's hair or DNA on my clothing, or if the souls of my shoes could be matched to footprints found at the scene of the crime/accident/suicide. I really don't believe it will come to that, but, ever the careful planner, it makes sense to err on the side of caution. Goodbye, favourite shirt.

"Tam, I'm off to the tip," I shout up the stairs.

She ambles down and joins me in the kitchen.

"How come?"

"I've been having a clear-out in the garage. There's loads of stuff I need to get rid of."

"About time too." She looks at me curiously. "Are you okay, Lee? You look washed out."

"Yeah, I'm fine thanks. I just didn't sleep very well last night."

"Anything on your mind?"

"Not particularly. Work stuff. Nothing important." I shrug.

"Okay. I'll see you later."

She jogs back upstairs and I head out to my car.

I load it up with all sorts of old junk I should have thrown out years ago. Amongst it, I conceal a tied-up plastic bag, which contains another tied-up plastic bag, which contains all the clothes I was wearing last night, including my shoes.

Through the light Saturday morning traffic, I drive to the waste recycling centre and dump the whole lot into a huge, partially filled skip. I stand and observe as other people throw their unwanted detritus on top of mine until it's no longer visible, and then thoroughly buried. No doubt, the bags and their contents will soon make their way to a landfill site, where they will rot slowly over the course of the next few thousand years.

I take a detour on the way home to get my car cleaned and valeted, in the hope of eliminating the last lingering traces of Sophia from my life.

I spend part of Saturday afternoon researching what happens to a body after it drowns. Reluctant to undertake any suspicious searches on my phone or home computer, I visit the public library for the first time in many years. After a fruitless ninety minutes of browsing through medical textbooks and periodicals, I abandon the old-school approach and instead use one of the public access computers. Fortunately, I don't have to provide any personal details to use this system. Thirty seconds later, I have all the information I require.

Practically without exception, a dead body lying on the bottom of a canal will come to the surface again. As the corpse starts to decay, bacteria within the body cause gas to develop within the tissues. When there's enough gas for the body to become lighter than water, it will rise to the surface. The length of time before this happens depends on two variables: the amount of fat contained in the tissues and the temperature of the water. If the water is warm, the body may rise to the surface in one or two days. If the water is cold, it may take several weeks.

So it looks highly likely that Sophia's body will be discoverable, possibly as soon as one or two days from now, when it inevitably rises to the surface of the canal. I need to prepare myself to answer questions about her disappearance, but other than that, there's nothing more I can do. It's out of my hands. From now on, I must wait and see what happens and react accordingly.

On Monday morning at work, it's apparent that something is afoot when all the staff at the office are summoned to the big conference room for a meeting with the boss.

When everyone has arrived, she closes the doors and waits for silence.

"Thanks for coming, everyone. I'm sure you're all wondering why I've gathered you here this morning. I've already heard rumours it's about staff redundancies, and let me reassure you, it's definitely not that."

An audible sigh of relief emanates from several people. Someone makes a sotto voce joke near the back of the room and the resulting laughter breaks the tension somewhat.

"I'll get straight to the point," she says. "The police have been on the phone to me this morning concerning our colleague Sophia Miller. Apparently, she didn't go home on Friday night, and no one has seen or heard from her since she left work on Friday afternoon. She hasn't made an appearance here yet either and, as you probably know, Sophia is usually one of the first people to arrive in the morning. Her husband believes she returned home at some point on Friday evening, and then went out again before he got home at nine-thirty."

She pauses, and the whispering begins. I listen to the people around me.

"That's weird."

"Oh my God! I hope she's okay."

"Sounds to me like she's left her husband."

"Alien abduction, I bet."

The boss continues. "Has anyone here had any contact at all with Sophia since last Friday afternoon?"

Everyone looks around the room, but there's no response from any quarter. I may be imagining it, but it feels as if quite a few people are looking in my direction. Is paranoia setting in? Can people tell I'm a murderer simply by looking at me?

"Okay. Well, the police have given me a contact number. They made it clear they're not overly concerned at this stage, but they'd like to be informed if anyone here has any information relating to Sophia's current whereabouts. If you know anything that might be relevant, please come to my office during the day and my secretary will let you have the contact number for the police."

She pauses and looks directly at me.

"Right, let's get back to work."

The rumours begin immediately:

Sophia's husband was beating her, and she's hiding at a women's refuge.

A body has been found in a shallow grave in the woods near her house.

She's embezzled a million pounds from the company and fled the country.

Someone was seen being bundled into a white van in town.

She's run off with her lesbian lover.

Several people approach me and ask if I know anything more. Apparently, it's common knowledge that Sophia and I were 'quite close'. I pretend I'm as much in the dark as they are. I try to match the mood and level of concern of my colleagues, but I can't help feeling that I've got guilt written all over my face.

◆ ◆ ◆

Shortly after lunch my cell phone rings.

"Hello?"

"Hi, Lee. It's Joe Miller here. Sophia Miller's husband."

Shit!

What should I say? 'I'm so sorry to hear your wife's been murdered'?

"Hi, Joe. Is there any news?"

"None, I'm afraid. I've been going through all Sophia's contacts and ringing everyone, in the hope she's been in touch with somebody, but I've had no luck so far. I'm worried sick to be honest. This isn't like her at all."

"I wish I could help, mate, but I haven't had any communication with Sophia since Friday," I say, remembering the last word she ever spoke: 'Lee ...'

"Has she said or done anything unusual lately? She talks about you a lot. I was hoping she might have mentioned something to you that might explain her absence."

"No. Only the usual work stuff."

"Okay. Sorry to bother you, Lee."

"No problem. Listen, I'm sure she'll turn up soon, safe and sound. Just hang in there."

"Cheers. I'd better go. I've got lots more calls to make."

"All right. Bye, then."

"Bye."

Well, that was awkward.

There are no further developments on Monday afternoon and I spend the evening worrying about the inevitable discovery of Sophia's body. I'm on edge all the time, expecting, at any moment, the police to smash down my front door, fill the house with tear gas and drag me away kicking and screaming in front of my bewildered family. I've decided not to mention to Tamsin anything about Sophia's disappearance for as long as possible. Presumably, the news will appear in the local papers at some point, but so far all is quiet. As far as I'm concerned, no news is good news.

On Tuesday morning, for obvious reasons, there's still no sign of Sophia, and some of my colleagues are increasingly concerned. I can't stop glancing towards her office, expecting to see her there, working away at her desk, and occasionally raising her head to smile at me; but it remains empty and defunct.

The police were here for a couple of hours, talking to the boss and a few other people, but they haven't released any new information. There's a subdued atmosphere in the office, with many people fearing the worst, but what is the worst?

Sophia somehow became locked in a derelict building and slowly starved to death?

She was decapitated in a car crash and her severed body is lying undiscovered in a ditch?

She was kidnapped, beaten, raped and murdered?

She was burnt to death after being struck by lightning?

She drowned after her lover pushed her into a filthy stinking canal?

The rumours get worse as time goes by.

I aim to stay out of these conversations as much as possible, striving to maintain a low profile and an appropriately anxious demeanour.

At 12:35 p.m. my cell phone rings once more.

I don't recognise the number, but I answer straight away.

"Hello?"

"Hello. Is this Mr Lee Bolton?"

"Yes, speaking."

I really hope it's a cold caller, trying to sell me something.

"My name is Detective Sergeant Brian Khan. I'm investigating the disappearance of your colleague Sophia Miller."

"Hello, Detective." I'm desperately trying to seem nonchalant, but my voice sounds unusually high. "How can I help you?"

"I was wondering if you could possibly come down to the police station. We'd like to ask you a couple of questions." He pauses for a response, but I'm temporarily tongue-tied. "It's possible you can help us with our enquiries."

"I'm not sure what I can tell you, Sergeant. Can't you just ask me over the phone?"

"It's Detective Sergeant. No, I'm afraid not. A face-to-face chat would be much better, if you don't mind. I'm sure you want to help us locate Mrs Miller."

"Yes. Of course. But I'm really not sure how I can help."

"I can explain that when you get here. Shall we say two o'clock?"

"Is this a voluntary interview? Would it be under caution?" I say.

"Yes. Just a voluntary interview at this stage, sir. You seem very familiar with the procedure."

"Not really. I just watch a lot of police shows on TV." And I've done a lot of research.

"I see. Then you'll be aware that you're under no obligation to help us if you don't want to, and you'll be free to leave at any time. However, we'd appreciate your input, as a colleague of Mrs Miller."

I can't see a way out of this. If I decline, won't that be highly suspicious?

"It's no problem at all, Detective Sergeant. I'll see you at two o'clock."

"Thank you, sir. Just report to reception and ask for DS Khan."

He hangs up before I can say goodbye.

# CHAPTER TWENTY- ONE

*The Interview*

I ask one of my colleagues to inform the powers that be that I'm not feeling well and I'll be taking the afternoon off work, then I drive to the police station and park nearby. Reporting to the reception desk, I ask for DS Khan and I'm told to take a seat in a waiting area. It looks grimy and there's a strong smell of disinfectant. Two other people are waiting to be seen: an emaciated young lady sporting a black eye and bruises on her wrists, and a restless teenager who keeps getting out of his seat and prowling around the room like a caged animal. High up, in the corner of the room, there's a CCTV camera with a blinking red light. Am I being spied on already? I try to assume the posture of an innocent man who's concerned about his missing colleague, but it's impossible to relax.

After approximately forty-five minutes, I'm about to approach the receptionist and ask if they've forgotten about me, when a buzzer sounds and an Asian man in his early thirties enters through a door marked 'No Entry'. He looks around the room.

"Mr Bolton?"

"Yes. That's me."

He comes over and firmly shakes my hand.

"I'm DS Khan. We spoke on the phone earlier. Thanks for coming in. Please follow me."

He uses a security card to open the door which buzzes again, and walks purposefully along a corridor with me in pursuit.

He stops at a door designated Interview Room 2, opens it and stands aside so I can enter first.

"Please have a seat," DS Khan says, pointing to a chair on one side of a large wooden table, opposite a woman who looks far too young to be wearing a police uniform.

"This is my colleague DC Colleen McBride."

She shakes my hand and nods, but doesn't speak. I sit on my allocated chair and try to find a posture that says 'concerned and happy to assist, but definitely not guilty'.

"Now, Mr Bolton…"

"Please, call me Lee." I want to appear friendly and likeable, after all, I *am* friendly and likeable.

"Thanks, Lee. Now, we'll be recording this interview, as is our normal procedure." He presses a red button on the desk and leans back in his chair, which I can't help noticing looks more comfortable than mine. "So, firstly, I'd like to do some introductions for the tape. In the room are Lee Bolton, DS Brian Khan and DC Colleen McBride. This is a voluntary interview. You're not under arrest and you're free to leave at any time. I'd just like you to take a moment to read this card which explains the rights, entitlements and safeguards that will apply to you during the interview."

He hands me a card and I pretend to read it, without taking in a single word. How did I come to be in a police station, being interviewed about the disappearance of a woman I murdered?

"Yes. That all seems fine." I hand back the card. "So, I'm definitely not under arrest?" I ask, trying to force a chuckle.

"No, Lee. If I arrested you, I'd have to tell you about the nature of the offence I thought you'd committed, when and where you'd committed the offence, and I'd have to read you your rights. As far as we're aware at this stage, no crime has been committed. We're just a bit concerned about Mrs Miller's whereabouts. Apparently, it's quite out of character for her to disappear like this, without getting in touch with anyone. We really appreciate you helping us with our enquiries."

"No problem. Before we go on, if you *were* to read me my rights, what would they be?"

"Good question. I'd read you the police caution: You do not have to say anything. But, it may harm your defence if you do not mention when questioned something which you later rely on in court. Anything you do say may be given in evidence."

At this point, DC McBride joins in the conversation, sounding almost as nervous as me. "Would you like a solicitor, Lee? You're entitled to one if you'd like." I think I can see DS Khan frowning at her out the corner of my eye, but when I turn in his direction, his face is neutral. "It's free," she continues.

"Thank you, that's very thoughtful. I do like free stuff in general, but in this case, as I haven't done anything wrong and I'm not under arrest, I don't think it's really necessary. I just want to help." I expect this to lighten the mood, but it doesn't seem to.

"Okay. Let's get started." DS Khan sits forward on his chair and DC McBride picks up her pen and a notepad.

"So, Lee, at the moment we're investigating a rather mysterious missing persons case, as you know. Mrs Sophia Miller has not been seen since last Friday evening, and her family and friends are becoming increasingly concerned. First, can I ask you about the nature of your relationship with Mrs Miller?"

"We're just colleagues. Sophia joined the company three or four years ago, and we've had a professional relationship since that time."

"I see. So, you'd describe yourselves as colleagues rather than friends?"

"Yes. I think so. We've always got on well, but we don't socialise with each other."

"Have you *ever* had any contact outside of work?"

"Not really. It's possible she's sent work-related emails outside of office hours and I might have responded to them, but that's all."

"Have you met her husband, Mr Joseph Miller?"

"I think he might have attended the office Christmas party a couple of years ago."

"What's your impression of him?"

"I can't remember him to be honest. I don't recall us saying much to each other at all. He seemed like a nice enough chap, but, as I say, I really don't know him."

"And that's the only contact you've ever had with Mr Miller?"

"Yes. Until this lunchtime."

"What happened at lunchtime?"

"Joe … Mr Miller rang me at work. He was phoning all the people in Sophia's contacts to ask if they had any information about her disappearance."

"What did you say?"

"That I hadn't seen her since work on Friday and I had no idea where she could be."

"Was he aggressive? Distressed? How would you de-scribe his mood?"

"He just sounded worried about his wife."

DC McBride writes something in her notepad.

"I see. When's the last time you saw Mrs Miller?" DS Khan says.

"Erm, I think it was at about five, maybe five-thirty on Friday, just before I went home."

"In the office?"

"Yes."

"Not in the car park?"

I pretend to be pondering.

"Actually, you could be right. There's a good chance we were in the car park at the same time."

"Did you speak to her?"

"Possibly. I may have said 'Have a good weekend' or something along those lines."

"And that's all?"

"As far as I can remember."

"Would it surprise you to hear that some of your colleagues have said they saw you and Mrs Miller embracing in the car park at about five-thirty on Friday?"

"Really?"

"Really."

"Gosh. I'd forgotten that. Yes, I think I asked after her cousin, who's recently been diagnosed with cancer, and Sophia looked a bit emotional, so I gave her a quick hug. It seemed like the right thing to do."

"Possibly the right thing to do if you were close friends, but you said you were just colleagues."

"We were... *are* just colleagues, but I'm a nice guy and I thought she needed a hug."

"I understand. And I guess it was also quite enjoyable to be embracing an attractive young lady?"

"That's got nothing to do with it."

"Are you attracted to Mrs Miller, Lee?"

"No. I want you to understand that I'm a very happily married man. I guess you could say Sophia is quite pretty in a rather obvious way, but I'm not attracted to her in the slightest. I love my wife."

"How long have you been married?"

"Sixteen happy years."

"And how many unhappy ones?"

I start to respond, but he interrupts me. "I'm just pulling your leg, Lee."

"Funny!" I'm not amused.

"According to Mr Miller, there *is* no cousin with cancer."

"What?"

"Mrs Miller doesn't have a cousin who has cancer."

"But that's what she told everyone at work."

"Yes. Several people have said the same thing. It's something of a mystery at the moment. Are you aware of any other times when Mrs Miller has said things that weren't true?"

"No. But, as I said, we weren't that close. We mainly talked about work."

"Yes. You did say that. So, after you embraced, did she say anything else before she drove away?"

"I don't think so."

"She didn't wind down her window and say anything to you?"

"Nothing that I can remember."

"Two people who were in the car park at the time claim she lowered her window and called out 'See you tomorrow, Lee' just before she left the car park."

"Is that a question?"

"Did that happen?"

"It sounds highly unlikely. As I've explained, we don't socialise and I've never seen her at the weekend. Perhaps they misheard, or maybe she was calling to somebody else."

"Yes, I suppose that's possible."

DC McBride nods in agreement.

"Is there anything else you want to ask me?"

"Just a couple more things, Lee, if you don't mind. It's important we get a full picture of the car park incident as it appears to be the last time Mrs Miller was observed by anyone before she vanished. One of her neighbours thinks she may have seen Mrs Miller's car outside their house on Friday evening, but she can't be sure, so your conversation is the last verified sighting of her we have."

"Didn't her husband see her when he got home?"

"No actually. Mr Miller says he arrived home at about nine-thirty and there was no sign of her or her car. A neighbour verified his time of arrival."

"That seems late to be getting home on a Friday night."

"Yes, we thought the same. The neighbours confirmed that his car is usually back on the drive between 7 p.m. and 8 p.m. every day. We're looking into it."

"Is he suspected of something?"

"Not at all. We're simply trying to locate Mrs Miller at this stage." He looks down at his notes and then continues. "Can you describe Mrs Miller's mood on Friday afternoon?"

"What do you mean?"

"Did she seem upbeat, thoughtful, anxious, depressed?"

"Just her usual self, really. She's got quite a bubbly personality, although she's been a bit subdued lately because of her cousin. Although, you're now telling me she made that up."

"She did, I'm afraid."

"Well, something must have been upsetting her. She's been crying at work a lot recently."

"Lee, do you think it's possible Mrs Miller May have committed suicide?"

"No way! She's not the type."

"Is there a type?"

"She's young, attractive, happy, healthy. Why would she kill herself? She's got so much to live for." I pause. "She was healthy, wasn't she? She hadn't been diagnosed with cancer or anything?"

"Not according to her G.P. He describes her as being in rude health."

"Well, I really don't know Sophia that well. I guess it's possible, but I can't imagine her committing suicide."

"Okay. That's useful information." He turns to DC McBride. "Colleen, have you got the map?"

She opens the briefcase at her feet, removes a map and unfolds it on the table between us.

"Where do you live, Lee?" DC Khan says.

I study the map, locate my street and point out the general location of my house.

"Just here."

"Ah. That's a nice part of town. You must be fairly well off. And where does Mrs Miller live?"

I nearly make a mistake. I'm just about to point at the map when I think better of it and use my pointing finger to scratch my nose instead.

"I don't know I'm afraid. I think she's local, but I don't have her address."

"Indeed. Her house is here." He points to a spot on the map and he's slightly off, but close enough.

"Uh huh."

"So, this would probably be her route to and from work." He takes a highlighter pen and draws on the map.

"Yes, that looks like the quickest way."

"Are you familiar with this road, Lee." He gestures with his pen.

"I've driven along it a few times, but not often."

"There's a lay-by just here. Do you know it?"

Here we go. They both study my face intently. They must have found Sophia's car or obtained her cell phone movements.

"No. I can't say I do."

"We have reason to believe that Mrs Miller may have been in this area on Friday evening; parked in the lay-by or possibly walking by the canal." He taps his pen on the blue line that represents the waterway.

"Was she seen there?" I ask.

"I'm not at liberty to say. Have you ever stopped in this lay-by or walked along this stretch of the canal?"

"No, I don't think so."

"Can you confirm the make and model of your car, Lee?"

"I can, but why do you need to know?"

"It's just routine. We collect all sorts of information at this stage of an enquiry. It all goes into a database and sometimes something useful comes to light. There were several vehicles seen in the lay-by on Friday evening, and we're trying to identify their owners to find out if they saw anything of interest."

"I see."

I tell them my car details and DC McBride writes them down in her notebook.

"One possibility we're investigating is that Mrs Miller might have fallen or jumped into the canal on Friday evening."

"Crikey!"

"It's unlikely, but it's possible. Are you familiar with the process of drowning, Lee? It's a very unpleasant way to die."

"No." I swallow.

DS Khan looks at his colleague who nods once, and then he begins a monologue which sounds wooden and rehearsed.

"Death usually occurs within two minutes, depending on the person's physical status. Once they're under the water they hold their breath until they're forced to inhale. At which point they gulp water. The water causes spasms of the larynx, which then closes off the trachea to protect the lungs." He points to his neck and then to his chest. "Not much water enters the lungs at this stage though. Once the trachea is closed, no fresh air can enter the lungs and the supply of oxygen begins to fail. This lack of oxygen, or anoxia as it's known, has a detrimental effect on the brain and within thirty seconds the spasms of the larynx begin to weaken as brain failure becomes imminent. The person then inhales again, this time aspirating water directly into the lungs, before the next spasm closes the trachea again, but for a shorter duration. With each successive inhalation, more water enters the lungs, anoxia increases, the larynx spasms get shorter and shorter until they finally stop and the lungs are filled with water."

"Oh my God! That's horrible." I'm trying not to imagine Sophia going through this ghastly process in a cold, smelly canal.

"I agree. That's why I never go out of my depth in water."

"Very sensible," I say.

"Lee, you've been here quite a while," DC McBride says,

interrupting. "Would you like to take a break?"

"Aren't we nearly finished?" I say, hopefully.

"Yes. We're almost there," says DS Khan, resuming control.

"Let's just get it over with then."

"Good plan, Lee. Would you like a drink or anything? A cup of tea? Coffee?"

"Actually tea would be nice."

DC McBride picks up the telephone on the desk and asks someone to bring three cups of tea.

After she hangs up the phone, DS Khan isn't happy. "You should have asked for biscuits."

"Sorry. Shall I ring back?" she says.

"No. Hopefully they'll take pity on us and bring biscuits anyway. I'm starving! I can't stop thinking about all that lovely food in Mrs Miller's fridge."

"What's that?" I say.

"When Mr Miller got home on Friday night, he found Mrs Miller and her car to be missing. Everything else in the house was exactly as it should be, apart from an unexpected amount of fancy food in the fridge. There was steak, lobster, caviar, champagne, truffles, expensive wine, gourmet cheese ... loads of stuff. Mr Miller had no idea what it was for."

"That's weird."

"I know."

The tea arrives, complete with a bowl of sugar, a spoon and a plate of biscuits.

"You're off the hook, Colleen, but make sure you ask next time."

"Will do, boss."

I'm able to relax a little as we drink our tea, but I haven't got the appetite to eat anything.

"Can you get the laptop out, Colleen," DS Khan asks DC McBride, his mouth full of biscuit crumbs.

She complies and takes a slim laptop computer out of her briefcase. I see a police logo on the top. She opens it and powers it on, then slides it across the desk to her colleague. DS Khan presses a few keys until he's found what he's looking for.

"What do you make of this, Lee?" He swings the laptop around so I can see the screen. They both gaze at me attentively.

There's a video playing. In the centre of the picture, I can see Sophia. She's in a dimly lit room, naked, blindfolded and tied with rope to an upright chair. Her hands appear to be secured behind her back. She's not struggling, but she keeps moving and tilting her head as if she's trying to pinpoint the location of a sound.

Nothing happens for a few seconds. Then I see the light change slightly as a shadow moves across the room. There's someone else there.

From the right side of the screen a naked man appears, and he goes to stand behind the chair. I can't make out his face, which is still in shadow, but I can see that he has something in his right hand. It looks like a small clear cube. He holds the cube above Sophia and, after a few seconds, droplets begin to fall from the cube onto Sophia's right breast. I see her stiffen in the chair and hear the hiss of a quick intake of breath as she arches her back as much as the rope will allow. It must be an ice cube. The man reaches forward and encircles Sophia's right nipple with the ice cube. Then he transfers it to his left hand and teases her other nipple. When he bends down to kiss her shoulder, his head leaves the safety of the shadow and his face becomes visible. I recognise the man straight away.

It's me.

There can be no doubt.

I look up at DS Khan and DC McBride in turn. It's clear from their expressions that they know it's me too, but DS Khan asks anyway.

"Is that you, Lee?"

I don't say anything.

He swings the laptop back around to face him, presses a few more keys and then points it back in my direction.

"What about this one?"

I glance at the screen for just long enough to see Sophia, on her hands and knees, in the middle of a creaking double bed. She's looking directly at the camera lens with a big smile on her face, while I pound her from behind, my features contorted in pleasure, oblivious to the camera recording my every move.

I don't say anything.

"Earlier I asked you about the nature of your relationship with Mrs Miller. In the light of what you've just seen, would you like to change your answer?"

"Am I under arrest?" I say.

"No."

"Am I still free to leave at any time?"

"Absolutely."

"Then I think I'd like to leave now." I start to get to my feet.

"Of course. That's fine. Is there anything else you'd like to tell us before you go?"

"No."

"Very well. We'll be in touch again soon, so please stay in the area."

I don't reply.

As I exit the room, I hear DS Khan say, "For the tape, Lee Bolton has terminated the interview at 17:20."

# CHAPTER TWENTY-TWO

## *The Loft*

I drive home, my head spinning.

The police know that Sophia's last location was the lay-by near the canal. They also know I just lied throughout my interview, and they're in possession of evidence which proves that Sophia and I were lovers.

If, or should that be when, they find Sophia's body, the four most likely possibilities will surely be: she committed suicide, she was murdered by her husband, she was murdered by her lover, or death by misadventure.

Presumably, a Post Mortem examination will be performed due to the suspicious nature of Sophia's death. The police will discover that she drowned. They'll find out she was pregnant. They'll come after Joe and me, their investigation converging on the most likely perpetrator as the evidence accumulates. I'm not going to be able to keep Sophia's disappearance from Tamsin for much longer.

As I'm driving, I try to plan what I'm going to tell her, but I'm struggling to come up with an approach that doesn't result in me being separated from my wedding tackle.

"Hey, Tam. You know Sophia from work?"

"Yes."

"Apparently she disappeared last Friday and nobody has seen her since."

"Really? That's weird."

"I know. Anyway, the police might want to ask me some questions about it."

"How come?"

"I was one of the last people to see her before she ... vanished."

"Is that all? You had me worried there for a minute."

"No. There's a bit more to it than that."

"Go on."

"The police have found evidence she was having an affair."

"How sordid! With who?"

"With whom."

"With whom?"

"Me."

"Can you pass me the gonad remover ..."

What if I put off telling Tamsin until Sophia's body is discovered?

"Sophia from work has been found dead in the canal."

"Oh my God! That's awful."

"I know. It gets worse. They discovered at the Post Mortem that she was pregnant."

"No! Her poor husband must be devastated."

"I'm sure he is. Anyway, the police might want to ask me some questions about it."

"Why?"

"They found loads of videos on her computer."

"Videos of what?"

"Sophia having sex?"

"With whom?"

"Me."

"Jesus Christ! ... Are you the father?"

"I don't know. I guess my DNA will be examined to find out."

"Just put your cock on this chopping board for a sec..."

I arrive home, have a shower and sit in the living room, waiting for Tamsin to return from work. To pass the time, I do some research into the length of prison sentences for murdering pregnant women. It's hard to obtain precise figures, but it's clear that if I'm tried, found guilty and sentenced, I'm likely to spend the remainder of my able-bodied years locked away. My hope is that there's not enough proof for a jury to convict me. There are no witnesses and there shouldn't be any physical evidence linking me to a crime. In the absence of proof, it would be hard for any jury to disregard the reasonable doubt that Sophia drowned accidentally or even committed suicide. Surely a jury would have enough uncertainty to not find me guilty.

I hear the front door open and close, and the sound of footsteps approaching from the hallway. The living room door swings slowly open, creaking on its hinges as it does so. It's Charlie. She slumps down on the sofa and rips open an envelope.

"Hi, Dad."

"Hi, pumpkin. Had a good day?"

"Meh! You?"

"I've had better, to be honest."

"Mum home yet?"

"No, not yet."

Charlie takes a sheet of paper out of the envelope and reads it. She looks confused at first and then her frown deepens.

"Well, this can't be right," she says.

"What is it?"

"My DNA results have come back."

"Huh?"

"You know. Nana and Greg bought me a DNA testing kit for my birthday. I sent it off a few weeks ago."

I'd missed that.

"They must have made a mistake," she continues. "According to this, I'm forty-seven percent European Jewish."

She hands me the piece of paper. I study it carefully as a hot ball of dread forms in my bowels and begins to expand within me.

"It's definitely got your name on it," I manage to say. In my head, random thoughts are firing and coalescing.

"I didn't think there was any Jewish ancestry in our family. Is it your side or Mum's?"

"Neither, as far as I'm aware. None of our grandparents were Jewish. Nor our great-grandparents."

"Well, for me to be forty-seven percent Jewish, wouldn't either you or Mum have to be practically a hundred percent Jewish?"

"Yes." I force a smile. "You're right, Charlie. It must be a mistake. They've obviously mixed up your saliva with someone else's."

"That's annoying. I'm not paying to do it again."

"Didn't Nana pay? I honestly can't remember her giving it to you. My memory's definitely getting worse."

"Actually, now I think about it, you're right. Nana came up to my bedroom and gave it to me there. She told me not to tell you or Mum so it would be a surprise."

Charlie screws up the letter and throws it in the bin.

"Waste of bloody time!" Charlie mutters as she stomps upstairs to her bedroom.

I retrieve the letter, flatten it out and inspect it, thoughtfully.

There's no mistake.

Charlie *is* nearly half Jewish.

I've never felt more certain about anything in my life. The moment the idea popped into my head, I knew it was true.

Jake is Charlie's biological father.

I sit in the living room and ponder, staring at the photos of Charlie and John on the walls and the sideboard. They certainly resemble each other quite closely, and Charlie looks a lot like Tamsin, but neither of them has inherited any of my features. My father and I have a distinctive nose which neither of the kids has acquired. I'm surprised I haven't noticed this before now. The longer I study their faces, the more of Jake I can see in them both. Can it really be true?

The front door opens and closes again.

"Hello?" Tamsin calls.

"In here, Tam."

She enters the living room, looking flustered, and deposits her handbag on the floor.

"You know the Year 6 residential trip tonight and tomorrow?" she says.

"No."

"Yes, you do. It happens every year."

"Okay."

"Well, someone's dropped out, so I've got to go instead. We're leaving in an hour."

Exasperated, she leaves the room and runs up the stairs. I assume she's going to pack, but it sounds as if she's having a shower first.

On the floor I spy her cell phone, peeking out of her handbag.

I pick it up.

Apart from my recent browse through the contents of Tamsin's laptop, I'm not one for snooping, but I can't shake my fear that Jake is the biological father of Charlie and John. If I'm right, and my gut is telling me that I am, then I'll need some evidence before I confront Tamsin. Perhaps I can find something on her phone.

I press the home button and the screen springs to life. It's not even password protected. What a schoolboy error!

I've looked at Tamsin's phone before. She's perfectly happy for me to use it whenever I need to. However, this time, I have a specific target in mind: Jake.

I begin with Tamsin's text messages. They're in order, according to who she's communicated with most recently. I don't find any surprises amongst the recipients: me, Charlie, John, Nilofer, her mum, my mum, colleagues from work, people from the tennis club, Jake …

I go straight to the messages Tamsin has exchanged with Jake. The most recent communication is several weeks ago:

"What time are you picking John up for the football?"
"12:30? I thought he might like to get some lunch first."
"Good plan. See you then. X"

This was followed, several hours later, by:

"Thanks for taking John. He had a great time. X"
"My pleasure."

This isn't what I was dreading to find. On the contrary, it seems more like the text message exchange between two friends with nothing to hide. I'm mildly concerned about the kisses at first, but, after a quick inspection of Tamsin's messages to other people, it's apparent that she uses kisses routinely with anyone she knows well.

I scroll back in time to the previous exchange between her and Jake:

"Happy Christmas! Xxx"
"Same to you. Looking forward to seeing you all later."
"What time are you coming?"
"Probably around 4 p.m."
"Ok. See you then. X"

I scroll back further.

There's nothing suspicious. Every few months Tamsin and Jake exchange innocuous text messages about routine things. Is it all in my imagination?

I search through Tamsin's recent call log. Again I find telephone calls to and from all the usual suspects, but I can't find any record of ingoing, outgoing, missed or failed calls between Tamsin and Jake. I'm relieved by this at first until I realise that I know for a fact that Tamsin has phoned Jake in the last few months; I've witnessed it. So, why is there no record of these calls? Has she deleted it?

Next, I try Tamsin's email. A quick scan tells me that they're fairly humdrum. There's lots of work stuff, but not much more. I try a search for 'Jake' within her email app, but it doesn't locate any emails from, to or about Jake at all.

The creaking floorboards above my head tell me Tamsin is out of the shower and moving around our bedroom. I figure that she's frantically packing, so I've still got a few minutes to snoop.

What about photos? There are 12,791 photos and 133 videos stored on Tamsin's phone. I haven't got time to inspect them all, but I have a quick look at some of the videos: mostly family events like Christmas, birthdays and holidays. There's nothing dodgy here. I scroll through the photos, but none appear suspicious. I locate Jake in a few shots, but can see nothing to be concerned about in any of them. There are a couple of restaurant photos of the seven of us from university, presumably taken by one of the serving staff, and Jake also appears in some of our Christmas day photos, but that's all.

Worried that Tamsin will come downstairs at any moment and catch me looking through her phone, I have a quick peek at the Maps app, but she's still got Location Services switched off, so there's no record of her movements around the country. I doubt I would have learned anything useful from that anyway.

I hear heavy footsteps on the stairs as Tamsin comes thumping down, and I barely have time to switch off the screen and throw the phone in the direction of Tamsin's handbag before she bursts into the room. Fortunately it was a good throw.

"Right. I'm off." She's breathing heavily as she places the strap of her handbag over her shoulder.

"Before you go, there's something I have to tell you," I say.

"I haven't got time, Lee. Can't it wait till tomorrow night when I'm back?"

"Yeah. I guess so."

Tamsin kisses me on the cheek, shouts a general "Bye!" up the stairs at anyone who may be up there and exits, slamming the front door behind her. I hear the tyres spin on the gravel as her car accelerates off the drive.

Sitting back on the sofa, I exhale an extended sigh. Either my hunch is wrong, or Tamsin has meticulously removed everything suspicious from her phone relating to Jake.

Unconvinced and undeterred, I decide to spend part of the evening searching the house for any evidence which implies that Jake might be the biological father of Charlie and John. I'm not exactly sure what I'm looking for, but I'll know it when I see it.

Beginning in our bedroom, I remove the top drawer of Tamsin's bedside cabinet and empty the contents onto the bed. I study each item in turn before replacing it in the drawer. There's nothing questionable. I repeat this process with every drawer in the bedroom, even my own, until I'm satisfied there's nothing untoward in any of them. Then I switch to the wardrobes, painstakingly relocating every item of clothing onto the bed, inspecting each garment, one item at a time, and checking any pockets, before replacing them in the wardrobe.

Still nothing.

I move onto the en-suite bathroom. Each object there is inspected and replaced, but I fail to find anything suspicious.

I continue my meticulous search, room by room: the kitchen, the dining room, the living room, the bathrooms, the spare room, the garage, the shed. All clear. My only reward is £2.73 in loose change.

By 10 p.m. I've painstakingly searched everywhere in the house except Charlie's room, John's room and the loft. There's no way I can examine these three remaining spaces without Charlie and John noticing what I'm up to, so I resolve to call in sick at work tomorrow and complete my search then, when I've got the house to myself.

I go to bed earlier than usual, but I suspect I won't be able to sleep. My mind is churning with unwelcome thoughts. I really want to talk to someone about this, but who? Sophia was my confidante, but she's dead, by my own hand. I'd thought Jake was my friend and ally, but now I'm not so sure. I can't just confront him or Tamsin without any evidence to support my life-changing suspicions.

I ring Nilofer.

"Hi, Nil. It's Lee."

"Hi, Lee. Is everything okay?"

"Yes, fine."

"You're phoning very late. I'm in bed."

"Sorry about that. I didn't realise the time. I just wanted to ask you a quick question. It might sound a bit weird, I'm afraid."

"What is it?"

"Well ... it's about Tam and Jake."

There's a brief silence.

" ... What about them?"

"Is there anything I should be aware of?"

"Like what?" I can hear an edge to her voice.

"Are they just friends or is there anything more to their relationship?"

"Oh, Lee. Please don't get me involved."

"Involved with what?"

"Nothing. Look, as far as I know, Tamsin and Jake have been no more than good friends since university."

"Did something happen at university? Were they more than friends then?"

"Well, they went out with each other for a few months in their first year. You knew that."

"I certainly did not! They were a couple?"

"Yes. Just for a while. It was common knowledge."

"This is the first I'm hearing about it."

"I don't think it was particularly serious. They got a bit hot and heavy for a while, but it didn't last long. In the second year, you got together with Tam, and Jake had several different girlfriends."

"Why didn't anyone tell me?"

"I've got no idea. Perhaps they just didn't think it was important."

"Were they sleeping together?"

"What do you think? They were first-year students at university. Everybody was sleeping with everybody."

I can't believe it. Jake had been shagging my wife the year before we met and they didn't tell me. Nobody told me.

"I'd better go, Lee. I'm tired and I've got to get up early tomorrow."

"Sure. One more question before you go. Did Tam seem okay to you when you saw her last Sunday?"

"Yes. Absolutely fine."

"Thanks, Nil. Sorry to bother you so late."

"No problem."

"Goodnight."

Bollocks!

Tamsin was at home with me all of last Sunday. Nilofer just lied to me. She thinks she's covering for Tamsin. I wonder how many times in the past Tamsin has claimed to be with Nilofer when in fact she's been with somebody else.

As expected, I get very little sleep. The police interview, and worries about my wife and our progeny, compete for my attention all night long. I give up trying to sleep and get out of bed when I hear the kids in the kitchen. I throw on some casual clothes and go downstairs.

"Morning, guys. Anyone heard anything from Mum?"

"Not me," Charlie says. "She's probably got no signal. They're staying in the middle of nowhere."

"I guess so," I say.

"Shouldn't you be getting ready for work, Dad?" John asks.

"No. I'm taking a sickie today."

"You okay?"

"Yeah. Just feeling a bit under the weather."

"Me too," he says. "Can I stay off school today?"

"Nice try, mate, but no chance."

"You're mean. That's child abuse." He picks up his book bag. "See you later, then. I won't be home till eightish. We've got an away match after school."

"See you, John. Good luck in the match."

"I'll be home late too, Dad," Charlie says, wolfing down a piece of toast. "Me and Jenny are going to study together for our biology test tomorrow."

I've never heard of Jenny, but this isn't the time to get into it.

Charlie and John head out of the front door together. As soon as they leave, I resume my search of the house. The process takes much longer in Charlie and John's rooms because they've got so much clutter, but none of it relates to Tamsin and Jake. I feel guilty about invading their privacy, but it has to be done. I make a mental note that I must have a conversation with John about pornography and I need to ground Charlie until she's twenty-five.

I've found nothing.

There's only one place left to search, and it's the place I've been dreading the most: the loft.

Our loft is dusty, cold, damp and inhabited by fearless spiders the size of my fist. Nobody ever goes up there except me. They've all got more sense. However, it's the only place I haven't searched, and I'm determined to leave no stone unturned. Once I've eliminated the loft, I can start to relax. If I can't find any evidence linking Tamsin and Jake in an inappropriate way, then maybe it's all in my mind and I can finally dismiss my paranoid suspicions.

I fetch a chair and stand on it to open the loft hatch, then get the ladder out of the airing cupboard and ascend into the darkness. On switching on the light, I swear I can hear at least thirty huge spiders scuttling out of sight. I look around. There's some wooden flooring surrounding the loft hatch, but it doesn't extend very far. Beyond it, there are just joists and insulation. That part of the roof space is pretty inaccessible unless you're particularly careful about where you place your feet.

A general dumping ground for rarely required clutter, our loft contains quite a few overflowing boxes: Christmas decorations, photographs, old school books, financial paperwork, toys that haven't been played with for years, camping equipment, Tamsin's wedding dress, unused electrical items and cables. There are also several empty suitcases and some sports equipment.

I search through it all. In the gloom of the single light-bulb, I examine the contents of each and every box. It's quite nostalgic. The photos, in particular, bring back many happy memories of the kids' childhood and our carefree family holidays together.

My phone rings loudly in the silence, making me jump. I take it out of my pocket and glance at the number, expecting it to be Tamsin. It isn't, but I've seen this number before and I recognise it straight away. DS Khan is calling me. I don't answer, and after a couple of minutes, it stops ringing.

I've examined all the boxes I can see, but it's possible there are more beyond the area illuminated by the ineffectual light-bulb. Switching on the torch on my phone, I shine it around the loft, into the darkest corners. There's nothing of interest to see, only a thin layer of fibreglass insulation, installed by the builders when the house was constructed.

Only one part of the roof space can't be seen from my current location. It's the gable above Charlie's room. In order to get a view of that part of the loft, I'll need to clamber carefully over the joists until I can shine my torch directly into it.

I'm pretty sure this is where the biggest, hairiest spiders hang out. There's hardly any point even looking there. It's the least accessible part of our property. On the other hand, it's the least accessible part of our property and thus the best place to hide something. Who am I kidding? Tamsin hates spiders even more than I do.

To my surprise, I find myself moving beyond the floor-boards, onto the narrow joists and carefully edging my way deeper into the loft. I'm holding on to the rafters for support and the rough wood is giving me splinters in my hands, but I persevere until I come to a spot from which I can see directly into the whole of the loft space. I shine my torch around and, as expected, there's nothing but joists and fibreglass insulation.

I'm about to make my way back towards the safety of the hatch, when I notice that the insulation is a few inches higher in the furthest, darkest corner, as if the builders have left two or three layers of fibreglass in a pile.

It's probably nothing.

I have to check.

After another ten minutes of uncomfortable manoeuvring and the acquisition of several more splinters, I reach the raised spot. Crouching precariously on two joists and holding a rafter with one hand to balance myself, I reach out with the other hand and press down on the pile of insulation. I'm expecting it to be soft and yielding, but there's something hard beneath the top layer. I lift it up, and below the fibreglass there's a concealed cardboard box. My heart sinks. 'I'll know it when I see it,' has become, 'I've found it.' Eureka!

I carefully manhandle the box to the hatch and carry it down the ladder. In our bedroom, I place it in the centre of the bed.

There's a reason it was so carefully hidden. I have my suspicions about what it contains, but I have to be certain. I realise that if I open this box, I may discover secrets that will change my life as I know it, and not for the better. What I see within, I will never be able to un-see.

I open the lid and look inside.

# CHAPTER TWENTY-THREE

*The Box*

I peer into the box.

It contains an assortment of items tidily arranged into groups. In one corner, there's a neat stack of diaries, possibly about twenty, with the year printed along the spine. The most recent is from last year. Next to the diaries, I can see bundles of envelopes, held together with elastic bands. They appear to be a mixture of typical hand-written letters and official brown-envelope business correspondence, the sort which usually contain bills and bank statements. Then there's a pile of photographs, neatly stacked, face down. Finally, there are eight cell phones and their accompanying chargers.

Where do I start?

I pick up the pile of photos and turn it over.

The first picture is of Tamsin and Jake. They're sharing an armchair in a cramped room that can only be student accommodation. Tamsin is perched on Jake's lap with her arms around his neck. They're smiling happily at the camera. I can tell from the hairstyles that the photo must have been taken during their first year at university, before I knew either of them, back when they were 'hot and heavy' as Nilofer had described it last night. It's bizarre seeing them together as a couple. I'd never thought of them in that way until now. Seeing it in a photo somehow makes it real.

The next thirty or so photographs look as if they come from that same year. Some comprise just the two of them, some include them as part of a group of people, most of whom I recognise, and some are of Tamsin on her own. Of the latter category, several feature Tamsin in bed, hair tousled and face radiant; apparently naked and partially wrapped in just a sheet; shading her eyes as the sunlight streams in through the window. I can't remember her ever looking so beautiful.

Thinking back to our university days, I recall that Jake often had a camera with him and he'd regularly take photos of our student larks. He must have had them developed, but I don't remember seeing many of the actual prints; only a few which he'd pinned to his notice board, featuring all seven of us.

As I scan the photos, one by one, I can tell they're in chronological order. After a while, there are fewer pictures featuring Tamsin and Jake together. When I reach their second year at university - my first year - I come across photos of Tamsin and me, holding hands or embracing. I've never seen any of these pictures before, and I'm entranced as I revisit the overwhelming sensations of falling in love with this wonderful woman.

My temporary joy is soon replaced by apprehension as I resume my obsessive search for the terrifying truth.

The next cluster of photos are, surreptitiously but undeniably, just Tamsin; candid shots taken at group gatherings. Sometimes they feature other people, but there's no doubt that Tamsin is the main focus of each picture, while other individuals are merely insignificant bystanders. It would appear that Jake still had something of a crush on Tamsin even though she was with me by that time.

Before long, I come to photos of our wedding. Tamsin looked so beautiful that day, her hair in loose ringlets and a big cheesy grin permanently plastered across her face. Again, Jake - ostensibly my best man - has taken lots of candid shots of Tamsin, and presumably then handed his camera over to someone else to obtain a few pictures of just himself with the bride. Incongruously, there's an unnecessarily large gap between their stiff bodies, and both Tamsin and Jake appear uncomfortable to be photographed together.

After our wedding, the time interval between photos increases, but the pictures become more damning. There are several shots of Tamsin and Jake - always with their arms around each other - at the seaside, in woods, on hilltops, in hotel rooms and in restaurants. Presumably, these were taken either with a timer or by some helpful passer-by. They make a handsome couple and seem very happy to be in each other's company. Nobody would suspect that, at the time these photos were taken, they were both married to other people. Jake's first wife had always suspected that he was having an affair. He'd vehemently denied it, but the marriage didn't last long. Here were pictures that would have supported her claim, but they aren't exactly proof of infidelity.

It's the next few photos that break my heart. They were taken in our old house in the living room. The camera must have been balanced on the mantlepiece. They're enchanting pictures of Tamsin and Jake looking directly at the camera, but for once they aren't embracing. This time, in his arms, Jake is cradling Charlie. Their daughter.

Shit!

I sit down heavily on the bed, in despair. I now know, without a shadow of a doubt, that my hunch was correct, but I've never wanted to be wrong so much in my life.

I can't stop myself from looking at the subsequent photos, even though it feels as if I'm torturing myself. After a few more pictures of just Tamsin and Jake, and the occasional one of the three of them, I finally come across the first picture of all four. There it is: Jake's complete unacknowledged family. The photo was taken at our current house in the garden. The camera must have been placed on the bird-table. They're sitting on the parched grass on a hot, summer's day. Charlie, who was about three at the time, is frozen in the act of throwing a football into the air. Tamsin is leaning against Jake and smiling at the camera while Jake is looking down at the baby on his lap. On his face, he bears the unmistakable self-satisfied beam of a father gazing at his baby son.

I put my head in my hands and weep. For my wife. For my children. For twenty years of deceit. My shoulders convulse for many minutes as I release all the pent up stress and emotion built up over the recent weeks. Finally, I compose myself and resume my self-flagellation.

The rest of the photos continue in the same vein - various combinations and permutations of the four of them - until they decrease in frequency and eventually stop about eight years ago. I guess that was around the time that most people abandoned the traditional camera in favour of the digital one on their cell phone.

The very last photo in the pile is a group-shot of Tamsin, Jake, Charlie, John, me and my mum; taken after Christmas lunch seven or eight years ago. We're all wearing paper hats from the Christmas crackers, except Jake, who always arrived sometime after lunch was completed. I should have realised before now that Jake visits all of his children on Christmas day, including the ones I had thought were mine.

Next, I turn to the letters, beginning with the more interesting looking handwritten envelopes. I recognise the spidery writing on the front as Jake's, and I notice the first few letters are addressed to Tamsin Cadwallader, her maiden name, either at her university accommodation or her parents' home.

I open the first one.

A quick glance at the contents tells me it's a love letter from Jake to Tamsin. It's handwritten and dated February of the first year they were at university together. It's four insufferable pages of immature, gushing, romantic drivel, and it's painful to read. Clearly, Jake was head-over-heels in love with Tamsin when he wrote it, and he didn't hold back. The intimate details about their lovemaking make my stomach churn.

The subsequent letters contain additional verbose, quixotic declarations of love, as well as responses to implied questions, so it's apparent that an exchange of written communication has begun between Tamsin and Jake. I can't bear to read more than two or three of these and I quickly skip ahead to letters nearer the bottom of the pile.

Now the tone has changed somewhat. Jake is still effusive about his undying love for Tamsin, but the contrite inflection makes it clear that he's done something to upset her and is now in her bad books.

The penultimate one describes how sorry Jake is that he cheated on Tamsin, and he begs her to forgive him.

The final letter in this selection contains a reiteration of Jake's eternal devotion to Tamsin, a promise he'll always be there for her, and a hope they'll someday get back together.

What a pussy! The schoolboy language would be painfully embarrassing to Jake if he was ever to re-read what he'd written as a smitten nineteen-year-old.

The next bundle of letters looks very dull. They're all buff-coloured business envelopes; the ones with the little see-through window that reveals the recipient's name and address. On each is typed 'Ms Tamsin Cadwallader' followed by our address. If I'd found one of these letters on our doormat, I would have put it straight on Tamsin's desk and then thought no more about it.

I remove the contents of the first envelope. Behind the initial piece of paper, which contains nothing except the type-written address, there are two more sheets of writing paper. These are hand-written pages and again are romantic in nature. I open another one. And another. They're all the same. They're all love letters from Jake to Tamsin. The most alarming thing is the first ones are dated from a period when Tamsin and I were living together, but weren't yet married. I had believed that this was the time when we were happiest and most in love, but it appears I was wrong. Throughout this period, Tamsin and Jake had found a way to send passionate love letters to each other in secret. I wonder, briefly, why they didn't simply text each other, but of course, this was about seventeen years ago, when emailing and texting were still in their infancy. I have to admire their ingenuity. There was no danger of me opening one of these missives and they could communicate with each other at will.

The detail within these letters enables me to confirm that Tamsin and Jake had resumed their sexual relationship at some point after we left university and were involved in a passionate affair even while Tamsin and I were engaged to be married.

While I'm impressed with their adultery skills, I'm beginning to despise them both with a passion.

There are still many more letters to read, but I'm impatient to discover what's written in the diaries, and I'm intrigued by the cell phones, some of which I don't recognise at all. I try to turn on one of the phones, but the battery is flat. However, it appears I have all the matching chargers too, so I spend the next ten minutes finding eight available plug sockets around the house with which to charge the phones, so I'll be able to switch them on and study their contents.

Once they're plugged in, I open the first diary.

From the year printed on the spine, I can tell it was written twenty-six years ago; the year Tamsin turned fourteen. There's an entry for each day of the year. Most of them are rather banal descriptions of her day: what lessons she'd had at school, what she'd had for tea, homework deadlines and so on. She'd obviously had a crush on a boy called Steve, who'd merited quite a few mentions. "Steve smiled at me in Geography … Steve told Julie he likes me!" and other comments of that ilk, with love hearts around his name.

I skip ahead a couple of diaries, looking for something a bit more interesting, and I find it on the date of Tamsin's sixteenth birthday. "Had sex with Steve in the downstairs loo!!! Standing up! Over very quickly and quite painful. No condom!" This surprises me because Tamsin has always maintained that she lost her virginity in her first year at university although she never told me with whom. She just said, "You don't know him."

I flip through the next few diaries, but there's nothing that catches my eye until Tamsin's freshman year at university. The first mention of Jake comes in late November and by the following January, they were sleeping together. She kept a record of every time they had sex and went into more detail when they tried anything new. Some entries simply said "Sex!" while others said "Sex! Doggie style. Nice!!!" or "Sex! Me on top!!! Very self-conscious!" or "Sex! 69. Pleasant, but hard to concentrate!" Tamsin had a lot of sex in those first few months of their relationship; probably the equivalent of ten years' worth with me.

The mood changed in May. Jake had slept with another girl after a party, and Tamsin had found out about it. She was devastated, and she'd dumped him. He begged her to forgive him and get back together, but she wouldn't, even though she was broken-hearted. Despite the relationship being over, there were still many mentions of Jake in the following months.

Keen to see my first appearance, I seek the relevant week in the same diary as the break-up, and there I am, in early October:

"Met Jake's new friend Lee. Kind of cute!"

That's promising.

A few weeks later I feature again:

"Slept with Lee to make Jake jealous. He was furious. Ha! Sex was average."

As I remember it, the sex was mind-blowing. I was a total stud! But Tamsin *was* rather drunk. Perhaps she didn't remember it as clearly as I did.

Two weeks later:

"Jake is shagging Beth. Slag! Nice chat with Lee. He's growing on me!"

The next day:

"Sex with Lee. Better!"

The following week:

"Seems like Lee and I are a couple. Not sure how that happened. Jake still wants to get back together with me. I keep saying no. Think he's finally getting the message."

After that, there are few mentions of Jake for many months. There's plenty of stuff about Tamsin's studies and her social engagements, but she's stopped recording her sex life. We finished university at the same time, after I completed my degree and Tamsin stayed on for an extra year and took a PGCE to train as a teacher, ostensibly so we could continue together at the same establishment for another year. It turned out that she rather enjoyed teaching, and we both found jobs in the same town and made the decision to set up home together. It's all recorded in Tamsin's diaries, but she doesn't go into much detail. I'm pleasantly surprised to discover how many happy memories come back to me after reading her brief diary entries, but I'm devastated that these memories have been tarnished forever by what I now know about the true state of affairs.

I had no idea Tamsin was keeping a diary all those years. Not once did I see her writing in one, or notice that she even possessed such a thing. She must have written it in private and kept it well hidden. Presumably, if you keep a personal diary, full of your most intimate thoughts, and you want to protect it from your nosy parents and siblings, it becomes a good habit to write it in secret and find a secure hiding place.

The year after we moved in together I proposed to Tamsin, and her immediate response was underwhelming to say the least. We'd been out for a romantic meal, and afterwards we went for a walk by the sea. As we'd sat on a bench, watching the waves crash against the shore, I'd got down on one knee and asked her to marry me. I'd expected her to be ecstatic and say yes immediately, but instead, she'd said, and I can still clearly remember her exact words, "Oh, Lee. You're so sweet! Do you mind if I have a couple of days to think about it?"

Two days later she'd said yes, but those two days were probably the longest of my life.

I look up the date of the proposal. In her diary, Tamsin had written:

"Lee asked me to marry him! It was windy and cold. I said I'd think about it."

The following diary entry reads:

"Phoned Jake. We had a lovely chat. He's madly in love with someone called Megan. She sounds like a right cow."

A day later:

"Said yes to Lee! He was over the moon. I'm going to be Mrs Bolton! Choosing a ring tomorrow."

There's nothing of interest in the next few months until Jake re-appeared on the scene:

"Jake has split up with Megan!"

A few days later:

"Jake phoned. We talked for ages. He said he misses me!"

The next day:

"Jake wants to meet me for coffee."

The following Saturday:

"Met Jake in town. He gets more handsome as he gets older! Lovely to catch up."

Two weeks after that:

"Lee away this weekend for a stag do. Jake coming round tomorrow to see our flat! Very nervous!"

The next day:

"OMG! Had sex with Jake!! Three times!!! Nobody makes me come so hard and so fast as Jake!!! He told me he still loves me! He's still here, in my bed!!!"

The day after:

"Jake stayed all weekend! Had sex twice more! In the kitchen and in the shower!!! He only left when Lee's flight landed. He wants us to get back together! So happy! Lee wanted to have sex, but I was too sore so started an argument. Lee sulking."

Three days later:

"Meeting Jake tomorrow to talk about 'us'."

The next day:

"Went for a long walk with Jake. Told him I want to marry him instead of Lee. Thought he'd be happy. He said he's 'not ready to settle down yet', but wants to keep having sex with me. Told him to fuck off!"

At the time, I was oblivious to all of this. Three weeks later, Tamsin and I chose a date for our wedding and sent out invitations.

The wedding day was a wonderful occasion. All of our closest friends and family attended, including our five best friends from university. Jake was my best man and Nilofer was Tamsin's chief bridesmaid.

I locate the relevant day in Tamsin's diary:

"Wedding day! I couldn't be happier. Jake made a lovely speech all about me and so did Lee. I felt really special. Near the end, Jake dragged me into a cloakroom for a snog!!! First one for 8 months and 17 days!"

I read the next entries very carefully, poring over every word until I find what I'm looking for. Less than three months after Tamsin and I were married, there it is:

"Jake came round. We had sex! Adultery makes me so horny!!!"

Three days later:

"Jake took me out for lunch. He says he can't bear not making love to me. Poor guy! He wants us to have an affair to see if we're compatible. If it goes well, he says we'll get married! Bloody cheek!"

The following week:

"Sex with Jake in his car! He begged me to have an affair. I said no, but I'm weakening! It would be rather titillating!"

The next day:

"Had a long conversation with Jake. We've agreed to a six-month trial affair to see how it goes!!! I really don't want to hurt Lee, so we must be very careful."

I throw the diary at the bedroom wall with all my might. It makes a slight dent in the plasterwork and falls to the floor. It doesn't take a genius to realise that Tamsin has been in love with Jake since before she met me. I was, and have always been, her second choice.

It's time to look at the cell phones. They won't be fully charged yet, but not far off. I find the newest looking one and switch it on. I'm not surprised to discover that it's passcode protected. I try a few combinations of numbers which I know Tamsin has used in the past, but none of them work. It's the same with the next phone. They're useless to me if I can't find the passcodes.

While I'm trying to think of alternative passcodes to attempt, I pick up the most recent diary and flick through it. The final few pages catch my eye. After the end of the calendar year, there are several blank pages for making notes. It's here I discover some very useful information. At the top of one page, Tamsin has written a secondary email address, one

I've never seen before, followed by a list of twelve passwords, each one crossed out except the last. On the following page, there's a list of twelve six-digit numbers, again all crossed out except the final one. My guess is that these are the passcodes to unlock her secret cell phone for that particular month of that particular year. I try the one at the bottom of the list and the phone springs to life. On the home-screen, I see a selfie of Tamsin and Jake on a hilltop, taken sometime in the last twelve months. Arms wrapped around each other and rosy-cheeked, they always appear to be so happy together, and I hate it. Why couldn't she be happy with me?

A quick look at the earlier diaries tells me that it's been Tamsin's habit to change her email password and cell phone passcode every month for many years. She's certainly more disciplined than I am.

The most enlightening entries in Tamsin's diaries are on the very last page of the notes section. Looking back over several of her diaries, she's used this page to write down her strategies for having an affair with Jake, without me, the kids or anyone else finding out about it. They're bullet points. Some of them are similar to my twelve rules, only better and more comprehensive. Her thoroughness is impressive. Nearly twenty years of practice at hiding her illicit relationship with Jake has enabled Tamsin to become highly adept in the art of deception. Here's a small selection:

"Delete all suspicious text messages and emails, but leave some innocuous ones. If there aren't any innocuous ones, then send some."

"Flirt with other men to throw Lee off the scent."

"Send letters disguised as business correspondence."

"Hide all photos and diaries at work in a locked cabinet."

"Set up a separate, private email address and change the password every month."

"Use a secret, locked, prepaid cell phone for all suspicious communication."

"Use work address for all itemised bills."

"Switch off Location Services."

"If Lee gets suspicious, promise to make an effort to work on trust issues."

"Be attentive to Lee's needs at least once a month." What a bitch! Just once a month?!

"Avoid eye contact with Jake if anyone else is present."

"No more meeting at home."

"Lie as little as possible, there's less to remember."

"Check for suspicious marks before returning home (wrists, ankles, neck)."

"Don't leave anything in Jake's bed or car. Do the HECK check: hosiery, earrings, condoms, knickers!"

"Use cash or a secret credit card for any purchases using work address for deliveries."

"Keep a separate bank account to pay off credit card and for cash withdrawals."

"Always be contactable. It's way too suspicious to be MIA."

I'm able to use Tamsin's passcode lists to access all of her secret emails and text messages on all eight of her cell phones. There are literally thousands of messages and emails on each one, exclusively to and from Jake. She must have stored her second phone at work, safely locked away with her diaries.

It's all here.

Everything I wanted to find out, but dreaded to know.

Using an amalgamation of the diaries, the letters, the emails, the text messages and the photographs, I'm able to piece together an accurate picture of Tamsin and Jake's affair from the very beginning until the end of last December.

What I discover breaks my heart into a billion pieces:

They've been in love with each other for over twenty years. Jake was honest enough to admit from the beginning that he could never be faithful to just one woman for the rest of his life, and that simply wasn't good enough for Tamsin. She always wanted them to marry, but not until Jake was prepared to commit to her and her alone. After the kids were born they agreed that the status quo was best for all concerned, but they've already discussed making a change to these arrangements as soon as Charlie and John have left home. They've talked a lot about growing old together. Bastards!

Deceiving me with ease, they've managed to meet in secret multiple times every year. Tamsin has employed several excuses for her absence from home: visits with Nilofer, tennis matches, residential school trips, shopping jaunts and many more. I had no idea she was so inventive. Jake has used work related fabrications to fool his three wives. The first wasn't convinced by his justification for frequent unexplained absence, and she divorced him acrimoniously, but he's confident that his current wife, Annie, is still completely in the dark. Perhaps I should give her a call.

I've been putting it off for as long as possible, but I must know for certain if Charlie and John are Jake's biological progeny or mine. Painstakingly, I piece together the events prior to Charlie's conception. From my perspective, roughly a year before Charlie was born, Tamsin, and I made the decision to have a baby. I remember her bringing up the conversation and I was over the moon at the prospect of becoming a father. Tamsin was using the contraceptive pill at the time and she stopped taking it straight away. Three months later, she was pregnant. Nine months after that, Charlie was born and my life changed forever.

Now for the real story:

Thirteen months before Charlie's birth, Tamsin and Jake began discussing the possibility of 'creating a child together'. Tamsin was the driving force behind the decision and Jake took some persuading. He was concerned that I would somehow be able to discern that the baby wasn't mine. Tamsin eventually convinced him by belittling his concerns and spouting some drivel about their child being the 'physical embodiment of their love for each other'. At this point, Tamsin stopped taking the pill and started tracking her fertility. They made a point of meeting up for sex whenever Tamsin was at the most fertile part of her cycle, and she also avoided having sex with me at those times, secretly using a diaphragm if she absolutely couldn't avoid my advances. She made up for it when she was least fertile, insisting I make love to her, so we could start a family, but still using her diaphragm as an extra precaution. For all that time, when I'd thought we were making a baby together, Tamsin was in fact taking action to prevent it.

Tamsin and Jake were successful in their endeavours, and their clandestine communications from that time are effusive with delight.

I have vivid memories of Charlie's birth. There was a small television in the maternity ward showing a football match. Keeping track of the game helped distract me from the exquisite pain of Tamsin crushing my hand. *She* was fine, *she* had gas and air, but I was in considerable discomfort. After three hours of labour, Charlie was born: a slimy, wailing, adorable baby. And I cried. Later that day, Jake came to the hospital to visit us all. Tamsin handed Charlie to him and he shed a tear too. I didn't think anything of it at the time. Shortly afterwards we asked Jake if he'd be Charlie's godfather and he said yes.

Three years later, Tamsin and Jake repeated the same technique and John was conceived and born, while I was again unwittingly left out of the process. They determined that two children was sufficient, and Tamsin had a coil inserted. I had believed that was a mutual decision between Tamsin and me, but apparently not.

It was even Jake who first suggested the name Charlotte, which surprises me because I thought it had been my idea, but it's all there in black and white. Days before we agreed on Charlie's name, Jake had proposed it in a letter to Tamsin, then she had fooled me into believing that it was *my* choice. They generously allowed me to call their second child John, after my maternal grandfather, despite Jake's preference being Isaac. Tamsin thought it would be a nice gesture and Jake went along with it. So magnanimous!

I'm deeply shocked when I read about Tamsin and Jake's sex life. For all this time, while I've been disappointed in Tamsin's lack of enthusiasm and effort in the bedroom, in reality, she's been creative, adventurous and permanently horny. They've been at it like rabbits at every opportunity. All the things I'd suggested, when Tamsin had practically called me a pervert, she'd done willingly and enthusiastically with Jake. Often she was the instigator of their more adventurous lovemaking. Apparently, Tamsin loves the kinky stuff. The more freaky the better. Every time they meet, she comes up with some new titillating foreplay. I can't believe how explicit Tamsin is in her emails. She uses words with Jake that I've never heard come out of her pretty little mouth. The classy, cool, housewife and mother was a role she played at home, but with Jake, she was a hot, insatiable, crude, lusty, sex machine. I had no idea until just now that my prim and proper wife likes to be tied up and fucked up the arse. No wonder she's always bereft of energy and ideas when it comes to having sex with her actual husband.

Tamsin acknowledged in her diaries that she has to be very drunk to initiate sex with me, but Jake is a surprisingly jealous man, so together they came up with techniques to reduce the duration and the frequency of Tamsin's lovemaking with me. I take cold comfort from discovering that Tamsin has lied to Jake on many occasions, claiming she wasn't having any sex with me for long periods when I knew that, in fact, she was.

My phone rings again. DS Khan is obviously very keen to speak to me. I wonder if the police have discovered Sophia's body and are already on the way here to arrest me. Once more I choose not to answer, and it stops ringing fairly quickly. If they've fished Sophia's corpse out of the canal, then it will be all over the news before long. However, I'm past caring about the publicity. I now realise that Tamsin must have known about my affair for many months. Jake would have told her about it straight after I'd told him, when I requested that he lie for me. She didn't let on she knew because she simply didn't care. If I was sleeping with Sophia, then at least I'd be requesting sex less frequently with her. No wonder my pathetic attempts to hide my affair appeared to be successful. Tamsin was simply pretending not to notice.

How dare she cheat on me for all these years? How could she pretend to have so little interest in sex when she absolutely loved it, but only with another man? How could she let me believe that the children I adore are mine, when in fact they were fathered by her lover, my supposed friend?

What have I done?

A few days ago, I murdered the only woman who ever loved me unconditionally, and my unborn child, only to discover that my wife is now, and has always been, in love with another man, and I've been bringing up *his* children for all these years.

My marriage is a sham.

I have nothing.

I have no one.

In my imagination, I picture Tamsin and Jake in bed together, naked and basking in a post-coital glow.

Then they're both laughing.

At me.

At my twenty years of ignorance.

At the lie I've been unknowingly living since the day I met them.

At my humiliation.

I walk downstairs to the kitchen.

I select the longest, sharpest knife I can find in the kitchen drawer.

I sit down at the dining table and wait for Tamsin to return home.

# EPILOGUE

"**H** i."

"Hi, Jake."

"You aren't going to believe this."

"Me first. Lee just told me he was with *you* last Saturday night."

"Go on."

"Well, correct me if I'm wrong, but weren't you balls deep inside me last Saturday night about two hundred miles away?"

"I was indeed, and very pleasant it was too."

"Agreed. So he's fucking lying to me. One of our Teaching Assistants saw him leaving a local hotel, but he certainly wasn't visiting you like he claims."

"Well, that brings us to my news …"

"Tell me."

"I've just hung up on Lee to take your call. He rang to ask me to lie to you about his whereabouts last Saturday. It seems he's having an affair with someone from work."

"Told you! I bloody knew it!"

"You were right again, my dear."

"I've known about it since the day it started. He was so fucking smug that evening; acting all weird. He could barely look me in the eye at first and then he was all affectionate. I knew something was up straight away."

"But that was months ago."

"It's that fat cunt Sophia from his office. They couldn't keep their eyes off each other at the Christmas party. I heard she's already fucked her way around most of the managers there."

"Well, I think he's a complete idiot. Why would he *do* that? There's no way she could be as hot as you."

"I know, right? He certainly wasn't very careful. It was so obvious! Always surreptitiously checking his phone. One time he sent me a text message he'd meant to send to her, then blamed it on one of his colleagues. Another time I walked in on him wanking over a nude photo she'd sent him, and he panicked and dropped his phone down the loo. What a dick!"

"That's a bit harsh."

"He was fucking cheating on me!"

"Have you ever heard the saying about the pot and the kettle?"

"It's different with us, Jake. We're soulmates."

"I love you, you know."

"I love you too. Always have. Always will."

"What do you want me to say to him?"

"Tell him he's a complete and utter twat for cheating on the best, sexiest, wife any man ever had. Make it clear you're extremely disappointed in him. Tell him if he ever does anything to hurt me, you'll break his fucking legs, pull out his fingernails and stomp on his balls. Then tell him, if I should ask you where he was last Saturday, you'll, with great reluctance, back him up and lie to me. But just this one time."

"Okay. He knows you've called me, so should I call him straight back?"

"No hurry. In fact, don't call him at all. Let's make him sweat."

"What are you going to do?"

"Nothing. I'll ignore it. Hopefully, that slag will tire him out and I won't have to sleep with him as often."

"Sounds like a good plan. There's no way he can find out about us is there?"

"Absolutely no way. We've been too careful."

"So we just carry on as normal?"

"Yeah. We're fine. There's nothing to worry about…"

# DEDICATION

In loving memory of:

Sophia

... and Tamsin

... and Jake.

To be continued in The Adulterer's Confession: A Novel

# AUTHOR'S NOTE:

The idea for this book came when I received a WhatsApp message meant for somebody else. It was innocuous enough, but it made me wonder: what if a 'happily' married man accidentally sent a suspicious text message to his wife instead of his lover? Is there a way out of that situation? Why was he cheating if he was happily married? How would he try to rationalise his unforgivable behaviour? Why was his lover having an affair with a married man? What steps could they take to minimise the chance of their affair being discovered? What else could go wrong? And what about his wife? What was her role in this story? Could there possibly be a happy ending?

So many questions, but I thoroughly enjoyed trying to get inside the mind of my main character as his life spiralled inexorably downward.

I loved writing it, and when it was finished, I loved reading it. I hope you do too.

Thank you so much for reading this book, especially if you made it all the way to the end. It was my first piece of creative writing for thirty-eight years, so I was a bit rusty! If you enjoyed it, I would really appreciate a review on Amazon or Goodreads.

To find out more about the further misadventures of Lee,

Tamsin and Jake, look out for the sequels in The Adulterer Series:

The Adulterer's Confession: A Novel
The Adulterer's Dilemma: A Novel

Till next time ...


Sam Anthony

Printed in Great Britain
by Amazon